A DIVINE'S RETRIBUTION

Rise of the Stria Book Three

TESSA MCFIONN

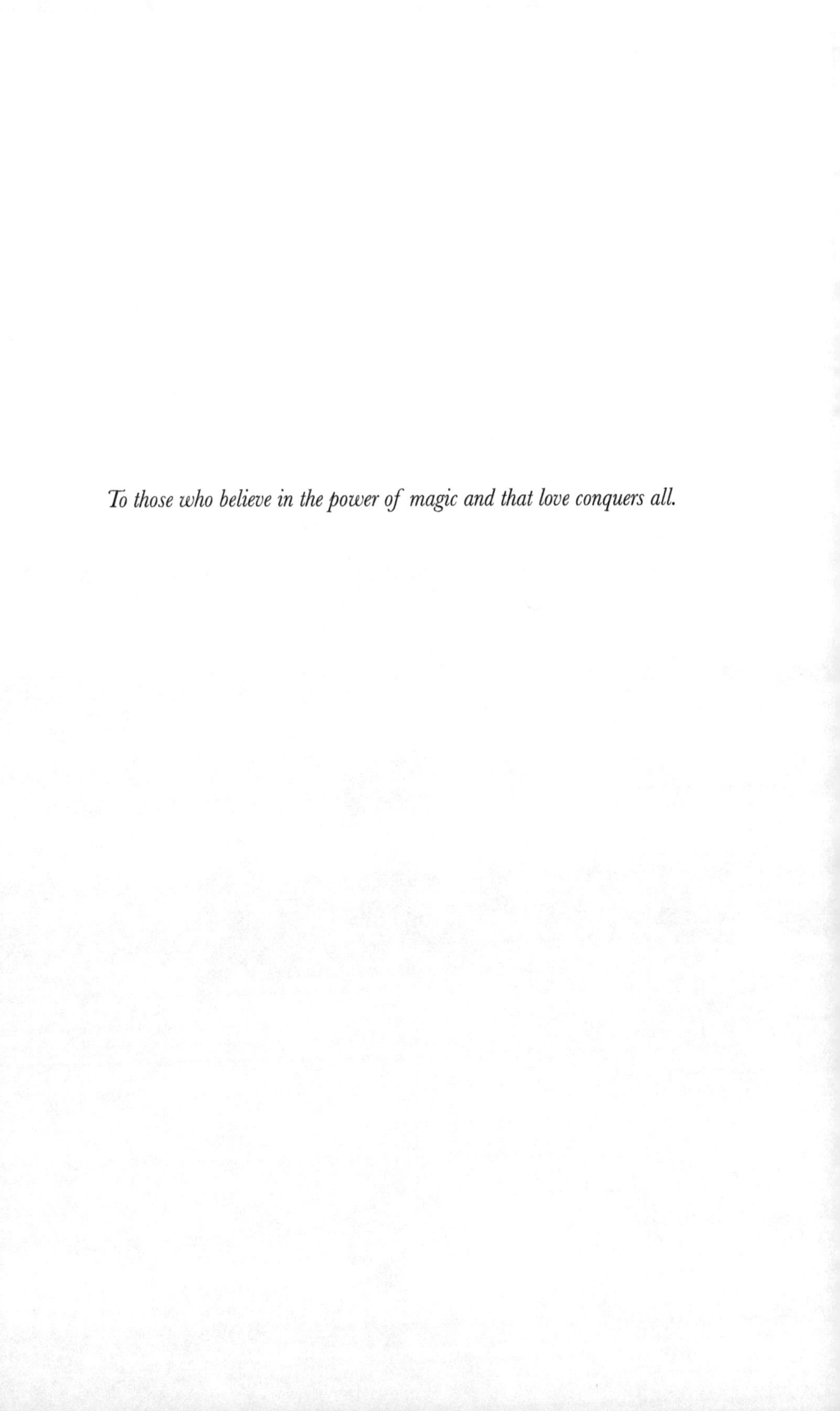

To those who believe in the power of magic and that love conquers all.

Acknowledgments

For as long as I can remember, I have looked to the stars and dreamed of life beyond our world. When I started writing *To Discover a Divine*, I began a journey that I had originally planned for the story to be a trilogy and last for only three books. However, once I sat in front of the keyboard to "finish" the saga, I was stumped. The words simply refused to come. My characters wouldn't talk to me and every idea only led to a roadblock.

I was at my wit's end. So I did what all smart writers do: I sought help. I got in touch with a fellow writer and wonderful friend, Lisa Kessler. The conversation started as most good brainstorming sessions do; reviewing the main events of previous two books in the series, looking at the cliff-hanger end of book two while enjoying a hearty breakfast.

As I was finishing my first cup of coffee, my dear friend looked over the table and asked the question that opened the floodgates.

"Does it have to end with the third book?"

That simple question. Did it? It was as if I had been given permission to stay in the world of the Dantaran galaxy. Once I realized the story didn't have to end, ideas poured into my mind and onto the page.

Sometimes just having someone state the obvious is enough to kick start things. Lisa, you are a diva!

To my wonderful betas; Denyce, Elma, Mary-Anne, and Ri, who are always willing to glance over scenes and listen to me prattle on at all hours of the day or night. Your kind words and spelling corrections help save my sanity.

To my cover artist and designer extraordinaire, Dani Julian; thank you for being able to read my mind when I babble about art and color and things way above my pay grade.

To my Romance Writers of America San Diego buddies, Tami, CJ, Cindy, Pam and Margaret; thank you for helping me keep my head above water.

To my friends and family, thank you for understanding why I sit in front of my computer for hours on end.

To my husband, who loves me even when my "office" gets so cluttered there is nowhere to sit.

And to Mom, thank you for inspiring me to believe in magic.

Chapter 1

"*Kahlym...*"

"Evainne?"

A strangely familiar voice had called through the dark of his dream, dragging him back toward consciousness. Kahlym did not know how much time had passed since he had lost his soul. Hours had melted into days, and every inch of his ship reminded him of her absence, brought back memories of her soft skin, her rich laughter, and her warm heart. They haunted his waking hours. Rage had fueled his daily routine, much to the chagrin of his crew. But alone with his thoughts in the silence of the night, Kahlym was tormented by the demons of guilt and anguish.

Each time he closed his eyes, a new incarnation of his angel would manifest—some appeared with her face, or of a mocking version of her musical voice—and all reveled in his suffering, refusing him even a little peace. They pleaded for him to stop, screamed at his stubborn stupidity, and cried in sadness. Each morning, he awoke, curled up in his chair high on the captain's deck, more exhausted than the night before, and the never-ending drain colored his foul mood even more. In his heart, he did not believe he deserved any respite, yet he yearned to steal what little solace he could.

"Kahlym … heed my words…"

He thrashed about, trying to banish this new devilment. "Evainne!" He refused to open his eyes; he only wanted to live in his fantasy world for a moment longer. "Forgive me, *ziat'xahn.*"

But the ethereal voice continued to pry into his mind until it took on an unexpected solid form. Shadows coalesced, and soon, Shezheer, the old Seer whose words had spared his life, stepped through the mists. Ancient at the time of his birth, she appeared frail, the ornate Divine robe nearly swallowing her hunched shoulders. A mysterious wind shook her spindly limbs as she shuffled closer.

"Near is the moment, Child of Prophecy, of my transcendence … Wrongs must be made right…"

"I don't understand. Wrongs?" Rooted in place, he struggled to ferret out meaning from her cryptic warning.

"The tasks to be carried are not yours to bear … Those shall rest … on the shoulders of…" Her image faltered, light threatening to break through the inky black.

"On the shoulders of who!" Kahlym shouted to the disappearing figure, whose mouth moved, whispering her secrets into the void.

"… Of your son…"

Chapter 2

"Bao! Open this door before I break it down!"

Evainne Wagner raged, pounding her fists against the smug barrier until her knuckles bled. She blatantly ignored the mutters at her back, hushed whispers about the "crazy round eye." It might have been a few years, and her Vietnamese might have been rusty, but she got the gist of their comments. Or maybe the space tech still implanted in her brain had simply switched all of the words into English.

Granted, she was still sporting her stylish attire of a smoke-stained, green-and-ecru gossamer gown that revealed more than concealed her assets, and ass-breaking sandals with a busted heel. She was certain she looked like an escapee from some toga party at Northeastern University. But her current goal was way more important than the perceived discomfort of passersby.

She continued to beat at the wood as the horror of her life replayed in her head.

Home.

She was back.

Boston, Massachusetts. Earth. Milky Way.

And she was pissed.

Her eyes drifted shut, and Kahlym's face jumped into the foreground, his tourmaline eyes glazing over with heartbreaking sadness before the chipped blue paint of her apartment door materialized before her. Tears pricked behind her shuttered lids, and she bit her cheek.

No. She would not give in to the loss or grief. Not yet. She still needed to use her anger to find the one person who could set this all to rights.

Growling, Evainne mashed the doorbell, sending out a furious Morse code signal of *"get the fuck down here,"* intermixing some kicking thumps as a strange downbeat to make her point even clearer. Time was of no importance; the sun was up. Good enough.

She paused, dragging down hot gulps of burning air and prepared for another assault, but stopped when she caught mumbles and footfalls on the other side of the door.

"Okay, okay. I'm—"

As soon as the door had cracked open, she shoved her way through, nearly knocking Bao to the ground. Startled and sleepy, he stumbled back, rubbing a hand across his eyes as he finished tugging on his white T-shirt. Bao had gotten even bigger since the last time she'd seen him, which was saying a lot since he was a champion heavyweight Sumo wrestler to begin with. A couple of frowning blinks later, his eyes snapped wide, surprise washing out his features.

"Evainne? Where the hell have you been? And what's with the getup?"

She shook her head as she drove him backwards through the hallway and into the kitchen. "Later. Where's sifu?"

Bao fell into the first available chair, screwing up his face. "What? Why the—"

Her glare froze the rest of his question. *Can this shit work here, too?* Taking her own advice, she'd think more on that later.

"Where. Is. Whetutoa."

Her heart raced as her mind spun in dangerous circles. How

long had she been gone? Did time work the same in both universes? What if only seconds had passed, or if in the time it took her to run the half mile to get to Bao's front place, Kahlym had already died?

That last screaming query had propelled her legs to Olympic speeds, and she fought back that ugly beast, using the panic to give her actions more purpose.

Bao frowned, the deep crease across his forehead rippling, disappearing into his thick, black hair. "He moved the dojo a couple days ago, which you would have known, if you had been around." Concern relaxed his stern countenance. "Evainne, what happened to you?"

With another frantic shake of her head, she grabbed his arm, intent on yanking him out of the chair. "Take me there." She tugged and pointed her toes back toward the entryway, only to be nearly pulled off her feet. The fierce glare returned to Bao's eyes as he stayed glued to the low-backed captain's chair. Trying to single-handedly drag three hundred pounds of solid muscle around like a kid's toy was maybe not the smartest thing she'd done all day. But she wasn't thinking straight, and time was not on her side.

She looked at him, swallowing past her growing lump of fear. "Bao, I promise I'll explain everything once we find him. Please." She added her other hand and backpedaled, offering him her most pathetic smile.

Precious seconds slipped by before Bao finally dropped his head and heaved an exasperated sigh. Reluctantly, he rose. "Fine. But you had better have a good explanation for waking me up at the butt crack of dawn on a Saturday."

The urge to throw her arms around him and squeeze the stuffing out of him was powerful, but if she let down her guard, tears would fall. Right now, she needed to contain those softer emotions, keep the darker ones at the forefront. Evainne nodded and continued to pull him toward the door.

Grumbling, Bao slipped on a pair of flip-flops and snatched up a set of keys from the bowl on the entryway table. "It's just around the corner, and driving would be a—hang on!"

As soon as they'd crossed the threshold, Evainne tapped in to her Divine skills. There. About two blocks over and halfway down the street, a pencil-thin column of deep lapis shot up like a rocket. Confident, she took off at a dead run, leaving in the dust Bao, who called out to her as he struggled to keep pace. But she was on a mission and refused to slow.

Now why the fuck didn't I think of looking for him like THIS in the first place?

The red light on Boylston did force her to stop, though, and if it hadn't been such a busy thoroughfare, she would have dared the crossing. Instead, Evainne paced and watched the cars zoom by, her predatory track short and dizzying. Huffing breath told her Bao had managed to catch up. He placed a hand on her shoulder, either to keep his balance or to hold her in place, or both.

"Shit, Evie. You'd think the devil was after you. What's the rush?"

Green flashed, and Bao tightened his grip. With a stern glare, he escorted her across the street. "Hey, are you gonna tell me, or what?"

She sped up as much as her physical leash allowed, her destination only a couple more storefronts away. "As soon as we get to sifu's place, I will. I honestly don't think I could repeat it twice. You'd probably call the local loony police and have me locked in a little rubber room with one of those self-hugging shirts." Up ahead, a simple sign announced the dojo of Jhuen Xaio Martial Arts.

Evainne scoffed, shaking her head sadly as the truth revealed itself. She shrugged off Bao's hold and stalked to the front door to give the black security gate the same loving care she had shown her friend's entry. A renewed sense of purpose added power to her knocks and shouts.

"Geez, Evainne. Go easy."

She snapped her gaze away from the groaning metal. "I don't have time to go easy."

Her knuckles bled as she continued to pound, until she opted for another tactic. She closed her eyes and prayed the embedded unicomm translator chip worked at such a distance.

"Xandar, I need your help."

Kahlym's musical language fell heavy off of her tongue as she rested her forehead against the frame, hoping to borrow strength from the building itself. Her heart stuttered, emptiness gradually taking over, and tears pressed hard against her closed lids, eager to make their escape, to bring her to her knees.

A *click* inches away from her face pulled her back to the land of the hopeful and she hurriedly dashed the back of her hand against her cheeks as the door swung open. Light haloed around the shadowy figure hovering in the entryway.

Focusing her blurred vision, Evainne marveled at the undeniable family resemblance. The strong jaw, and wide, almond eyes were almost an exact match, though his intriguing facial tattoos carried a new meaning beyond unique geometric patterns. She had attributed her instructor's unusually dark skin to either Middle Eastern or African descent, yet now, all she could see was a taller version of Kahlym. But the eyes were wrong.

Never had she seen her sifu's eyes; all while she was studying, he had always worn thick, black, wraparound sunglasses. Also, he walked with a long staff, so she'd assumed he was blind. Only now did she realize she was the one who had been wandering in the dark. Pools of the most unnatural shade of blue stared back at her. Long, black lashes brushed the tops of his cheeks as he blinked slowly.

"You learned my language easily, *learom-xahn.*" He took a step back, his gaze traveling from her curl-tumbled hair down to her barely encased feet. "The Divine robes suit you well."

"Can it, bucko. No amount of compliments are going to save your ass on this one. Trust me." Painful tingles pricked, needle-like, along the length of her arm, centering around the aching edge of her hand where her nails dug into her palm. A couple of flicks of her wrist, and the sensation began to recede.

A sad sparkle danced through his piercing midnight blue orbs. Then concern drew his brows together. "But why—"

"Why am I here?" She shouldered past the silent sentinel, needing the safety of inside. "Well, gee, sparky. How about we start with the plain and simple fact that your brother is a fucking imbecile. He's stubborn and bull-headed and ... and ..."

And I love him more than the next breath I take.

Shock washed out from the shimmering ebony complexion. "How do you know Brel?" he asked.

"Not just Brel. I know Kahlym, too."

Her senses flew into overdrive as a pair of arms approached, but she stumbled away, angered, and stalked farther into the dojo. Chairs. She needed someplace to sit down while her brain raced toward the next possible solution. Time was ticking, and she had to get back. Soon.

"They all think you're dead. You know that, right?" She spun around, pinning her teacher with an angry glare. "All of them— your parents, your brothers, your friends. Hell, your father is sporting your ship like a kid who stole Dad's Ferrari. And you've been kicking back here, hiding out and sipping sake, while Kahlym's been carrying the guilt of your death for ... how many years now?"

This time, she was pulled to a gentle stop and, unable to look away, Evainne stared into the fathomless, dark blue eyes towering above her. "How is it you know of my family?" he said.

"Maybe, genius, because your brothers were the first people I ran into when I got tossed halfway across the friggin' universe? After getting dropped on my ass in the middle of a prison ship, that is. Any other questions you want? Current events? The weather report from Raedyn Primus?" Her razor-sharp tongue refused to slow, even as she stared into the confused faces of her friends. "Things are a complete clusterfuck, and don't even get me started on the shitstorm of political crap still swirling since you didn't marry Princess Bitchface."

The man she'd known for so long as Whetutoa ran his hand over his smooth head and wandered to the folding chair against the wall. "I was not meant to rule. Nothing I could do was going to make any difference."

"Okay, hold on," Bao piped up. "Will someone please share with the rest of the kids?" He tossed up his arms as he crossed the space. "Who is this Callum you guys keep talking about? And what's this about a princess? Help a guy out here, eh? Does this have anything to do with where you've been for the past two weeks?"

Evainne looked over. "He's his—wait, what? How long?" Her heart leapt as she ran up to Bao, grabbing on to his white shirt. "Are you sure that's how long I was gone?"

If her counting was accurate, it had been at least three weeks since she'd first appeared in that long-ago hallway. How much time had passed for her journey home? Panic rose, and she felt the urge to throw up.

Bao frowned, moving her out of his personal space. "Yeah, give or take a day or two. After you didn't show for class again on Thursday, I headed to your place, looking for you. Your flat was all locked up tight, but the junk mail and newspapers were starting to pile up. Hey, you don't look so good."

Her vision swam, and a pair of strong hands steadied her. *No, no, no. This can't be happening. He can't be dead. They can't be dead. I can't be alone.*

The litany became a continuous loop, and she refused to believe things had taken a turn for the worse. Some part of her sensed both Kahlym and Brel still lived; a tiny voice in the back of her head said she would have felt something—a stabbing loss; the sound of a thousand voices crying out in pain, then silencing. Something, anything. No matter how Obi-Wan she made it seem, she had to keep alive that belief.

<You are correct, Evainne. Even at this great distance, you would know if

those to whom you have forged a deep connection have passed. > She raised her chin, craned her neck to peer into the deep lapis eyes above her. When she was sure her legs weren't going to crumble, she shuffled back.

"Time moves at a different pace on our two worlds. What you call a day here is more like three days in the Seventh Quadrant."

Bao groaned. "I feel like I stepped into the middle of some anime cosplay scene. Will one of you please clue me in?"

"It is all right, my friend. She knows."

Evainne stiffened, ice shooting down her spine at the surprising words filtering through the silent air. With a deliberate slowness, she swiveled her head from one sheepish giant to the next. Her confusion must have been pretty obvious, judging by the relieved expression on her friend's face.

"Thank God. Now I won't feel like the only crazy one here," Bao said, though his sad smile did not give her any comfort.

"You knew?" Betrayal laced her voice. "All this time, you knew he wasn't what he claimed to be, and you never thought to say anything?"

Before another word was spoken, an eerily familiar voice echoed in her head.

<Do not be angry with him, learom-xahn.> She snapped her gaze toward the man she once trusted. He cast his face down. Resting his forearms on his bent knees, he supported his weary head in his huge palms until, with effort, he raised his chin to level his sorrowful, lapis eyes on hers.

"He has guarded my secret for many years."

The world around her tilted, and her stomach dropped once again. Air seemed to vanish from the large, open space as if her lungs had forgotten how to work. Something solid bumped against the backs of her knees, and she happily collapsed. A large hand rubbed her back, encouraging her body to resume its normal functioning. As she repeated the litany of "breathe in, breathe out,"

Evainne stared at nothing on the padded floor, her vision refusing to focus on any one object.

How long had she been living in the dark? Had they been planning this from the start?

"Is this why you're here, Xandar?" Feeling detached, she let the words tumble out as hot tears burned trails down her cheeks. "To groom me for my intended fate? Was Bao your contact, the front man to grab unsuspecting girls off the streets while you mess with their heads?"

Venom had dripped from each hated word, and her heart shattered.

Used.

Betrayed.

Helpless.

Darkness threatened to consume her, when she was forcibly dragged out of her aching pit of painful melancholy, unable to resist the magnetic pull of a pair of impossible blue eyes.

"No, Evainne. You have to believe—"

"I don't *have* to believe anything!" she roared, the onslaught of conflicting emotions more than she could bear. She leapt to her feet, the chair skittering across the floor as if it had anticipated the impending breakdown and decided to get the hell out of the way. "I've just spent the last three weeks being told what I had to believe and what I had to understand. Was all that bullshit, too? Am I nothing more than a fucking tool to the universe?"

She was crying in earnest, but she didn't care. Too much had been piled onto her already-chipped and shattered plate. She needed to let go.

"I get yanked off my front porch and tossed halfway across the fucking stars to find out I'm supposed to be the answer to a prophecy, that I'm either some kind of magical baby factory, or the one who's supposed to save the whole damned world." Gesturing wildly, she swung her gaze in the general direction of her companions. Even though the two faces were blurred, she felt embarrassed guilt radiating off of the pair. "Now, I end up back in the place I never thought I'd ever see again, to find out the only two people I thought I knew, people I trusted, have been lying to me!"

The darker figure rushed in and pinned her arms to her sides, a gentle yet effective restraint.

"Evainne. No." His accented voice had cut through her tirade with surgical precision. He sounded exactly like Kahlym, and she struggled to contain the building ache. Only a tiny, heartbreaking hiccup slipped through her ironclad grasp.

His expression, but not his hold on her, softened.

"Please, do not let these dark and dangerous thoughts consume you. None of this was done out of spite, and neither Bao nor I have ever meant to hurt you."

Even though her inner child was throwing a monumental temper tantrum, her rational mind still functioned. She appeased both with a sharp, mirthless laugh and a tired shake of her head. "Yeah, well, you're gonna have to forgive me if I'm a little cautious right now."

A compassionate smile touched her former instructor's face, and her tightly restrained resolve shattered. Grief, anger, and soul-draining exhaustion poured out with each heavy sob, and she stood on her own for only a moment before two brotherly behemoths enveloped her. Needing to let someone else shoulder her burden for a while, she dropped all pretenses and continued to bawl. She didn't care about appearances. It didn't even bother her that neither of them had ever seen her shed a tear in anything other than overwhelming anger.

She had reached her limit of giving a shit when Kahlym had disappeared from her sight.

Though nothing was said, waves of understanding brushed against her soul, and the two giants stood as silent sentinels, protecting her from the world, giving her time to sift through her feelings as if permission had been granted for her breakdown.

Her heart's raw emptiness ached the most. She had grown

accustomed to Kahlym's presence in her mind, the sensation like butterfly wings tickling her spirit. Even when she was held prisoner by his evil father, she knew she was not alone. She had believed, no matter what, that he would find her. Now, a vast nothingness sat in that spot; a void she feared would never be filled again.

Do not give in to the darkness, Evainne.

Remembered words from the old doctor filtered through the chaos in her head. If she was to figure out how to return to the only place she truly called home, return to the man who held her happiness, she had to be stronger than her fears.

As her catharsis wound down, her thoughts began to sort themselves into logical piles. Like clear skies after a sudden storm, its waters washing away the clutter and mess, Evainne found clarity, and it steeled her.

"I think we broke her."

Bao's stage whisper had earned a muffled chuckle from her, and she turned her head to rest her ear on the damp shirt in front of her, taking in a stuttered breath. As if sensing the bonding moment was done, the warm presence at her back disappeared. Evainne stood on her own, raised her chin, and met the firm gaze of her ticket back to her real home.

Her teacher smiled down at her, pride reflecting back. "No. She is much too strong for that."

Using a corner of the long, flowing sleeve as a makeshift handkerchief, Evainne dabbed her eyes and shook her head. "I wouldn't bet the farm on that one today, uhhh…" How was she to address the man she'd known so long as Sifu Toa?

"Please, call me Whetutoa. Xandar died in that shuttle crash all those years ago." He led her back to her vacated seat. "Somehow, the blast sent me here. I know there is much you need to hear, and I will tell you all I can."

He dragged another over to join her, then began. "While I was still a boy," he said, "I watched my father connive and scheme his way into the good graces of the very man against whom he should have been fighting all along. Currying favor of a vicious tyrant was not how I wanted to live my life. You see, I was a scientist of some sorts on my homeworld. Studying the ways of the universe had long since held my mind."

He sank down, his eyes never once moving away from hers. "I am sure you were made aware of the decline in the birth of Divines and the dangerous ramifications of this loss of power for the Thrall Emperor. I began to wonder if, somehow, those qualities could be found in worlds much farther than our own galaxy. I consulted as many star charts as I could get my hands on."

Evainne scooted to the edge of her seat. While his voice had a trace of Kahlym's musical accent, it wasn't the same. It didn't set her blood on fire, nor did his eyes pierce the darkness engulfing her soul. She blinked away the tears threatening to fall and refocused on the important story.

"For years," he said, "I pored over data and thought I had found a possible system to explore. But the destination was too far and it would have taken decades to arrive. So, I began searching for a way to combine the technology of our short distance transport chambers with the hyperdrive engines on a shuttlecraft. I was conducting an experiment that day, certain I had discovered the solution."

With a shrug she immediately recognized, he grinned sheepishly. "What I got was transported through space; somehow, my ship disintegrated, and I alone traveled through the portal I had inadvertently created. Confused, and with no way to get back home, I wandered in a daze away from my landing site. Bao was the first person I encountered."

"Nah," said Bao, "I think 'ran into' is the more correct phrase." Her longtime friend added his own chair to the party, spinning the metal folding seat around and resting his hefty arms across the narrow back. "I'm jogging through Winthrop Square, turn the corner onto Devonshire, and WHAM!—next thing I know, I'm sitting on my ass, staring up at this guy." He grinned, thumbing over his shoulder to Toa. "Long ol' dreads going every which way, dripping blood, and babbling on. He looked like some crazed mental patient." He chuckled and, glancing over at Toa, shook his head slowly. "But something told me not to leave him. Maybe it was the fact that not many people can knock me down."

Whetutoa shrugged innocently. "Ishtanti smiled on me when She placed him in my path. He was patient and kind, teaching me his language until the translator chip was operational once again." He tipped his chin in her direction. "But to be honest, his language makes more sense than your English."

Evainne had to give him that one. As she'd pored over the ancient tomes back on Raedyn Primus, she'd noticed most of the languages of the Dantaran galaxy had more in common with Chinese logograms than standard English writing.

"Yeah, I think I threw everyone there a loop, too." She smiled weakly. How flustered Yhan'tu had become when she flew into a tirade. The stray thought triggered another question. "Wait. If you were a scientist, what's up with the facial tats?"

Bao frowned, his gaze swiveling between them. "I took him to get them. Why?" he asked. "Is that bad?"

"No, my friend." Toa shook his head, trailing his fingers against the indigo-and-yellow interlinked lines and angles. "Where I come from, those trained as clerics in the healing arts were marked by geometric designs. The colors here are much duller than those of my homeworld, but the message is the same." He pursed his lips. "Somehow, I hoped—that is, I believed—by reinventing myself, I could escape everything I had lost. Yet, it seems Ishtanti had other plans for me."

She listened to Toa's resonating timbre; the musical rise and fall brought to mind a haunting pair of tourmaline eyes and she swallowed hard. She longed for Kahlym's touch, to feel the soft press of his lips against hers. She replayed his voice, focusing on the reverent way he'd first said her name.

"Evainne? We can talk later, if you would prefer."

She bit the inside of her cheek to hold back impending tears, and when a dark hand covered hers, she nearly lost her battle of control. With a quick shake of her head, she reined in her feminine side and brought the rational part of her psyche to the forefront.

"No, none of this can wait," she said. "I have so many questions needing serious answers." She pushed away the comfort and sat up straight. "Why me? I still can't shake the feeling that, for all these years, I've been trained and groomed like some circus animal."

Toa violently shook his head. "Evainne. Please. You must understand—" She snapped up one finger, eyes narrowed, and the words stopped. He sighed heavily, apparently searching for another way to explain. "I am sorry if you are tired of hearing the phrase, but it is the best I can do, *learom-xahn*."

A curious movement flickered at the corner of her eye and, frowning, she turned her head to find Bao with his hand raised. She arched a brow. "Really? What are we, back in friggin' high school?"

Her old friend shrugged, grinning impishly. "Hey, I didn't want to be rude and interrupt. But … what the hell do you keep calling her?"

"Little sister."

Toa's deep, resonating voice had supported hers as they answered in perfect harmony.

"And she hasn't handed you your nuts yet?" Bao gave a soft whistle. "You're a braver man than I."

"Really?" she quipped. "This, coming from the man who called me 'weirdo' and managed to make it sound like a compliment."

A sad smile touched her teacher's lips, and Evainne saw the ghost of her lover coalesce before her eyes.

"Language can be both a weapon and a comfort when wielded correctly." Toa turned his face to her. Her brow furrowed, and she folded her arms across her chest. "As I said," he continued, "Bao found me and helped me to acclimate to this new world. Your home is much different than mine." He laughed weakly at her bland expression.

"Gee, ya think?" Evainne snorted. "At least you had a translator."

Bao's arm started to rise again and Evainne's sharp look froze his movement, but not his tongue. "Wait. Translator?"

Toa shook his head. "Not at first. The trip had knocked it out of commission. But eventually, yes, I was able to get it to work." He shifted his attention to Bao. "Because there are so many languages spoken throughout the Seventh Quadrant, all members of any ruling family are implanted with a universal translating chip while we are very young. It makes negotiations and other dealings much easier, less of a chance for misunderstandings."

Evainne glared at him, unconvinced, and Toa lifted a shoulder with a wan smile. "In theory."

"What?" Bao said. "And here I thought I was just a really great teacher." He popped Toa in the meat of his shoulder. "Bastard."

Evainne dropped her face into her hand as the pair of mammoth men continued to act like twelve-year-olds squabbling over the last cookie. "Children," she said, "could we please focus?"

Bao chuckled, returning to his chair. "Now *you* sound like a teacher."

She scowled as best as she could, hiding her surfacing smile. "Yeah, well. I kinda have something else on my mind right now."

With the pass of her hand, both faces shifted from playful to pensive. Remorse tapped her on the shoulder, and she murmured a half-hearted apology; she didn't mean to be a wet blanket, but she had to keep her eyes on the prize. Earth was no longer her home, and fear continued to nag at her soul. She gruffly shoved her panic back into its box as she returned her attentions to the two sheepish faces.

"You still haven't answered my main question: Why me? Or 'how' might be better, or maybe just as good. Aw, hell, I don't know. Please tell me why all this is happening to me. Was it chance, or fate, or nothing more than dumb fucking luck?" Her voice trembled and she shivered, rubbing her hands against her bare arms, hoping to cloak her actual terror with the mild annoyance of the chilly mid-morning air. Bao excused himself and stood as Toa pinned her with a curious stare.

"I must ask you this first," said Toa. "Which answer would set your mind more at ease: The fact that it was random chance, or that you were destined to save the universe?"

Fuck. She hadn't thought of it that way. Did either of them make any difference? The longer she pondered his rhetorical point, the more she relaxed by fractions. "Neither," she replied. "But it still won't stop me from asking."

A strange twinkle danced in the unearthly blue orbs. "And that, *learom-xahn,* is why the choice could be none other than you."

She screwed up her face at his cryptic fortune-cookie wisdom. "Huh?"

"When I first met you, Evainne, you were nothing but a dangerous blend of rage and self-doubt, held together by a string. But it was that bond that drew me to you." Toa leaned in as Bao returned and laid a heavy blanket across her back. She glanced up, nodding in thanks to Bao as he rejoined the circle. "And it was hope. Somehow, given all that life had taken from you, you refused to be broken. You persevered and never lost your true self, no matter how hard your family or others tried to take it away from you. It had already been many years since I had seen Kahlym, but I saw something of him within you. He had that same spark, the need and the desire to prove he was more than a … a…" He halted as his vocabulary failed him. "What is that word?"

"A freak," she mumbled, grief coloring the hateful sound as her mind pulled forth images of her lover, his exotic tourmaline eyes gazing down at her as their bodies slid against one another. Chills crept over her arms as his imaginary fingers tantalized her skin. For one brief moment, her heart leapt, believing her connection had reached across the stars to find him … yet it was nothing more than a memory.

"Yes." Toa nodded heavily and slumped into his chair. "Freak."

He shifted his gaze, guilt haunting him. "But, returning to your question: At the time, did I know you were destined for more than this world? No, I did not. I saw the potential in you, though; I saw, within you, a chance for you to rise above and to go beyond what this world had to offer. Your fierce courage, as well as your compassion and intellect, were qualities found not only in the Divines, but were also the hallmarks of a Divine Adept. I did my best in sharing with you the teachings I had received as a boy. I only wanted to do right by someone else, since I had failed my own brother so miserably."

Now it was her turn to offer comfort. She reached across the gap and rested her hand on his knee. "But you didn't fail him," she said. "Not really. Kahl still looks up to you. I hear it in his voice when he and Brel would talk about you. You'd be proud of how he turned out. He's caring and compassionate and fights to protect his friends and…" Toa's strange expression cut off the rest of her thought.

"Is it Kahlym you love?" he whispered, his voice hushed and wary.

Her eyebrows tugged together. "Well, yeah? Why would that—"

The rest of her words, along with her breath, vanished in a whoosh as Toa jumped up and hug-attacked her. Toa's surprising enthusiastic response had managed to coax a tiny smile from her.

"Thank the Goddess! She truly has blessed him this time."

She patted the big guy on the back, scoffing. "Sometimes I'm not so sure either of us have been blessed. It hasn't been easy, that's for sure. And I thought I had trust issues."

Toa released his stranglehold and sat back on his heels. "How much have you learned of my brother?"

With a sad smile, she shrugged. "A bit, but I'm sure there's tons more I don't know." *Like where his heart truly lies.* Anger and grief tangled in her gut. He knew she could fight and that she wouldn't leave his side. Her heart dropped as she focused on that one truth: She would never leave his side. And being the overly chivalrous jerk he could be, Kahlym would see that as a danger.

She silently cursed him, even as she worked out a way to return to him.

"How much do you know of the prophecy?" Toa asked.

The sudden question snapped her back into the now, her brain spinning to determine the correct response. "Uh, a little. I mean, I heard all the words, but like any prophecy, the details were pretty unclear. And let me tell you, it took a friggin' act of Congress to get the information out of anyone. Is there some kind of rule that says you can't repeat the scary words or something?"

The filtered sunlight bounced off of Toa's shaved dome as he shook his head. "I would not call it fear. For my people, we have lived, and died, for as long as we can remember, because of ancient decrees. It has simply been assumed the words were known by all." His brow gained a deep crease as if he were searching for some vital piece of information. "I believe you would call it 'common knowledge.' Like, as if you tried to explain to someone why the sky darkens at night."

She rested her chin on her knuckles, pondering his explanation while Toa returned to his chair. It would make sense that news about a universal Armageddon would have traveled through all of the systems.

"Was fear of the prophecy the reason you have returned?" Toa asked, but his innocent question struck a dangerous chord.

"Huh? What makes you think I'm here because I want to be?" she said. Her patience was beginning to wear thin. Either that, or exhaustion was starting to get the better of her. Whichever, she was inches away from another breakdown, though this one had all the signs of catastrophe written on it.

"Then why did you come back?" Bao chimed in.

His confused words had landed like gasoline on a dying ember, sparking her once-forgotten rage. "Oh, I don't know," she said. "I thought I'd drop back in to grab my phone charger." The sarcasm gave her strength to make light of her own pain. She leveled her unapologetic gaze at Toa, locking eyes with the one person who could help her return. If only to beat the ever-living shit out of Kahlym.

"You make it sound like this was my choice." She jabbed her finger in Toa's direction. "The last thing I remember is running from the fucking enforcers after your dad called in the big and bad. Then your dumbass brother zaps me back here."

Toa blinked slowly, digesting her anger. Part of her nudged at herself to apologize for yelling, but a much larger part was pacing at this lack of activity, the squandering of precious seconds. Her thoughts spun in frantic circles. Did everyone get away? Were they safe?

Did Kahlym even miss her?

She gnashed her teeth at her teenage reaction. She needed to keep hold of her rage. It gave her some semblance of strength, feeling in control of something, even if it was only her temper.

Evainne took to her feet, gaze darting between the apprehensive faces.

"Whetutoa?" She took a deep breath, calling on a bit of needed courage. "Xandar. I need your help to get me back there."

The bluest eyes vanished under the curtain of black lashes. "That place is no longer my home and—"

"But it is mine!" She dropped to her knees in front of Toa and clutched one of his large hands. His black talons had been filed down, and an odd manicure had given them a paler hue. "For me, I can't think about it as anything else. This place, here? This is no longer my home. My ... my heart is there." She stumbled over the painful truth but forced the words out. "Look, I love him. And even though I want to strangle him right about now, I have to get back. You said you were a scientist. There has to be some way to figure out how we can get back."

He arched a curious brow and eased his massive shoulders away from her. "We?"

"Oh, hell yeah, sparky. That's definitely a 'we.' I am not going back empty-handed. You have two brothers who need to know you're still alive."

She continued speaking even after her listener had gotten out of his chair and had started to walk away. Undaunted, she climbed to her feet, scooping the flowing robes into her arms, following a half-step behind.

"Look," she said, "I get you don't want to get back into that screwed-up mess of politics. So don't." She trailed him, fighting to keep up and not trip over the squishy mats until, with a frustrated sigh, she captured his shirt tail and yanked him to a halt. "Just go back and face your brothers. After that, you can come back here and be done with it."

"Just go back?" He spun, glaring at her with a familiar fire in his eyes. But she had a good idea how to handle it. "You think it will be so easy?"

Her burgeoning smile vanished and she gripped his hand tighter. "No, I really don't. All I know is we have to try." She paused, adding the one word she hoped would tip the scales in her favor: "Please." *And why not? It had worked on the rest of his brothers.*

Her heart flip-flopped as the stern lines that had cut deep into the shimmering ebony complexion melted into the forlorn look of defeat. "That is not playing fair, *learom-xahn.*"

She shrugged a shoulder, smirking at her hollow victory. "I have far too much to lose to play nice, *kherdes.*"

Their eyes locked in the lengthening silence, her stance unwavering as her breathing took a time out. If he didn't answer soon, she might pass out. She was right, though; she did have too much to lose. Her sanity had long since checked out and her heart no longer resided in her body. That, as well as her soul, were halfway across the universe being held captive by a pair of bi-colored eyes.

"I do not even know if I can—"

"We," she added quickly.

"Bro." Bao entered the frame, propping his elbow on her sifu's shoulder. "You know you're gonna help her. Might as well just admit it now."

"Fine." The word filled the air—an exhausted exhale with sound. Not wanting to waste another second, she threw her arms around him, his frame much larger than Kahlym's but with a similar build.

"Thank you, Toa." She rested her cheek against his chest, stealing a little strength from the steady beat beneath her ear.

"Xandar," he said, and she leaned back, staring up in surprise. Her teacher focused on some far distant point, replaying memories she could only imagine. "If I am going to return, I might as well get used to hearing my name once again." Then he shifted his gaze down, pools of deep azure boring straight into her soul. "But I must warn you: We may not be successful."

Evainne shook her head, undaunted. "Now I must warn you: Failure in this is definitely not an option. Before we start, though…" She flashed them a timid smile. "Could I please first get something else to wear?"

Chapter 3

Kahlym glared at the black skies, staring into the abyss, the deep night echoing the emptiness within him. He was hollow, a shell of a man, simply propelling his body in some kind of forward direction. Time had long since lost meaning, but he was fairly certain at least nine moon rises had passed since he had banished his soul.

Gone was the warmth and comfort that had given his days purpose and his nights pleasure. Instead of trusting the strength and power of pure love, he listened to the evil whispers of his own insecurities and ingrained fear. He had been terrified of being unable to protect her, so he had sent her away. Sent her far from the reach of his scheming father and the lecherous plans of the Thrall Emperor.

But that also meant he had sent her far from him.

He dropped his gaze, the pain and anguish of her absence sucking the air out of his lungs. The choice had been his, and now he had to live with the consequences, no matter how much it hurt. He pressed his palm flat against his chest, forcing the pumping muscle beneath to continue its appointed task, and as his eyes drifted shut, he was tormented by the last memory he had of his angel. The deep green in her gown had brought out the rosy tones of her pale complexion, her deep brown eyes wide as realization had sunken in. The thick curls he wished he could wrap around himself like a living blanket had shaken frantically from side to side as tears had streaked down her cheeks. Time had frozen for an instant, giving him one final glimpse at paradise, and then nothing.

With each passing second, his rage had swallowed his grief and his friends had paid for his unstable emotions. He'd lost count of the number of blows he and Dhaerin had traded since returning to the ship, as well as the barbs he'd slung toward every other crew member.

Now, a buzzing off to his left demanded his attention, and he begrudgingly let another into his world of self-loathing. Not that he would get any rest tonight. Sleep hid from him for more reasons than his empty bed.

"What is it, Brel?"

He knew it was his brother, the only crew member who dared to check on him, and even his visits were brief and superficial. The others kept a safe distance, opting to remain alive. Kahlym wished he could apologize for his uncharacteristic mood swings, but the words would be meaningless. He'd doomed them along with himself when he had lost his heart.

"We'll be landing on Ontaxa soon. The last three jumps and false trails seem to have done the trick. All scans show no signs of any other crafts in the area. Looks like we managed to get away clean…"

Brel stumbled over his words and Kahlym lifted his gaze. A tic twitched along the square jaw, teeth gnashing in contained silence. The sight of his only current supporter on the verge of a break had finally unlocked a small, sensible part of Kahlym's mind and, with a heavy sigh, he leaned forward, cradling his head in his hands.

"Brel, what am I doing?" He hated the pathetic question, but he hated himself more at the moment. Some of the tension in the room had vanished, allowing fresh air to filter in.

"You're leading your crew to a safe haven." The flat delivery crushed his spirit, though it was nothing less than what he deserved. Could he repair the deep damage he had wrought?

A chair scraped against the floor and a steadying hand landed on his shoulder. "You're getting us to the nearest friendly port so we can figure out a way to get Evainne back to us."

Kahlym barked out a mirthless laugh. "You were right. Both you and Dhaer said this was a bad idea, but I—"

Brel yanked him out of his pity party, locking eyes with him. The normally warm citrine orbs of his brother brimmed with anger and unshed tears. "Yes, I did," he said. "And as much as I want to tell you 'I told you so,' it won't make any kind of difference. But you were the only one thinking of her safety and not what the rest of us wanted. With the death of the last Divine Seer, the emperor won't be able to find her again."

Neither will I. The words spun in hateful spirals in his mind.

A sharp slap jerked him back to the present. He reached a hand to his stinging cheek and stared slack-jawed at Brel.

"I know what you're thinking, *kherdes-xahn,* and I'm not gonna let you do this. R'uan has the coordinates from the first transport. If they have the right equipment on Ontaxa, and if she hasn't gone too far from where she was dropped, we can—"

"Dammit, Brel. Did you hear how many ifs you just said?" These same scenarios played out each time he closed his eyes, but hearing them spoken aloud made them somehow more unattainable. He rose, needing to direct his anger into physical action. "If they have the equipment. If she's still there. What about this one: What if she never made it to her destination in one piece? Did you think of that one? How about these: What if she never made it home? What if time flows faster on her homeworld and we find she's lived and died before we even got to her? What if she hates me so much she refuses to return?"

Fear ramped up the volume of his voice and his breathing climbed as he paced in frantic circles, too terrified to mention to his brother the newest wrinkle, the bizarre message from the ancient Seer still ringing in his ears.

"I wouldn't blame her one bit if she did," Kahlym said. "Do you know what she asked of me?" He spun round, nearly running headlong into Brel as his brother trailed after him. "One thing. She asked only one thing from me: She asked to be my strength and not my weakness." His throat tightened, choking on the last word.

He still pictured that exact moment with crystal clarity: Her legs wrapped around his waist as he plunged deep inside her warm sheath; all of her bloodwine curls cascaded around her flushed skin and her short nails dug into his chest; sweat created tempting trails between her lush breasts, the drive to capture the stray drops with his tongue too much to endure. His heart had knocked against his rib cage as he looked down at her. Tears had streamed down her face even as she shuddered in post-coital bliss. She had pleaded for him to not give up on them.

Brel gripped Kahlym's biceps, jerking him to a halt. "Well, she told me she was afraid you would do something stupid over her." This time, the slap was not physical, though the blow just as surprising. "Now, do I think what you did falls into the category of monumentally idiotic? No. Baby steps dumb? Definitely." A slight smile warmed his lips, and he released his death grip on Kahlym's arms. "But you had to make the tough call none of us could have. She needed to be out of Father's hands as quickly as possible, and if she had remained, I doubt we could have gotten her away in time."

"I have to get her back, *kherdes.*" Though he despised vocalizing his fear, perhaps once spoken, the emptiness would subside. The words of the ancient woman from his waking dream spun in furious circles in his head, yet he was unwilling to voice them. "I … things have changed. Things about the prophecy."

"Ontaxa in five."

Dhaerin's voice had cut through the ensuing, heavy silence. Seconds continued to tick by while Kahlym waited for an answer to appear out of the heavens.

"Changed?" said Brel. "Changed how?"

Kahlym leveled his gaze, meeting curious citrine. "I'm not sure if it was nothing more than another nightmare, or a portent. Either way, I must find her again."

"I promise we will never stop trying."

Absolute certainty rang through Brel's determined words and Kahlym's heart echoed the sentiment, cheering and beating with renewed purpose. Even his pragmatic mind latched on to the tiny beacon of hope and held on for dear life. He listened again to the short statement inside his head. His brother's voice held no guile, no feigned sympathy, no obsequious bolstering. Only truth filled the space between them.

In a very short amount of time, Evainne had become such an important part of their tight-knit crew. Her open acceptance and fresh perspectives had touched each member in a deeply profound way. Although nothing about her projected weakness, the big-and-burly bruisers on his crew immediately took her under their wings, donning the role of overbearing big brothers with delight. Even his grouchy tech, Falka, had warmed in the presence of his angel.

The connection between her and Brel went far deeper, though it didn't hold a candle to his own feelings. Time and again, with every action, Evainne crawled further into his soul. Blood debt be damned. Even if she had never picked up that blaster what seemed like a lifetime ago, he would still love her with a depth that terrified him.

Brel placed his hand on Kahlym's shoulder, dragging him out of his thoughts. Kahlym met his brother's confident stare with a painful trepidation. The days without her had been sheer hell; he dared not think what years of searching would do to him. With a weary sigh, he dragged his hand across his stubbled cheek. He'd been hiding from his razor, since he had no real reason to look presentable. He was sure he didn't smell like a flower, either.

"Clean up, Kahl. It'll help clear your head." With a comforting pat, Brel moved toward the entry. "Besides, you stink like a tulmak's ass."

Kahlym dropped his shoulders as Brel's laughter echoed off the walls before fading behind the closing door.

Blessed Ishtanti, may time be on my side, and please bring my angel back to me.

Chapter 4

"Wait. Explain this to me again. How the fuck is this going to work?"

Evainne groaned as Bao repeated his question for the umpteenth time. After borrowing a much warmer outfit, she'd begun working on a way back. Xandar had reluctantly agreed to help, though his decision on returning with her was still in flux. But, not wanting to waste another second, Evainne had launched into her rather harebrained yet simultaneously brilliant plan. Granted, the whole physics thing was never her strong suit. That's why she needed a scientist.

For every suggestion she'd made, Xandar had found some reason for it not to work. Little did he know, however, she wouldn't be deterred. In fact, all of her former teacher's naysaying simply invited even more creative solutions. If she didn't figure out this whole time/space problem, and soon, God only knew what kind of trouble Kahlym would get himself into.

She dug her thumbs into her throbbing temples, forcing down the blurring tears. Instead of giving in to her fears, Evainne channeled them, clenching her jaw as she growled out her response.

30

"It will work," she said, "because it has to. I got there." She threw her arm toward the sullen figure leaning against the wall. "He got here. There has to be a way to open the door on command."

She tugged up the sleeves on the enormous, faded charcoal sweatshirt that swallowed her, her legs wrapped in a pair of slightly too small leggings she'd found in the dojo's lost-and-found bin. If she could get into her apartment, she could raid her own wardrobe. Instead, she paced around the room in silent, socked feet. As soon as they had a viable solution, she could go back to her place and grab a change of clothes, plus a crapload of weapons, and return to the only place she called home.

Bao pinched the bridge of his nose, his great head shaking back and forth. "There has to be a way? You sound like my mother when she's got the remote in her hand: 'There has to be something decent on TV,' she says. 'No, Ma,' I say. 'There doesn't have to be some- thing *decent* on; there just has to be *something* on.'" He jumped up from his chair and halted her current circuit. "I'm not trying to rain on your parade, Evie, but—"

"Bao, you don't get it." She aimed her pleading gaze at her friend. "I can't … I can't stay here." After a moment, she shifted her focus to Xandar, peering deep into his unearthly blue orbs. "So, come hell or high water, I will figure out how to get back."

Her rebuke must have done the trick; both men had the decency to search the floor for answers, though their admonished behavior did little to nothing in the way of finding a solution.

"Evainne," the silent shadow spoke, his tone soft yet steady, "it is growing late…" He raised a hand, forestalling any retort. "I am sure you are hungry and in need of rest."

"I'm fine, really, I—"

"But I am not. It may take hours to sort out the details." Xandar glided across the room, his long legs covering the scant distance in a handful of simple strides. She'd seen another move with such unconscious grace, and she choked back a sob. As much as she wanted sleep and its welcoming darkness to consume her, if she dared to dream, she knew what she would see. She couldn't banish the tourmaline eyes haunting her every step. Not until she was once again in his arms.

After I beat the crap out of him. Reality tapped her on the shoulder, and her warm-and-fuzzies vanished. He'd pushed her away, taking the easy way out. Evainne ground her teeth as anger roiled in her gut. Maybe she should just stay here.

A pair of large hands enveloped her shoulders, and Xandar pressed his forehead against hers, encouraging her eyelids to slip down.

<*Do not think too harshly of my brother. I am certain he believed he was doing the right thing.*>

She barked out a bitter laugh and wrapped her fingers around his wrists. "Which makes it even that much stupider." After a quick squeeze, she let go and leaned back. "Nothing good ever came out of people trying to do the right thing."

But the regally arched brow over one lapis blue eye told another story. "Evainne, you do not really believe that, do you? You have kept your courage and faith until now, and I do not think you are going to give up."

She opened her mouth to refute him, but his gentle head shake froze her tongue. "Please, give me a few hours to think."

Disheartened, she wanted so much to argue with him. But he was right. Again. For her, sleep was a pipe dream, though, and she didn't feel much like eating, either. But she wasn't the only passenger on board this crazy train. Maybe they did need a break. Was time enough of an ally to allow them a couple of few minutes to regroup?

Chapter 5

From his safe vantage point outside of the cockpit, Kahlym watched the deep black surrounding *Tiamat's Revenge* melt away as the bright silver sun of Ontaxa flared to life. Years had passed since he'd seen the black sand beaches and thick forests of his friends' homeworld. Only those loyal to the Stria were given clearance codes to land in the safe zones, and the natural vegetation blanketing the planet's inhabitable surface made Thrall scans impossible. Both his pilot and current co-pilot knew this land better than he did, and he knew his own presence was neither wanted nor needed at the moment.

Hovering over the already agitated pair of Ontaxians would not be his best choice. Dhaerin had made his disdain quite clear about Kahlym's earlier decision to return Evainne to her home, from the moment their ship slipped from Raedynese space. The fading yet still tender bruise on his cheek sat as a bold testament to how eloquently his pilot had made his point. Fists and insults had flown from both of them whenever they stood within arm's reach of each other since then, their barbs sharp and deadly accurate.

But his ship could not have been in better hands, so Kahlym left them to the task of reaching the landing dock while he clawed his way through the thick tension in the narrow confines of the cockpit, still hesitant to speak the necessary apology.

"Captain?"

He stalled his escape, stunned by the voice he'd avoided for the past few days.

"Yes, R'uan?"

He wanted to hate R'uan; wanted it desperately. He wanted to blame him for putting the original idea into his head, pointing his finger and screaming about it all being someone else's fault. Upon reflection of his recent actions, that's exactly what he'd been doing: cursing and blaming R'uan for his current plight.

Yet he couldn't hate the man for doing what he had been ordered to do. *And by you, specifically, you ass.* R'uan was his friend, and his friend deserved more than his silence. He turned around and clutched the door jamb for support, glimpsing only the shadowed reflection of sorrowful eyes, a thick, black-and-silver mane hiding the rest of R'uan's face.

"Dhaer is taking the ship to the closest and strongest transport hub." The normally deep and resonant voice was nothing more than a whispered hush of air, and Kahlym cringed at the damage his projected rage had wrought. After his much needed talk with his brother, Kahlym now discovered he had much more work to do, with the first bridge to be rebuilt standing before him.

Swallowing hard and choking on his pride, Kahlym sighed and placed a hand on R'uan's shoulder. "Thank you, my friend."

"Friend," Dhaerin scoffed, muttering under his breath. "That's rich, coming from you."

Kahlym scowled, a spiteful retort poised on the tip of his tongue. He could let them fall, then curl back into his hole. But they were more than his crewmates; they had all fought and bled, laughed and cried with, and for, each other for far too long.

"Just spit it out already," Kahlym growled. "I screwed up. Is that what you want to hear?"

Dhaerin swiveled the suspended grav chair to face him, his orange-and-brown eyes cold, and they held him fast. "It's a damned good start." He folded his burly arms across his chest, his angered gaze launching daggers across the narrow space.

Kahlym felt like a child standing in front of his father after some imagined slight, and the triggered memory set his teeth on edge. The urge to lash out was dangerously tempting. His pilot, sensing a misstep, relaxed his guarded posture, his stare sliding away.

"She's one of us, Kahl. She didn't deserve—"

"You know as well as I do exactly what would've happened to her," he yelled. "She would've been handed over to the emperor, after my father was done with her, and she would've been forced to birth the next generation of Divines for him." He glared at his friend, daring him to object. "You know it, I know it, and she deserved a whole hell of a lot more than that. That's why Ishtanti placed her in all our paths; we were chosen to protect her, and that's exactly what I did."

But rage gave way to hollow laughter, and Kahlym shook his head as he released the tight hold on his emotions. "Fuck, Dhaer, do you think this has been fun for me? I see her face in every shadow, and hear her voice even in the silence. I keep expecting her to come around a corner, taking Yhan'tu to task about wearing the regal robes."

And I haven't slept in my own cabin. That little gem, he kept to himself. None of his crew needed to know he had spent every night on the captain's platform, as far from his quarters as he could be and still be on board. He couldn't step into his room, knowing her scent still clung to everything—the bed, the shower, the very walls. Her presence, and its profound loss, rippled through the entire ship.

After a moment, Kahlym found his voice as well as his courage. "I … I trust your brother to be able to bring her back to us. To all of us. I have to." He shifted his apologetic stare to R'uan, whose snowflake obsidian eyes sat haunted. "I never should have taken my anger out on you, and I hope you can forgive me someday."

Kahlym dipped his chin and moved toward the open hatch.

"Kahlym?" R'uan again froze Kahlym in his tracks, although this time, his tone's familiar confidence had returned. Kahlym looked over his shoulder at his co-pilot, grateful to see a hint of a smile on his friend's face.

"We'll get her back, *kherdes-xahn*, if it is the last act in this life."

"Let's hope it doesn't come to that," Kahlym answered, with a weak grin of his own. "Our miracle is what we seek, and I can't afford to lose another brother."

"I just want her back so you'll stop being so much of an asshole," Dhaerin added, his playful tone returning, before he spun around to maneuver the ship into its final approach pattern. "I thought you were bad before she showed up. Now?" He *tsk*ed, shook his head, and chuckled as he followed the glowing beacons pointing them toward the open landing bay. "Come to find out, you only needed to get laid."

Kahlym smirked, grumbling as the brothers joked and bantered at his back. One heavy burden had been lifted off of his shoulders. Now to make amends with the rest of his crew. Unbidden, a beautiful memory slipped into his mind: Evainne curled in his lap as they sat in the med bay. With grace and ease, she'd deflected the unwanted advances of his treacherous navigator and had accepted his eclectic band of friends without batting an eye.

Blinking back threatening tears, Kahlym made a hasty retreat from the cockpit. His angel still needed his strength. This quest was far from over.

Chapter 6

Sub-Confidant Anaxar du Jhuen slammed his fist against the innocent table, scattering his gathered men as well as the papers on his desk. Rage seethed beneath his skin; he needed an outlet for his growing desire for violence.

Ten moons had risen since his abortion of a son had stolen away, like a thief in the night, taking the emperor's prize. No. "Taking" was not the correct word. "Throwing away" might be more apt. When the debris had settled, they'd discovered the transport terminal had been smashed beyond all hope of learning the traveler's final destination. Had he sent her to one of the Stria's strongholds?

The systems still loyal to the Rimmarian empire remained as a solid number, yet some homeworlds held a fool's hope for a shift in power.

Pathetic.

As long as the emperor maintained control of the Divines, the authority of the Thrall was unshakable. Anaxar knew this, and once he retrieved that bitch and handed her over to M'Uubair, his own future would be firmly set into its proper ranking.

37

"Perhaps you should have waited to make your deal with Gha'-jahn, husband."

Anaxar bared his teeth at his lady wife as Jaleen sauntered uninvited into the war chamber, refusing to be bullied by a look alone. Instead, she crossed the cracked marble inlaid floor, stopping only when she stood toe-to-toe with him. Condescending anger brimmed in her diamond white eyes. "I told you it was unwise to chase the Divine. Had you listened to me and waited until—"

The back of his hand across her mouth stopped any further tongue lashing. "Take care how you speak to me, wife," Anaxar growled out the once-loving term. "You tread on dangerous ground."

Jaleen cupped her cheek, angered shock reflecting back for a moment before self-preservation tempered her wounded pride.

"I do not care to hear how I should have waited. I only care about where to find the little … Divine," he spat. That frightened young female who'd used her wits and her wiles to lull him into a false sense of victory before turning the tables on him with a sway of her ample hips. He'd learned too late of her sharp intelligence, having believed her to be nothing more than a simpering child.

Only his wife had witnessed the Divine powers she wielded, and from the shadows still darkening her eyes whenever she spoke of the event, he did not doubt the truth of it. Jaleen had been so much more intelligent when he'd courted her in their youth. Did birthing three sons steal all of her mental capacities?

"A thousand apologies," she mumbled, "but I might have found someone with helpful information."

Anaxar arched a brow. "Some one?"

Jaleen gestured toward the open doorway, motioning in the servant cowering in the shadows. "Come forward, child." His wife's maternal tone did little to encourage the girl. Instead of a second request, though, his wife snapped her fingers, and the stooped maid shuffled closer. "Tell my husband what you told me."

The bowed shoulders bobbed up and down, the barely audible whispers directed to the floor, boiling Anaxar's anger.

"Speak up!" he and his lady wife barked out in perfect harmony.

"I-I-I overheard the c-c-cursed one speak of sending th-th-the Divine home."

Home. Anaxar's stomach lurched as that nugget sank in. He'd heard the Divine Haseunn, the last Traveler, had plucked the girl from her homeworld far across the vast expanse of space. Her home could be anywhere.

"Did they say more?" He already knew the answer, but it didn't hurt to ask the question. The frantic head shake solidified his instinct. "Go. If you remember anything else, come to the lady immediately."

Scuffling footfalls raced toward the exit, while Anaxar drummed his talons against his fisted knuckles. Home. He churned the concept before dismissing the notion. "As protective as the bastard acted toward her, I sincerely doubt he would truly blast her across the stars." *But where is she?*

"Husband?"

His wife's odd tone had captured his attention, and he shifted his gaze in her direction. She tapped her steepled fingertips lightly on her lips, barely hiding the devious grin, and he arched a brow, intrigued by her sudden excitement. "Yes?"

"I do recall news that one of the crew members from your son's..." His growl paused her words for only a moment. She leveled him a bland glare. "From your son's vessel had betrayed them."

Anaxar waited, gesturing for her to go on when his patience wore thin. "Perhaps," she purred, slinking closer to drag a finger along his jawline, "dear husband, you could make contact with such a potential ally? Money is always a strong incentive, don't you think?"

A wicked smile curled the corners of his lips, and he wrapped his arms tight around Jaleen's waist, pulling her against his chest.

"Do you wish to see your youngest one final time before he crosses the final threshold?"

She cupped his cheek as enticing shadows danced in her diamond eyes. "Remember, to kill him would defy prophecy." With a tempting sway of her hips, she leaned close, whispering into his ear. "Bring him back alive and let fate have her way with him."

And if that bitch of a Divine is with him, she will make a fine gift for the emperor. The returned prospect of his seat on the High Council stirred his blood, and he plundered his wife's parted lips.

Chapter 7

Darkness had long since swallowed the room, plunging Evainne into a downward spiral of self-doubt, anger, and frustration. Her heart screamed at her to run through the place, yelling, demanding everyone wake up and get back to figuring this out. Her body, however, had no interest in doing much more than improving upon its current impression of a piece of furniture. If she could get her mind to even function, she might be able to find some compromise.

Until then, though, she remained glued to the padded floor, her arms holding her tucked-in legs close to her chest as she stared at nothing. She knew she'd pay for this uncomfortable position in the morning, but right now, she didn't have the desire to move. Sleep hadn't been an option, as she discovered, when the silence had become deafening hours earlier. Each time she closed her eyes, she was immediately transported back to that horrible room, pounding her fists against the shimmering barrier, calling out to Kahlym.

Dammit. Can't I catch a break?

With a heavy groan, she once again dragged the damp sleeve across her eyes. She was so tired of crying and had opted to blame her breakdowns on the lack of rest. Soon, voices cracked the quiet, and she lifted her head. Seemed the universe still spun, with the first morning's light drifting in through the narrow windows overhead.

"Hey, Evie. Did you sit there all night long?" Bao's sleepy-yet-accurate appraisal of the situation drew a weak smile from her. "Tell me you at least got a little shut eye?" he said.

Evainne uncurled her cramped legs to force the muscles out of their hours of disuse and, joining in with the sunrise stretch crew, she climbed clumsily to her feet, shaking out the pins and needles below her knees.

"I got a little shut eye," she parroted back dutifully, refusing to glance in his direction.

An exasperated sigh echoed through the open space. "You know you suck at lying, Evie."

"What time is it?" She feared the answer, though not knowing scared her more. She refused to try to compute the amount of time that must have passed for Kahlym and his crew; the math hurt her brain too much. So, rather than face her growing fears, she opted to hide in the mundane rolling and unrolling of her baggy sleeves.

"It's time for you to slow down and eat something." Bao crossed into her space and waited for her to stop fidgeting. "I mean it. You're gonna blow a gasket if you continue on like this."

On cue, Xandar strolled into the room with a tray of familiar fruits and cheeses. As she stared at the normal red apple, Evainne stuttered, swallowing down her rising sadness. He set down the platter and leaned in, his words meant only for her ears. "Have you tried to reach out to Kahlym?"

Really? If he weren't standing so close, she could have hit him more easily.

"What do you think I've been doing?" she hissed out between clenched teeth.

Her mentor pulled away with an enigmatic smile. "Hiding, so lost in your anger and hurt that you have not been listening."

Evainne stared, slack-jawed, at nothing in particular as the pair of footfalls faded into the distance, vaguely aware of a door opening and closing. Alone again in the silence of the empty room, she mulled over Xandar's simple response.

The moment of truth had arrived and she stood mutely before it. She'd been so focused and determined with her own agenda, she never thought to give him a call. Was she punishing him for his actions? Was she secretly reveling in tormenting him?

Her fragile trust had taken a heavy blow as she stood in front of the chipped blue door she never expected to see again. Was she that lost in her sense of betrayal, unwilling to give him a chance to explain his reasoning? Had their roles been reversed, would she have done any different?

She growled, disgusted with her Monday morning quarterbacking. Sure, it was easy to sit back after the fact and say how things could have gone. *Every story has three sides: yours, mine, and the truth.* She had her version of the events, but his side was missing, with the final piece a twisting combination of both. Without all of the details, she was spinning her wheels in dangerous circles.

All of these logical theories, though, did nothing to make her any less upset. Her lover had tossed her into the nearest cage and locked the door to keep her safe from the big bad monster outside, and the longer she pondered his actions, the more she discovered the exact nature of her anger. He'd not only felt the overpowering need to shield her, but he also hadn't believed she could protect herself. And that's what hurt the most. Just like everyone else in her past, Kahlym had viewed her as weak and incapable of surviving on her own.

She reflected back on the moment they had first met. When had things changed? As they had run hand in hand down that endless corridor, watching each other's back, she had been an equal. He'd placed his trust in her, and she'd felt wanted. They had moved perfectly in tandem; even their legs pumped in synchronous harmony. In that dangerous moment, they'd solidified their role as a team. As soon as her special stature had come to light, though, everything had shifted. No longer were they two people with an undeniable attraction; she was now the exalted Divine and he was the deformed outcast. Evainne had had glimpses, stolen moments, where she'd seen the possibility of a lasting love. Yet, for each declaration of affection he made, he was back to cowering in the shadows with the next breath. This irked her so much, she wanted to wring his neck.

Or kiss him so hard, it would chase away the pain.

She sniffled and dashed the escaping tears with her overlong sleeve. She needed a clear head. Sleep and a decent meal had sounded tempting, but at the mere thought of food, her stomach knotted. Even the innocent apples and grapes before her sat unappealing.

"Evie? You still here?"

She furrowed her eyebrows, swinging her gaze around the bright room to find the speaker. Bao munched on a burger, the scent of charred meat tugging at her gag reflex. A couple of coughs and some tough swallows later, she was able to walk toward him without the urge to vomit on his shoes.

She shoved the stretched-out cuffs over her elbows again and shrugged. "Didn't really have anywhere else to go."

Bao offered her a sympathetic grin, as well as his burger, which she waved off, though she did step in for a needed hug. Wrapping her arms around his wide girth, she was transported back to a darker time in her life: After being kicked out of the latest boarding school for asking why, or refusing to toe the line without a good reason, her parents had changed the locks on the main house.

She'd huddled under the great eaves of the family mansion, shivering as the freezing rain had slowly drenched her. The feeling in her feet had long since vanished and she'd pounded her knuckles raw, her insides nearly as cold as her outsides, with despair and defeat consuming her. The people who were supposed to have loved and supported her had cast her aside—again. The spiteful words swirled in her mind, attack after attack laced with a bitter resentment and constant disappointment. Nothing she ever did had pleased them. No matter how hard she tried, they had been unwilling to accept she simply had other interests, other passions that drove her, none of which could be tied to wealth or pandering to the city's elite. She hadn't been what they'd expected, and they despised her for it.

As if a light bulb had appeared over her head, its dim glow illuminating the way to a painful truth, Evainne had realized she'd never again set foot inside the cold stones before her. That place was no longer her home, only a building where she kept a few of her things. She had refused to let this knowledge break her, though, and she'd known her parents stood just beyond the bolted threshold, listening with malicious glee. So, with her remaining shred of dignity, she'd squared her shoulders and stepped off the porch.

Before long, a voice had called out, its timbre completely wrong for either of her hateful parental units. She'd nearly continued on her trip to nowhere, but a thick blanket, as well as a pair of beefy arms, had wrapped around her and hurried her into the shelter of the servant's quarters. She must have looked like a pathetic drowned rat, hair in knotted dreads, school uniform plastered to her body. However, the silent giant had kept his comments to himself as he and her parents' cook had scurried to find her something dry to wear and something warm to eat.

Since that dark night when she was thirteen, Bao and his mother had been the only real family she'd ever experienced.

"Don't worry, *củ chuối*," Bao said. "We'll figure this out."

Evainne barked out a laugh at the nickname she hadn't heard for so many years. At first, she'd been honored by the title, assuming it was something reserved and given with great respect. When she'd discovered he was basically calling her a weirdo, she'd popped him in the arm. But his infectious laughter, and his relentless tickling, had brought an unaccustomed smile to her face and the term stuck.

"We have to." She gave him one final squeeze, then let go. "No ifs about it."

"This Kahlym guy must really be something for you to be so eager to get back to him."

Thank you, Captain Obvious. Instead of her go-to phrase slipping from her lips, a strange warmth pricked her cheeks and she nodded, the corners of her mouth pulling up even as she tried to bury her true feelings. "I wouldn't go that far right now."

Bao's dark, slanted eyes crinkled, joy seeping through the narrow space between them. She knew that look, and she knew what was coming next. Either her reflexes had slowed, or part of her wanted the impending show of affection, but whichever the reason, Evainne managed only a feeble sidestep before being enveloped in a bone-crunching bear hug.

"I am so happy for you, Evie." He bounded around the room with her, flinging her about like a child's rag doll. Boisterous peals of laughter rang out through the padded space as Evainne gasped for air, a smile on her face.

"Geez. I should've known better than to say anything to you." Her words had squeaked out in time with each bounce. When oxygen deprivation started to look like a reality, she tapped Bao on the shoulder and her feet found the floor again.

"Damn, this is just so great." His smile faltered. "Wish I could meet him."

Her heart stuttered. She hadn't even considered that. "You could come back with us?" That which started out as a statement ended up with a question mark. As long as Bao had his mother, he wouldn't leave.

An idea crept into the fringes of her mind and she took a deep breath, then stood on her tiptoes to cradle Bao's head. "How 'bout we split the difference?" she asked.

Bao hesitated, but then followed her lead and leaned down. Evainne closed her eyes and, conjuring up an image of Kahlym, pressed her forehead against Bao's.

"Whoa."

A weary smile touched her lips and butterflies fluttered to life deep within her, rekindling the dormant fire. The memory was so visceral, she thought his breath tickled the back of her neck. Tourmaline eyes blinked at her, happiness sparkling within the bi-colored depths.

"Is that … were you on a real spaceship?"

His astonishment encouraged her to share a little more. She picked out other moments, keeping the private things hidden: She paraded R'uan and Dhaerin laughing, Yhan'tu and Falka trying hard not to drop down in reverence, and even a stray peek at some of the nastier folks she'd encountered. Views through various windows, and scenery of unreal beauty, flowed in the background, each otherworldly color popping in vivid detail, and her captive audience gasped, oohed, and ahhed in all right places.

"Holy crap! Does … does that person have three arms? Way cool."

When the details of her return voyage had begun to run, Evainne found the off switch and ended the playback. Now alone in the dark of her own mind, she prayed for the strength to find a way back.

"Come, Evainne. It is time for you, and for me, to go home."

She pried open her eyes and lifted her gaze. Her teacher had transformed before her; no longer did she see the blind man who'd so patiently guided her to find her inner power. No, now she saw a Raedynese warrior in full, resplendent glory. The gearsuit still fit him like a glove, and she shook her head, dismissing the visage of her lover as his brother stepped closer.

"Now?" she croaked, coughing to restart her vocal cords. Her brain fired in twelve thousand different directions, with one prime question banging on the inside of her skull: *Why now?*

His long legs made short work of the distance between them, and soon, he stood tall before her. "Because now," he said, "you are ready to lead the way." He offered her a pair of cross trainers, then waited.

An exasperated sigh slipped from her lips and she frowned,

struggling to ferret out meaning from his latest fortune cookie response. She tried to reply, but a sharp nod froze her tongue.

"Once you shared your experiences with Bao, you discovered the most direct pathway back. For whether or not you believe in destiny, Evainne, you are the Divine foretold on the day of Kahlym's birth. You can bring us back to the Dantaran galaxy, and you can stop the endless years of Thrall tyranny."

She forced her eyelids to blink, though it took some effort. Only one option seemed like a viable solution.

Evainne tossed her head back and bellowed out great waves of rolling laughter. Sleep deprivation must have finally caught up with her. Not to mention the whole idea was pure insanity. Nothing made any sense, and her emotional outburst threw her back into a sterile room with much different company. Without warning, the peals of laughter turned to sobs as she fought for control.

Someone shook her with a gentle yet centering force. "*Learom,* I know how this may sound. I—"

"No, you don't know how this sounds!" she shouted, frustration grounding her. "It sounds like complete and utter bullshit. That's all it sounds like to me. First, you tell me you don't want to go back, and now, I'm supposed to be the knifepoint of an interstellar rebellion." She glared into Xandar's unflinching midnight blue eyes, daring him to contradict her.

"You are as you were always meant to be."

She yanked free her arms, needing some breathing room. "Cut the metaphysical crap, Toa. Why now? Why the change of heart? And don't bullshit me. I'm really tired and I'm just looking for a straight answer."

She planted her feet, locking her fists onto her hipbones as she stared at him. Her old teacher's face remained unreadable, though she could pick out some of the louder thoughts firing through his mind—family, amends, destiny, and redemption all rose in peaks and valleys. Her muscles lost some of their determined tension, and she dropped her arms down to her sides and studied the floor, spying the discarded sneakers at her feet. They looked like they'd fit, but in her heart, she'd have rather been slipping into another ziploc gearsuit.

Xandar placed a hand onto her shoulder, and she met his sad smile. "By sharing your memories with Bao, you have opened the door."

"And let me guess," she said, huffing out a weary laugh, "it won't stay open for long."

His grin tilted, and the family resemblance tripled. She gave herself a mental shake so as not to plant a huge kiss on his lips. Instead, she knelt and gathered up the shoes. Her brain might have been rusty with the shoelaces, but her fingers flew through the task. Xandar nodded, offering her his hand.

Moment of truth. She paused, her fingers hovering above his.

"Ugh. Fine." She gnawed on her bottom lip, then glanced down at her current attire. "Don't suppose I have time to stop at my place for a change of clothes?" Part of her knew the answer already, but it never hurt to ask.

The admonishing eyebrow arch spoke more than any words. "Would you prefer to return to the robes?"

Grumbling, Evainne slapped his palm before gripping his hand and climbing to her feet. "I am so gonna kick someone's ass, as soon as I get a better pair of pants."

Chuckling from nearby reminded her of the room's other occupant, and she turned her gaze to her oldest friend. Bao stood like a sentinel, wearing a broad grin as he guarded his chest with his folded arms.

At that moment, Evainne knew she would never see her adoptive brother again. She released Xandar's hand and dashed over to Bao. Unlike the members of Kahlym's crew, he welcomed her enthusiastic hug with one of his own. Her joints popped and her breath escaped, but she didn't care. She wanted to tell him how much she'd miss him, how much his family had saved her.

If only her brain could get her mouth to function.

Instead, she wrapped all of her unspoken words into one embrace. Her message must have gotten through—he pressed his cheek against the top of her head and patted her back.

"Go on, Evie. Go back to that man lucky enough to love you." Bao's strong voice was thick and hushed. She squeezed her eyes shut, walling the impending tears behind fragile lids.

"Gah, don't you start," she croaked out past the lump in her throat, and the big guy laughed, dissipating the sorrows. He released her and, holding her at arm's length, grinned broadly. Evainne responded with a less-than-convincing smile of her own. "I don't want to look like a friggin' raccoon when I finally get to beat the crap out of his brother."

She tossed a thumb in Xandar's general direction, then dragged her sleeve across her eyes. The faded gray fleece didn't darken with wetness too much, proving her grip on her emotions was getting better. Her heart cracked a little, though, as she set his face to memory. Warmth radiated from the looming presence at her back a moment before a hand rested on her shoulder.

A faint trace of electricity sizzled beneath her feet even as her gaze stayed riveted on her friend. Her return trek must have been priming to begin. Even though this world was no longer home to her, the thought of leaving Bao tugged on her heartstrings. As she mouthed a final farewell and waved, a tender squeeze as well as the whispered voice in her head centered her.

<*Find Kahlym. Draw on your memories and reach for him. The journey will guide itself.*>

Tingles crept up her legs, and her heart began to pound. Then panic froze her blood, and she gulped down short swallows of air. Was she now afraid of leaving?

<*You have nothing to fear,* learom. *I have faith in you.*>

The voice in her head reminded her of another, one far away. One whose touch she craved with each passing second. Her mind latched on to the last memory of Kahlym. Every detail jumped to the forefront, images so vivid that she reached out, hoping to brush her fingertips along his coppery skin. Pain and sadness swirled in his bi-colored eyes, and a stray tear slipped down her cheek.

A second hand gripped her shoulder, anchoring her to the shifting ground.

"Hold on tight." Evainne was unsure if the words had been spoken aloud or had been spinning around between her ears. Whichever, she closed her eyes and took a deep breath.

"I'm coming, Kahlym," she whispered.

A silent pulse boomed, and the world vanished.

Chapter 8

"Kahl? We're clear to go."

Kahlym blinked out of yet another lapse in concentration and looked up, meeting Dhaerin's curious frown. How long had his friend been waiting for him to respond?

"Sorry." He locked his jaw and groaned at his growing inability to focus. His salvation was finally within reach and all he could do was moon about like a lovestruck kid.

Dhaerin grinned, extended his hand. "Thought you would have run outta here, chasing after R'uan."

"I didn't think he wanted me breathing down his neck again," said Kahlym, taking the offer and following his pilot out of the cockpit. His apology had patched the rift between himself and his crew, but his head was still stuck in its dangerous rut of deadly questions.

What if she didn't reach home? What if they were unable to bring her back?

Kahlym hissed, pain crawling up the inside of his arm, and he glanced down to spy the trickle of blood from his clenched fist, his talons cutting deep into his fleshy palm. More growling, and he shook out his tense hand, wiped away the evidence on the leg of his gearsuit. Anger would not help this situation. He needed a clear head.

Boot heels clacking on the metal floor cut through the deep quiet as they passed through the ship in silence. He had to say something before he lost both his mind and his nerve.

"We'll get her back, Kahl." Dhaerin had beaten him to the punch, his profile confident as they arrived at the back of the ship. Kahlym paused as his pilot tapped the ramp release, then he clasped him on the shoulder. The conviction in Dhaerin's tawny-swirled eyes was infectious; an answering nod and a slight grin touching his lips warmed his heart.

"I pray Ishtanti will hear you, my friend."

"She'd better. Because if this doesn't work, I think the line to kick your mopey ass will loop around the planet twice."

Kahlym rolled his eyes as Dhaerin flashed a shit-eating grin, thumping him on the back as they stepped down the loading ramp. Air, thick and heavy, drifted in, along with the mingling scents of flowering trees and recent rains, banishing the stale, recirculated air from his vessel. He had forgotten the lush beauty of his friend's homeworld, the planet's perfect distance from Ontaxa's sun keeping the vegetation blooming throughout the year. He scanned the surrounding verdant canopy, the landing pad high above the treetops.

Pinpoints of light dotted the distant, bright violet mountains, leading the way to the cavernous cities and underground villages that housed the peace-loving Ontaxian populace. Long ago, the people of the greenest planet in the Seventh Quadrant had discovered the best way to ensure harmony was to train your entire race for war. Not even the Thrall Emperor himself dared to bring violence here. The man might have been a megalomaniacal overlord, but he was no idiot. Every Ontaxian—young and old, male and female—was well versed in various manners of combat, and no off-worlder knew all of the tunnel systems.

Kahlym inhaled deeply, pulling the fragrant calm into his soul. Yet the heady aroma did nothing to abate his mind's panic. He could only think of how much Evainne would have loved the tropical gardens and rain forests making up most of Ontaxa's lush landscape.

Frantic voices drew him out of his thoughts, and he snapped his gaze to the receding back of his pilot. He chased after Dhaerin, not wasting another second, ducking to avoid the low-hanging branches.

"Fuck, R'uan. Are you sure?" Dhaerin yelled into his comm link, and Kahlym's blood turned to ice. Something had gone wrong. He forced his legs to keep pumping. Dhaerin swore under his breath again and slammed on the brakes. Unable to stop his momentum, Kahlym collided with his friend as the big Ontaxian spun around.

"They moved the bloody transport hub." Dhaerin climbed around Kahlym and headed off in the opposite direction, while relief nearly dropped Kahlym to his knees. Instead, he remembered how to breathe and followed after his pilot.

"I leave for a little bit and look what happens." Grousing comments continued to bleed from his guide, but Kahlym paid these little mind, too busy trying to return his internal organs back to their places—his heart pounded against his rib cage, and his stomach was now neighbor with his kneecaps.

She still lives. She is not lost.

The words set pace for Kahlym's feet and he focused on nothing else while their twisting path crossed and crisscrossed the terrain. He hoped they were not desperately lost.

"Don't worry, Kahl." Dhaerin had tossed the shouted disclaimer over his shoulder as they chugged on. "From what I got from R'uan, the jungle decided to reclaim the new facilities, so they moved the equipment back to an older site."

A quick sidestep saved Kahlym's face from a whipping frond, but his heel caught a slick step. He windmilled his arms, throwing his weight forward, and managed a less than graceful series of slides to remain on his feet. If he remembered correctly, the

Ontaxian High Counsel chamber was very close to the central landing bays. Praying his memory was right, he zeroed in on the veiled entryway.

Dhaerin reached the door and triggered the release, just as Kahlym stumbled inside. Blinking rapidly, he carved out recognizable shapes from the flooding brightness. R'uan ordered Falka about, directing the tech around the narrow room, while Brel and Yhan'tu did their best to stay out of the way.

Tension clung to the walls, and Kahlym's panic returned in force.

"Then reset the fucking homing tracker."

R'uan rarely swore. This was not good.

"What happened?"

Kahlym's question fell like a death knell, freezing all occupants, his own heavy breathing the only sound cutting through the encompassing silence. His gaze roamed the chamber, but not one of his friends were willing to meet his eyes. Kahlym steeled his spine and stepped farther inside.

"I said. What. Happened?" His cold voice had mirrored the ice creeping through his veins, preparing him for the worst. He clenched his teeth and glared at his crew.

Movement from the control panel caught his attention, and he homed in on his nervous co-pilot.

"We … we can't find her."

Kahlym stared as his heart withered. Then he blinked, re-engaging his vocal cords. "Excuse me?"

"The coordinates are correct," R'uan said, quick to fill in a necessary blank, but Kahlym was lost. He still breathed, though he no longer had a reason to. "She did reach her destination," R'uan added, "but she simply is no longer anywhere near that area."

"That's because *she* didn't feel like waiting for a ride back."

Colors flared to life around Kahlym. Surprised and confused, he blinked repeatedly as his vision adjusted, unaware of their original disappearance until now. He whirled about, refusing to believe what he was hearing, praying that his mind had not snapped and was simply creating another elaborate hoax.

Standing inside the room was his angel. Her clothes were somewhat similar to the ones she had been wearing at their first meeting —flimsy, black material caressed her legs, while brightly adorned short boots protected her feet, though most of her body was engulfed in an overly large and loose-fitting tunic, its sleeves brushing her fingertips. Her long hair had been hastily secured in a twist, a couple of stray curls slipping free to tumble about her shoulders.

"E-Evainne?" he whispered, afraid anything louder would shatter the illusion.

A full second ticked by before her gaze locked with his. Pain, visceral and heartbreaking, reflected in her deep brown eyes. Other emotions swam in the troubled pools, but he couldn't see beyond the hurt he'd wrought.

"Yeah. Surprise." Her voice, both a salve on his soul and a slap on his face, had filled the quiet room, its rich tones coating the walls.

Brel whooped in delight and launched himself across the room. Relieved laughter warmed the somber mood as the rest of the crew sprung to life to join Kahlym's brother in the celebration. But Kahlym remained glued to the floor, legs unable to move, heavy heart struggling to beat.

"How in the name of Bleakhell did you manage to make it here?" Brel said. "And before us, by the looks of it." Then he laughed, having asked the question waiting on the tip of Kahlym's tongue had he been brave enough to speak.

She was here—true and real—standing in this very room, and his guilty conscience refused to let him go to her.

Her accusing gaze remained fixed, the voice in his head shouting every manner of hate directed inward. "I did have a little help," she said, and she leaned back on her heels to glance over her shoulder. "You coming out or what?"

Out from a darkened alcove emerged a looming shadow, and

once again Kahlym had to remind his lungs how to breathe. Gone were the long warrior locks, and his shaved head glistened in the captured glow. Twisted geometrics in faded gold-and-plum marked the left side of his face, while faint scars spiderwebbed along his exposed throat. Broad shoulders filled out the older-generation gearsuit, seams straining against the extra muscle. But as long as he lived, Kahlym would never forget those eyes. The deep, perfect lapis blue orbs had tormented his days, simultaneously reminding him of better times and unbearable grief.

"How … How can this … Xandar?"

His sibling's long-forgotten face grew larger and closer, but he spied no movement from the impossible statue guarding the corner.

"Did she bring you back from the grave?" Kahlym asked. All rational thought had fled, leaving only numb confusion in its wake.

"Dorchester, actually," Evainne chimed in, wriggling free from Brel's enthusiastic embrace. "But close enough."

Kahlym's head swiveled between the two faces—one he thought he'd never see again, and one he was sure he'd never see again.

"Hello, *xahn'cal.*" The childhood nickname threw him into an emotional tailspin, and the wheel of responses landed on rage. Kahlym launched himself at his long-missing brother, fists flying unchecked.

He was vaguely aware of arms pulling him off of his prey, but he wasn't yet ready to give up on his confused anger.

"All this time. All this fucking time, I've been blaming myself for your death, and you've been—" Nothing was real any longer. His dead brother lived. His angel despised him. He was lost, adrift on a turbulent sea of doubt and senseless existence, so wrath seemed the only viable course of action.

"Kahl! Stop." Brel's voice had sliced through the madness, adding to the vice-like grip on Kahlym's shoulder. "How about we all sit down and talk, huh?"

Kahlym snarled out a guttural response, beyond consolation and nearly beyond reason, as Brel continued to drag him away, moving toward the center of the room.

Kahlym's eyes remained fixed on the apparitions, his pride hidden in an unreachable corner of his heart, embarrassed by his childish tantrum. He should have been happy beyond words, relieved by the reappearance of those dear to him. Instead, he had rebelled, lashing out in any and all directions.

Was his control so far gone there was no turning back?

He had expected to see disgust in the dark blue orbs of his brother; rather, he saw acceptance and contrition. Sorrow had cut long furrows into his soft ebony forehead, banishing Xandar's laugh lines from Kahlym's memory.

"No, Brel," he said. "Let him go. He has more than earned his anger." With a deep sigh, Xandar shifted his gaze and offered a sad smile to the stunned group. "And I do have some explaining to do."

The moment frozen, Kahlym's eyes darted, landing briefly on each face. Silence in the room was like glass; no one seemed ready to throw the first stone.

"Oh, for fuck's sake," Evainne said, her exasperated voice shattering the stalemate. All heads swiveled in her direction. "I swear to Christ, I have no idea how you stubborn, dumbass men ever got as much power as you have in any universe." She stalked over to Kahlym, who tensed, preparing for her impending attack. As surprising as ever, she grabbed his arm and led him to the nearest chair. He could do nothing but follow and collapse in the seat as ordered. "Always thinking with the head in your pants instead of the one on your shoulders," she added. His gaze locked on to her natural grace, his heart aching as she moved around the room, grumbling under her breath as she retrieved his crew, one by one.

"Falka, you deserve a goddamned medal of honor for sticking it out with these testosterone junkies." After a couple circuits, Evainne had corralled everyone present, including their unexpected visitor, into the available chairs, before claiming the last open seat. "Now, I don't have time for any more bullshit. I'm tired, starving, uncomfortable as hell, and in desperate need of a shower. So, who's going first?" She plopped down and glared at the group.

Kahlym gaped, words failing him, but one of his crew had a solution. Brel tossed back his head, his laughter filling the cavernous space. It took only a moment for his crew to join in the frivolity.

"I cannot begin to tell you how much you have been missed, *learom-xahn*." Brel swiped his sleeve against his face, wiping away the mirthful tears. While Kahlym wished nothing more than to share in the happiness, the haunted shadows darkening his angel's eyes prevented his heart from leaping with joy, and shame shifted his gaze to study the floor at his feet.

"Yeah, yeah." Her husky voice sent forgotten electricity through Kahlym's veins. "You know me; never one to mince words." Her sigh brushed across his soul and he swallowed back the agony. His brother had told the others Kahlym was allowed his anger. Now, he must give the same allowance to his angel. If their connection was real and worth saving, she would need time and space.

He glanced across the short distance separating them, wanting nothing more than to gather her into his arms and kiss away the pain in her heart. Yet the dangerous darkness in her eyes had warned him against his desired course of action. Though he desperately wanted to test their link, he feared her rejection.

Again, Brel broke the tension with a simple query. "How did you guys get here?" He took a deep breath. "And were you here before us?"

Xandar paused from rubbing his jaw, his gaze scanning the apprehensive faces. "I believe that story is for our Divine."

Chapter 9

Evainne blinked as all heads swiveled her direction and seven sets of inhuman eyes focused on her with laser-like precision. She hadn't even had a chance to get her bearings yet. She'd simply been standing in the dojo before it melted and morphed into thick jungle. None of the faces she longed to see were around, and she'd begun to panic. She'd expected to be dropped back into a smoldering room, or maybe even materializing on the ship. But green as far as the eye could see?

She was extremely grateful to have dragged Xandar along for the ride, though, since he was definitely more familiar with this part of the universe. Ontaxa. The name had rung a distant bell but nothing she could hold on to. Confused, she'd opened her mouth to ask what went wrong, only to hear R'uan's voice, followed by more of Kahlym's crew. Xandar had ushered her into the shadows as they waited for all parties to arrive.

In truth, she'd hoped her reappearance would be in the cockpit of Kahlym's ship. *Just to see the look on his face.*

Yet even with him now close enough to touch, he was still on the opposite end of the universe. The usual spark in his tourmaline eyes was absent, as was the soft caress of his voice in her head. How much time had passed since their last meeting? Only a handful hours had been lost for her—less than a day—but how much more for him, she could only guess. She didn't remember the dark stubble shadowing his jaw, or the rugged facial hair and wild mane solidifying the family resemblance among the three brothers. He also appeared leaner than the last time. Must have been a trick of the light.

Well, if he could move on, then so can I.

A lie, but what else could she do? She was beyond exhausted, and her heart ached the longer she sat near Kahlym without ripping his clothes off. Or beating him senseless. Tough call.

"Huh?" She blinked, vaguely aware of the surrounding conversation, suddenly realizing a response from her was required.

Brel chuckled and, leaning forward, rested his hands on his thighs. "The first question was: How did you guys get here before us? But I'm beginning to think a better one would be: When was the last time you slept, *learom*?"

She shrugged, giving him half a smile. "Beats me, hon. How long has it been since, um … well…"

Her voice dried up as she struggled to speak aloud her feelings of betrayal.

"Ten moon-risings have passed since you were returned to your home," Kahlym replied. Chills marched along her spine, her blood fleeing south even as her heart threatened to break. The rich tone that once turned her insides to mush was sadly missing, cold indifference having fallen from his lips.

Her defense mechanisms kicked into gear, eager to protect her shattered soul and to inflict a little damage in return. She glared at Kahlym, arms tensing as if preparing for battle.

"Gee, don't sound so broken up," she said. "Next time you throw my ass out, I'll stay away longer."

The second the hateful words had slipped from her tongue, regret strangled her. She could blame exhaustion as much as she wanted, but she was hurting and she needed to spread some of that ugly wealth around.

"Told you she wouldn't go easily."

She pivoted to Brel, who wore a confident smirk. Evainne's brows tugged together as she pulled apart his cryptic message. "You're goddamned right," she said. "And why the hell was that even an option in the first place?"

Her inability to censor her language was a warning sign; she only lost complete control of her profanity meter when she was beyond rational function. But, as beat as she was, if she didn't get some answers, sleep would never find her.

She waved off the impending explanation, certain it would start with those famous words: *You must understand.* She was done understanding, and she was done with waiting for someone else to take the reins of the conversation.

"You know what? Screw it. I don't have time for this." She looked at Xandar. "Your turn, chief. Besides, I think they want to hear your story more than mine."

Her diversion technique worked and the spotlight swung away from her. No longer under the microscope, Evainne breathed a sigh of relief. Only one pair of eyes remained unchanged and unmoving, and her heart picked up a beat or two the longer she felt the heat from the unyielding, bi-colored orbs. It would be so easy to turn her face the scant inches needed to capture his gaze.

Too easy. And she was in no mood to make things simple.

While Xandar's lips moved and heads nodded, nothing pierced the blanket of tense silence wrapped around her and Kahlym. She observed, from a distance, arms gesturing as story hour continued beyond her quiet bubble. A faint breeze ruffled the hairs on the back of her neck, imaginary fingers brushing her sensitive skin. She locked her jaw and blocked his further comforts with a determined one-finger salute. Her head ached as she fought against the urge to slide her narrowed glare toward him.

For as long as she lived, his tourmaline eyes would forever call to her soul. His voice whispered to her and her alone, pleading for a chance to be heard. In those fuchsia-and-jade depths, she'd seen all the things she'd dreamed of for herself but never believed she could have: happiness, love, a future with someone by her side.

But she now realized the most important element was missing: trust.

Until he could accept her as an equal, she would keep him at arm's length, no matter how much her body and her heart rebelled at the idea. Even now, she fought against her baser self, the part craving to feel his lips on her skin, as well as the sensation of his throbbing shaft filling her so completely. Clamping down on her raging libido, she shook her head and dropped her gaze.

"So, are we all caught up enough?" she grumbled, not caring if she'd interrupted right at the good part. "Is this place safe?"

Dhaerin stood, a proud smile on his bushy face. "No place safer in the whole of the Dantaran galaxy. You're on my homeworld and one of the Stria's most loyal strongholds. We can remain here as long as you'd like."

Evainne stretched out her legs before joining the leonine giant in the mush pot. For a split second, her knees buckled, and she swore to cover up her fatigue, grabbing the back of her chair to stay on her feet.

"*Dym Char'ann*, are you unwell?"

She gnashed her teeth and shook her head. "Ah, Yhan'tu. Always the master of the obvious." Tensions had dissipated, surely from Xandar's explanation of his whereabouts for the past decade, but the true comfort she longed for was still a pipe dream. "Nah, I'm good. Just needing to sleep for the next week or so."

R'uan rose to stand beside his brother. "We can find lodgings for everyone within our family's grotto."

Dhaerin grinned proudly as he folded his arms across his chest and leaned back against his denmate's shoulder. "Hell, there's enough room there to house half the rebellion and still have everyone with their own bathroom."

The longer Evainne remained vertical, the more she doubted her ability to get anywhere under her own power. Adrenaline had run its course and left nothing but fumes in the tank. *Dammit, why now?*

"Well, I hope they're close," she said. The figures around her blurred along the edges, and she struggled to focus her eyes. "'Cuz I have no idea how much farther I can—"

She could have sworn she'd finished her thought, but the world tilted and spun. One minute, she was standing; the next, she was staring up at the ceiling, the living ground soft beneath her. A pair of lapis eyes flashed into her field of vision before being replaced by the intoxicating tourmaline depths of her dreams. Empty tears slipped down her cheek, grief gripping her heart, as she let exhaustion and its comforting darkness consume her.

"I have you, *ziat'xahn*." The words brushed against her soul, tapping lightly on the flimsy armor protecting her fragile love.

But will you keep me?

Chapter 10

Kahlym swallowed hard, the accusatory question in the mind of his angel striking a blow more deadly than any wound. He shifted his gaze from her sleeping visage to the face of his long-absent brother.

"She refused to rest until she returned to you, *kherdes*." Xandar rested a hand on Kahlym's shoulder, sad wisdom reflecting in his deep, lapis blue eyes. "She truly does love you."

"And I cast her away at the first sign of danger." Stark resignation choked him. His beautiful Divine, who had braved all manners of trials and tribulations with grace and spirit, including facing down his father … and he tried to hide her under the nearest table when the tide began to shift.

"Do not be so hard on yourself, Kahl," Xandar said, his quiet voice cutting through Kahlym's anguish. "You only did as you saw fit in the moment. But do not discount her abilities. She is much stronger than any of us give her credit."

He contemplated his brother's epiphany and could find no fault in his logic. He sighed and nodded in agreement. "How do I make this right? If our places were reversed, I don't think I would ever trust me again."

Brel bumped against Kahlym's shoulder, forcibly yanking him further out of his pit of self-loathing. "Then I guess we're all lucky you are not her." Kahlym shifted his gaze from Evainne to glare at his smirking brother as Brel passed by. "Personally, I think you'd look like shit in a dress."

The rest of his crew stood poised at the doorway, waiting for their newest party members to join them. Everyone needed rest, but Kahlym was still frozen in place, unable to will his body into motion. He shifted his gaze back to Xandar, so many questions rattling around in his mind with one jumping to the head of the line.

"How … how is it that you found her on Terra? Was it chance, or fate? Were … were there others in her life before you?" Too many demands fired through Kahlym's head. Doubt and envy swirled in dangerous circles, and he hoped the fierce jealousy ringing in his own ears did not reach his voice.

Xandar smiled and stood up, offering his hand. "You have no need to fear, Kahlym," he said as Kahlym gathered Evainne into his arms and regained his feet to stand next to his brother. "She has been nothing more than a pupil of mine. And of the others of which you speak, they only brought her tears and grief. Her heart has never belonged to another before you, and she has chosen to give it to you alone."

Kahlym cradled the tender bundle against his chest and took comfort in the hope she could forgive him. With a deep inhale, he dragged her scent back into his soul, betrayal souring the flowers-and-spice he longed to taste again. He was thrown back to the first time he'd held her like this—she'd awoken in the med bay, sobbing, heavy emotions pouring off of her like rain against a slanted roof.

He'd promised to protect her then, and those words still held true. Kahlym closed his eyes, blocking the further stroll through his memories, and placed a soft kiss atop her thick tresses.

"You have grown taller than I had imagined, *kherdes-xahn*." Lifting his lids, Kahlym realized he now stood eye-to-eye with his older brother. As the youngest, Kahlym had been dwarfed by both his siblings, and Brel had towered over both of them. Time had allowed Kahlym to play catch-up, and now he surpassed Xandar by a fraction or two.

"And moodier," Brel chimed in from across the room.

"And stubborner," added Dhaerin.

"And don't even get me started on his temper," R'uan said, intently focused on shutting down the transport controls.

Kahlym growled under his breath as his crew continued to enthusiastically point out his many faults. "All right, all right." Laughter broke the heavy tension, and even he dared to crack a smile. "R'uan, where are the closest rooms?" It was easy to ignore the good-natured jabs at his back when his salvation was curled against his chest. Xandar was right. He would need to do some serious penance to earn back her trust.

Hard to believe it had only been ten moon-risings since she'd slept by his side, and each second away from her had been agony. That, however, paled in comparison to the guilt that had wracked his soul when he'd seen the heartbreaking flatness in her eyes. Gone was the fire that had ignited his blood, its absent spark dragging the air out of his lungs. A sanctimonious voice in his head whispered venomous words.

What did you expect? Her gratitude?

He'd made a decision in haste, and now, he'd suffer the consequences of his knee-jerk reaction.

Just plain jerk is more like it. The corners of his lips tugged up as he imagined the uncensored response from Evainne.

With a heavy sigh, he followed R'uan out of the transport hub, hugging close his sleeping female. As her even breathing fanned against his exposed throat, he vowed to do whatever it took to prove himself worthy of her love and her trust.

His gaze darted around the dense jungle, distant sunlight

filtering through the thick canopy, keeping the planet's floor in perpetual twilight. The trees swallowed the sounds of the surrounding world, with only the musical songs of hidden birds breaking through the comforting silence. He spied the flash of brightly colored feathers as their group continued down the winding path.

As they trekked through the thick vegetation, Kahlym began a mental list of destinations for Evainne to see as soon as she was awake; he set to memory each twist and turn that brought them to a beautiful vista or a secluded grove. She'd asked for visits to the gardens on his homeworld, and due to his father's treachery, she'd been denied the full experience. Now, in the comfort of their allies, he'd show her all the beauty she deserved to witness.

Soon, the trail poured out into a vast, open space, one of the many massive courtyards serving as the gathering places for the Ontaxian people. The footpath spiraled down past small shops and fruit vendors, the heady aroma cramping his empty stomach. As much as he wished to stop and grab something to eat, Kahlym had more important business to tend to, namely the bundle in his arms. He vaguely recalled Xandar's explanation, remarking on how his angel had neither rested nor ate for…

Exactly how long had they been separated? Had she gone hungry for days on end?

"Xandar?"

Kahlym glanced over his shoulder as his older brother joined him, Xandar's legs straining to keep up with Kahlym's determined pace. "Yeah. What's up?"

Kahlym's brows tugged together at the strange phrase, then he groaned in recognition of the determinedly Terran colloquialism. "You have been gone from us for nearly two decades. How much different did time pass for you?"

The smile Kahlym remembered from his childhood warmed the face next to him. "Our moon rises, or 'solar days' as they call them on Earth, are not as long. Or maybe it would be better to say time does not flow with quite the same pace there as it does here. So, to answer your unvoiced question and to my knowledge, she was only without food for a matter of a day. I am not sure how long after she returned that she found Bao, and he——"

"Bao?" Jealousy flared to life once again at the sound of the male pronoun, and on instinct, he clutched Evainne closer to his chest.

Another laugh and a brotherly pat on the shoulder eased his death grip on her.

"Please relax, Kahl. Bao is nothing more than another overprotective big brother. Is it so hard for you to believe she remains loyal to you and you alone?"

"Yes," he groaned, embarrassed by his own fear. "Because I do not know what I would do if I truly lost her." The confession had fallen from his lips before he could stop the words, and Kahlym cringed in self-loathing, preparing for the recrimination regarding his actions. Instead of the accusatory rationale, his brother gently squeezed his arm and offered him a sad smile.

"Then trust in your love for her. Trust her."

His eyes and his mouth popped open. Had she told him of their intimacy?

Xandar tilted his head, a knowing grin warming his lapis eyes. "She did not divulge any details, but her responses spoke far more than her words ever could. However, little brother," he added, his voice losing its earlier mirth, "let me ask you this: Was the world lacking when she was far from you?"

Kahlym pondered the question, swinging his jaw shut before he coaxed his voice into action. "Color only returned when I saw her again."

Xandar lifted one shoulder, nodding in understanding. "Then you have your answer. She is your true match and your soulbond remains unharmed. Now, do not misunderstand," he said, shifting his calming tone to a sharper reprimand, "she has been hurt by your perceived betrayal and is still angry. And rightly so. Remember, I trained her myself and I know there is nothing she cannot handle."

Kahlym replayed the dark moments prior to their parting of ways. "You don't understand, Xan. Father had sold us out to the emperor, with plans on defiling her before handing her over to be used as a broodmare for the remaining Divines. I—" Kahlym swallowed his disgust, trailing his hand along her arm to tamp down his anger, and met his brother's shocked face. "I couldn't let that happen."

"Bloody hell."

Leaving the open-air market behind them, they veered toward the caverns nestled deep in the foothills. Tunnels traversed the whole of Ontaxa, making it an ideal base of operation—so many landing docks were invisible to the uninitiated observer, several linking with arsenals and vicious traps designed to keep out unwanted guests. Had R'uan or Dhaerin not been with their group, they would not have made it past the edge of the tarmac, much less deep within the living heart of their cities.

A comfortable silence descended as they continued on their journey, and a long-missed tranquility seeped into Kahlym's soul. He craned his neck upwards, looking into the distant treetops as a soft mist began to gather, soothing and cooling. He held his angel closer to his chest, shielding her from the gentle damp.

Dhaerin grumbled from behind him. "Crap. This could get ugly fast, but we're almost there. Home is just around the bend."

As if on command, the rain began in earnest, and Kahlym jogged as carefully as possible, trying not to awaken the bundle in his arms. Rounding the corner, he spied the welcoming glow of the nearby dwelling and, not wasting a step, Kahlym continued his quick pace until he passed over the main threshold.

One by one, his crew were led down narrow paths to their own lodgings. Xandar touched his shoulder before peeling off, and Kahlym glanced up, locking eyes with him. Words were meaningless, so they were simply bypassed. With a gentle squeeze, Xandar nodded and ducked into his alcove.

A guiding hand pressing into the center of his back urged Kahlym forward, and he let Dhaerin direct his steps. "Come on." Their odd dance lasted only a few moments until Kahlym stood in a large sleeping chamber, the bed prepared, a small pile of firewood waiting and ready to warm the cozy room.

"This is my sister's place whenever she comes around." The big Ontaxian glided through the space with a graceful ease, quickly triggering the hearth. "Don't worry, Kahl. We have plenty of space here, and Zybella is off with her latest boy toy."

The sweetwood ignited and the damp chill vanished in tendrils of fragrant smoke that coiled up toward the chimney. Kahlym searched the room, spying an overstuffed chair and matching footrest, with a dresser rounding out the furnishings. But one thing was missing. His brows tugged together until Dhaerin tapped him on the shoulder, pointing toward an inset doorway.

"Each room has its own bath, so you don't have to worry. There's plenty of clothes in the closet. Zy is a bit bigger, but——"

Kahlym shook his head with a smile to stop the rest of the explanation. "This is more than I could ask for. Thank you."

Dhaerin smiled back. "I was kinda looking forward to tranqing your ass if we couldn't get her back." And Kahlym groaned as his friend's laughter rang out. Then the mood shifted, and Dhaerin placed a comforting hand on Kahlym's shoulder. "But honestly, I'm just glad she was smart enough to find us."

Kahlym nodded, words failing him as his pilot headed out and closed the door behind him. Now alone, he took a moment to send a grateful prayer to Ishtanti as he beheld the exquisite face of his sleeping beauty. She murmured and shifted about in his embrace, but did not awaken.

His eyes drifted shut, and he rested his cheek against hers. "I hope you can find it in your heart to forgive me."

Kahlym inhaled deeply, her fragrance wrapping around his

heart. In the dark of his thoughts, he saw her, her head thrown back in pleasure, and his mouth watered, savoring the recollection of his tongue across her sweat-dampened breasts. His palms tingled, and his cock jumped to life at the vivid memory of her welcoming body and of her passionate soul.

But the chill in the air yanked him back to the present. He crossed to the bed and gently laid down his tender bundle. Knowing time was of the essence, he quickly stripped her of the drenched clothing. Her thick shirt still held the earlier rainfall, and he tossed the heavy fabric onto the floor. Her porcelain skin glowed with a disquieting bluish tint. He made short work of the painted-on leg coverings, peeling away the clinging material and exposing more creamy flesh.

Had it not been for his impulsive actions, he'd be curling up beside her, losing himself in the comfort of her presence. Now, he faced an uphill climb to earn that right once again. His close proximity to her sent his blood racing down to his aching erection, and with a pained groan, he wrapped the blankets around his angel to drive away the chill. After limping over to the inset closet, Kahlym grabbed two items of clothing, not bothering to give them more than a passing glance, and his shoulders drooped in dejection when he took a better look at his selected garments. A sad smile touched his lips and he returned the bright pink ensemble to the closet, rummaging through the cluttered attire until he found a deep green-and-black mottled tunic.

Satisfied, he shuffled back to the sleeping bundle and laid the borrowed wardrobe across the narrow chair facing the bed, then he watched over her a moment longer, trailing his fingers through her silken tresses until his eyelids refused to stay open.

After placing a tender kiss on her forehead, Kahlym stood, defying his aching muscles, and planted himself in the semi-comfortable chair. His neck would hate him in the morning, but it would be worth it. And so, leaning his head back against the soft cushion, Kahlym forced his muscles to relax enough for sleep to become a possibility.

Chapter 11

The tinkling sounds of rain on a tin roof drew Evainne out of her deep slumber. She vaguely recalled the hard look on Kahlym's face at her unexpected appearance. After that, things got a little blurry, though she wasn't sure if it was due to a lack of sleep, or because her heart didn't have much of a reason to beat anymore. Learning that more time had passed for him had only made things worse. For her, the mere hours on Earth had been like a lifetime apart, and yet, Kahlym seemed even further away now than when she'd been on the opposite end of the universe. Tears pricked behind her closed lids and she swallowed back her emotions.

Did she expect him to run across the room and kiss her sense-less? *Actually, yes.* She'd at least hoped he'd look happy to see her. Instead, his face had been an unreadable mask of indifference.

Evainne opened her eyes and opted to take in her immediate surroundings from the comfort of a soft bed. Natural light streamed in through a loose knit canopy of bright green fronds. No water had leaked through the woven ceiling, and she marveled at this fact a moment longer until, with a soft sigh, she turned her attentions to the rest of the room. Living walls surrounded her; even the blanket tucked under her skin felt alive. As she stroked the warm fur covering, she amended her earlier thought. Everything seemed to pulse with life and breath, cocooning her in a deep serenity unlike anything she'd ever felt before.

Forest green with swirls of black adorned the garment draped carefully against the chair directly across from her, while somewhere beyond the verdant walls, children giggled and played in the downpour. Smells of meat roasted over an open fire wafted through the air, and her stomach cramped at the tantalizing aroma. Part of her wanted to stay a bit longer in this tranquil moment, but the heat from a nearby stare refused to allow her any peace.

Her breathing sped up, shallow and angry, and Evainne clenched her jaw, reaching out for the offered attire. She turned away from his piercing gaze. Not that he hadn't seen everything before, but she still did her best to keep her nakedness under wraps. She punched her arms through the wispy sleeves and yanked the long gown over her head before she tossed away the comforting covers. The gossamer fabric flowed down, its excess pooling around her bare feet. Without a look backwards, she stormed out through the open archway, tugging the extra length about her waist.

"Evai—"

"No." Her answer was sharp, its harsh edges cutting her heart deeper than she had expected.

Let him stew.

Her steps traveled in no particular direction. She needed some distance to get her head screwed on straight. She had a fuzzy recollection of passing out from exhaustion and her body remembered the feel of Kahlym's arms around her, and as much as she wanted to return to that sensation, her brain was dead set against it, her heart too battered to fight back.

Chugging along on an unknown path, she struggled to bring her warring internals back into focus. Against all odds, she'd managed to find her way back across the universe, only to be rejected by the one person she'd wanted to see the most.

"What are you doing up?"

She lifted her gaze to glare daggers at Xandar as she motored toward him. Her mentor had traded his traveling ziploc for a set of robes similar to Yhan'tu's. "What? Was I supposed to stay in bed like an invalid?"

"You were *supposed* to spend some time getting reacquainted with your lover." Xandar's honest tone irritated her, especially since a large part of her wished she was doing that very thing. Only her wounded pride kept her upright and moving away from the object of her current anger.

"Nope. Not happening. I give up. It's over." She shouldered past him, needing to find the nearest doorway leading to the outside.

"Bullshit."

She froze, stunned. "Excuse me?"

Xandar, catching her arm, turned her about to face him. "You heard me. And you know how I despise the use of such profanity. I know you better than that. You do not give up easily. Besides, if you knew it was over before you returned, why were you so eager to get back?"

"Because I stupidly thought he might actually give a shit and … Hell, you saw his response," she spat, tugging her arm, to no avail. His iron grip refused to allow her to escape.

"Actually, I did not. I was too busy staring at people who have believed me to be dead these long years."

Oh. That took some of the wind out of her self-righteous sails. But, unwilling to release her anger, Evainne shook her head and braced her aching shoulders against collapsing under the weight of her crazy emotions.

"Well, you didn't miss much," she said. "He didn't have one. Not even an, 'Oh, hey. Good to see you.' He's obviously done with me, so I'm gonna return the favor."

Silence drew her gaze up to an unamused pair of lapis blue eyes.

Then her vision blurred and she broke off the staring contest to find an interesting spot on the wall just to the left of his beefy arm. "Don't look at me like that. Besides, I know when I'm not wanted."

Xandar *tsk*ed. "I do not believe that for one moment." He shuffled around until he was in her direct line of sight. Her focused gaze drilled a hole through the center of his chest and the regal robes, but she refused to look up. "Do you remember what I told you when we first met?"

Evainne wiped at her watery eyes. "Get out?" she croaked.

The fingers around her bicep loosened. "And what about the time after that?"

She huffed out a tired breath, rolling her eyes. "Which time?"

"Exactly." Xandar guided her out of the middle of the walkway, and she was helpless to do anything but follow. "I lost track of how many times I kicked you off my doorstep. I remember telling Bao to stop bringing you to see me. Do you know what he told me?"

She scuffed her feet on the smooth flooring, shyly lifting a shoulder. Words refused to come, so she waited for Xandar to continue.

"He told me he tried. In fact, he said he told you, after the first day, to give it up; that perhaps I was not the right teacher for you. But you didn't. You wouldn't. Every day, I woke up and looked out the window to see you sitting on the stoop. Cold. Rain. Snow. Nothing mattered. You were not going to take no for an answer. Do you wonder why I finally agreed to train you?"

Not liking where this conversation was going, Evainne continued to study the soft and spongy ground beneath her toes. "Because you got sick of me bothering you?" she mumbled.

A gentle touch on her chin encouraged her eyes upward, and she studied the rich gold-and-purple cloth beyond her nose, counting the thread weave while postponing the inevitable final destination. When her gaze had completed its journey, she met a warm smile and an understanding pair of lapis blue orbs. Standing this close, Evainne noticed the undeniable family resemblance—Kahlym was just the newer version of the model in front of her.

Her breathing grew shallow, grief closing like a fist around her heart.

Xandar shook his head. "I could have continued to throw you off my porch. No, the reason I agreed was because you were determined. Each time I said no, you refused to hear it. You showed up again and again and again. When I first met you, all I saw in you was rage and anger at the world. I knew those emotions well and I did not want to have any part in aiding anyone along that path. But after Bao told me of your family, I looked at you in a different light. I looked at myself in a different light, too. Instead of a loud, obnoxious, smart-mouthed child"—he offered her a soft smile—"I saw a scared young girl who had never been given a fair chance at a normal life. In that moment, I knew I had to help you."

His gaze softened, his grin wilting. "In your eyes, I saw the brother I had left behind. The brother I'd left to a hellish fate without me. Once I realized that, I could not say no any longer."

Evainne blinked, and the ghosts haunting her friend and mentor vanished. The corners of his lips lifted, and he gripped her shoulder.

"It was your tenacity that convinced me to teach you. You would not give up. And I do not believe for an instant you would give up this easily on love."

Evainne choked out a mirthless laugh, biting her lip in an attempt to curb her threatening tears. "Dammit, Toa. I was so close."

He leaned in, frowning at her harsh, quiet words. "What do you mean?"

"I almost had it." She swallowed past the tangle of emotions stealing her voice. "It was right there, so close I could taste it. I ... I almost knew what it was like to be happy, really happy, and ... and now it's gone."

"There, you are mistaken. You have not lost anything, *learom.*"

"Yes, I have. I've lost everything. My resolve, my ... my..." She shook her head, determined not to cry. "I can't give my heart to someone I can't trust."

Xandar's smile warmed as his gaze shifted to a point behind her, and before she could turn to see what held his attention, a strong pair of arms curled around her. The heady scent of heaven flooded her senses, and she grabbed on to the anchoring bands as they coiled around her body. Her eyes fluttered closed, and safe in the shelter of her lover's embrace, Evainne sobbed.

____

Chapter 12

____

Kahlym rested his cheek on the bloodwine waves of silken curls, savoring the feel of his female once again in his arms. His own tears flowed silently as she openly cried, her body trembling at the outpouring of emotion, while in the solitude of his own mind, he railed at his idiotic actions. She was right. He never should have doubted her, nor should he have sent her away. She was strong and more than capable.

So strong, in fact, she'd discovered a path back to him before he could rescue her.

He'd spent most of the night watching her as she slept. Deep within, a battle had raged between his brain and his body, neither part willing to concede its own moral high ground, so he'd been helpless to do more than keep a respectable distance from what he desired. It had also meant sleeping options were either the narrowly confining oval chair, or the floor. The ground wouldn't have offered him a view of his beautiful female, and in his heart, he knew he would get no rest that night.

Time wore on as he stood vigil, staring on as an impotent outsider, and he sensed the moment she woke, his eyes popping open at the first sound of movement. She rose swiftly and vanished just as quickly. He attempted to lurch to his feet, planning on giving chase, but his muscles had refused to comply. Instead, he gasped as his legs spasmed and locked in rebellion.

<Kahlym. You need to come here. Now.>

He grit his teeth at his long-absent brother's commanding tone. The urge to tell him to fuck himself was tempting, but his missing angel had stopped him from the childish response. Grumbling instead, Kahlym unfolded his cramped limbs and encouraged the blood to return to his tingling extremities.

<Did you hear me, skan'tah?>

Kahlym froze, memories flooding in.

"Did you just call me an asshole?" He rolled through his shoulders and shuffled toward the door, dragging a hand through his knotted hair. "Since when did you learn to swear?"

<Just get out here. We can debate appropriate language later.>

Voices in the corridor halted any further argument, and Kahlym quickened his pace. Evainne had her back to him, making his eavesdropping much easier, and he listened until his heart nearly broke. In his mind, he pictured her crouched in the pouring rain outside of a dingy, gray building, while time and time again, his brother had opened the door, shaken his head, and disappeared back inside.

Tears blurred Kahlym's vision, and he'd silently stepped closer to join them.

Now, hearing her mournful plea, he'd closed the final distance to take her into his embrace. She melted against him, and he flexed his sore muscles, tightening his hold. Yet, as her tears fell in earnest, panic seized him. Had she been injured and his strangling hold was now causing her pain?

Had this been any other time, he would have pulled away to ask if she was okay. But he was in no mood to release her. An eternity had passed since he had last felt her touch. Instead, he readjusted his grip, sliding his palm across her collarbone. His plan was to give her some breathing room, but apparently she was not interested in space. She dug her nails into his arm, keeping him firmly in place.

<Perhaps it would be better if you took her back to your chambers. I will have food delivered to you later.>

Kahlym opted to take his brother's wise advice.

With delicate care, he slid his hand down Evainne's back and scooped her up to rest against his chest. She continued to sob, trembling, folding in on herself. He cradled her in his loving embrace, kissing the crown of her head, losing himself in the welcoming waves of her velvety-soft tresses.

<Thank you, kherdes. Thank you for bringing her back to me.>

A chuckle echoed in his mind. *<She was the one who did all the heavy lifting, Kahl. I simply came along for the ride.>*

Kahlym closed his eyes for a moment and sighed. *<There is so much for which I need to make up to her. I ... I don't know if I really can.>* He stepped away, only to be pulled to a halt. He glanced up to his brother. How long had it been since he'd stood this close to him? Even with the passing of so many years, Xandar's presence still managed to instill him with hope.

"Do not think in those terms, Kahl. You only need to believe in her."

Kahlym nodded sharply, teeth clenched to hold in any continued stupidity. Now was not the time to wallow in self-pity and useless internal recriminations. So, steeling his nerve, he strode back toward the vacant room. In his arms, Evainne tensed, kicking her legs out and reaching her bare toes toward the ground.

"No. I'm... Please. Let me down. I can walk myself."

A large part of him wanted to argue, blood racing through his veins to pool below his belt line with the innocent contact. He gaped, but no sound fell from his lips as his brother's sage words echoed through his head: *Believe in her.* Even if his body would rather deny her simple request. Unwilling to relinquish all connection, Kahlym set her carefully onto her feet and brushed his fingertips down her arm, stopping once he'd reached her elbow.

What should he say? *Where do I start?* They walked on in silence until they passed beyond the threshold and, with a light touch, Kahlym triggered the living curtain to seal the opening. Since most Ontaxians lived in familial colonies, there was little need for privacy; only during mating rituals were doors used. Even though that possibility might not be the final outcome, he was still grateful for the option should things get … animated.

Kahlym turned about and stared, transfixed. Evainne kept her back to him, her wild burgundy tresses trailing down to the lush globes of her ass. He sensed the conflicted emotions raging through her. Within his heart, he heard her spirit crying out in despair, confusion, and frustration. The proof of their true Soulbond resonated through his bones, and soon, he stood close enough to feel the tickle of her long hair against his bare chest. His hands trembled as he willed his arms to move. He exhaled slowly, then covered the final distance between them.

She flinched as his palms cupped her shoulders.

"I … Evainne, I never meant you any harm."

Her mirthless laugh chilled his spirit. "Oh, gee. Then I guess that makes things all right. I mean, you didn't hurt me on purpose. Just by accident, right?"

A sad smile tugged at the corners of his mouth. "I have missed your direct words, *ziat'xahn*." Her scent invaded his senses, calling to mind hours spent tangled in her arms, bathing in the intoxicating softness of her skin. His eyes drifted shut, his head hanging heavy. "I have missed you."

"Is that why I got such a cold reception, because you *missed* me?" She jerked out of his loose hold and spun about. Red rings circled her deep brown orbs and silver streaks glistened along her pale cheeks. Her chin quivered as her gaze darted over his face. "Call me funny, but if you hadn't tossed my ass out in the first place, we wouldn't even be having this conversation."

She was due her anger, and he struggled not to draw her into his embrace. "You m—"

"If you even think about saying 'You must understand,'" she growled, "I will make you useless as a man." Fire burned in her eyes, and pride filled his heart. Here was his passionate mate, prepared to battle any and all foes. She paused, a curious frown pulling together her slender brows. "Okay, maybe not useless. But you will limp for a while."

"You are upset and"—he raised a hand to halt her expected interjection—"I will not deny you your anger." Daring fate, he approached her, arms open. She remained out of reach, cautious and rigid. "Do I regret my actions?" *Moment of truth.* "I only regret your ire."

Evainne threw her hands toward the skies and stalked away, muttering under her breath.

<You know I can still hear your thoughts.>

"Good." She spun about, glaring. "Then I won't have to repeat myself. Dammit Kahl, why didn't you trust me enough to fight beside you?"

Her grief-stricken tone chilled his heart, and he swept in close. "Evainne, I trust you and only you with my very soul. But I *know* my father." A tic started at the corner of his lip, and he forced down his horrific memories. "In order to get to you, he was willing to sacrifice everyone living within the palace walls. It was the only way to truly keep you safe."

"Oh, come on. Do you really expect me to believe that?" Even though her words lacked the vehemence of her earlier outbursts, she still sounded unconvinced. "Instead of listening to what I might have to say, you decided to bundle me up and ship me off to that craphole that was my old apartment, locking me away where it's 'safe'?"

The temperature in the room dipped, and an odd blue glow emanated from behind Evainne. Kahlym frowned, reconsidering his original observation—she wasn't standing in front of the light; she was the source of it. Silhouetted, she stood bathed in the strange hue, one fisted hand resting on one shapely hip.

"I'm not some helpless, frightened waif, needing her big, strong man to fight off the monsters. I'm a damned good fighter and I can kick anyone ass."

Alarmed voices crowded into his head as the room continued to chill. "Evainne? Beloved?"

"Oh, so now it's words of love you're gonna try, huh?" She paced around the room, leaving behind trails of searing blue. "Those might have worked better yesterday when you saw me."

Don't hate me. Kahlym rushed toward her, heart thundering in his chest. He cradled her face and pressed his forehead to hers.

<Please, ziat'xahn. I need you to calm yourself.> He squeezed shut his eyelids, burying his panic, sending only love through their link. As he entered her mind, chaos and howling winds battered him. Somewhere, lost in the turmoil, was his beloved, and he refused to let her slip away.

Her fingers gripped his wrists and yanked away his offered comfort. But there was more at stake than her wish for space. He'd willingly pay for his forward behavior when they were safe. "What the hell?" she said. "No, you don't get to tell me what do to and what not to do. Let me go, dammit."

<Evainne, my heart. You are in grave danger and I must ask that you trust me.>

Her struggles ceased even as the temperature dropped into frigid levels. "Danger? Trust? That's rich coming from you. Kahlym, what kind of fucked-up game are you—"

In the distance, a cacophony of frantic voices filled the room. He picked out Brel and R'uan above all of the others. Thankfully, they were smart enough to hold the crowd away. Risking her further wrath, he pulled her close even as she fought to escape his embrace.

<This is no game. Evainne, I know you are confused and angry, but I beg you, please listen to me now. If you continue on this path and let your rage rise, your powers will call out to the other Divines. And believing one of their own to be in mortal distress, the Divine Light will guide them, and the emperor, as well,

directly here. To you. To all of us.> He prayed his words conveyed his concern for her safety.

<What? What! Omigod! No! What do I do? What do I do?> Guilt cut through her frenzied hurricane of emotions as her nails dug into his forearms. *<Oh, God. I'm sorry. I'm so sorry. I don't, I mean, I didn't...>*

<Shh, ziat'xahn.> A relieved smile touched his lips. *<I have you, Evainne. I will not leave you to face this alone. Can you feel my hands on your skin?>*

In the darkness, he searched for her. The storm in her mind had abated, but she remained hidden. His head bobbed in time with her jerking nods. *<Let it center you. Can you feel my breath against your cheek?>* He took in a deep breath, pulling her fragrance into his blood, and let it out slowly. His breath fanned her cheek and he repeated the process.

She curled into his embrace and answered with a stuttered inhale. Degree by degree, the heat returned around them.

<Let it guide you.> As he exhaled a measured and controlled stream of air, he directed her lungs to follow his lead. Her staggered breath tickled his chest, and he forced his mind to stay on task. With each paired breath, he searched for her in her mind's growing quiet, and in the distance, her pure light gleamed—a beacon leading him straight to her. Her barriers shimmered as she hid, her arms and legs pulled in tight. Armed only with love, he strode toward her.

<Can you feel the beat of my heart?> He held her locked fingers to his chest, his body jolting at her innocent touch, and carefully traced lazy circles with the tips of his talons across the back of her hand. *<Let it bring you back to me.>* Gradually, Evainne loosened her clenched fist. The tension slowly seeped from her arm and he stepped in closer, while the throng gathering at his back added waves of encouragement outside of the intimate circle. Deep in her mind, Kahlym knelt beside her trembling spirit, then gathered her into his embrace. In the physical world, he pressed his palm against her pounding heart. Seconds ticked by in comforting silence, Kahlym unwilling to break the tender spell.

<Kahlym? Is she okay?>

Xandar's voice had echoed in his head, its deep tones long-absent from all but his memory. He still recalled his brother's commanding timbre. Remembering Evainne's plea for trust, Kahlym opened the familial link, including her in his responses. *<She is strong, kherdes. She will be fine.>* A nervous thought rocketed through his mind. *<Are we safe?>* The instant he'd sensed her loss of control, he'd swooped in. Now, he worried his actions had been too slow.

<Yes, Kahl. We are safe. The only reason I felt her call was because I was close by.> Kahlym sensed Xandar, as well as Brel, as they stood inside the threshold at a respectable distance. *<I do not think the signal made it any farther than the hallway. The canopy was not breached; on that I am positive.>*

<C-c-canopy? Oh, God. Please tell me I didn't do anything monumentally stupid?> Her timid query warmed his soul. Certain she had returned to her normal self, Kahlym slipped from her mind but did not relinquish his hold on her. He peeled open his eyes, gazing down upon her pale countenance.

"You were angry and lashed out, *ziat'xahn*. I was the one who, as you so aptly put it, was 'monumentally stupid.'"

"Don't worry about it, *learom*," Brel chimed in. "He's a pro at the asinine awards. You're still an amateur."

Kahlym frowned. Shifting his gaze away, he smirked at his brother's less-than-complementary interjection. "Thanks for the vote of confidence."

A goofy grin split Brel's face, light dancing in his citrine eyes. "Are you kidding me? I'm totally in her corner." He thumbed at their silent companion, beaming proudly. "She's gonna surprise the shit out of the emperor, and that, I cannot wait to see." After a strong cuff to his brother's shoulder, nearly knocking Kahlym off of his feet, Brel winked and headed toward the exit. Kahlym sighed, shaking his head, opting to keep his attentions on the cascading curls of deep bloodwine rather than on the receding voices at his back. Soft material pressed against his palm as it cocooned her steadily beating heart. Her breathing had evened out, but she refused to meet his eyes.

The final pair of muffled footsteps vanished down the corridor, leaving him alone with his confused lover and, needing to reassure her, and himself as well, Kahlym pulled her toward his embrace. She moved woodenly at first, her steps tense and jerky. Once in the shelter of his arms, though, she melted, and he tightened his hold to keep her on her feet.

"*Ziat'xahn.*" Any other words failed him.

With careful shuffles, he guided her to the bed. Her hands were cool against his bare skin, and he buried his face into the waves of tempting, fragrant tresses.

"Kahlym," she whispered, "what did I almost do?"

He threaded his fingers through her loose, thick mane, savoring the forgotten silken texture between his rough digits. As his knees bumped against the edge of the bed frame, he sat down, carrying her to rest in his lap.

Evainne, however, had a different idea. She paused before she swung her leg over his to perch on his thighs, facing him. "I know this protective hold. I promise I won't lose it, but I really need some answers." She lifted her soulful brown eyes to lock with his. Entranced, he fell into the fathomless depths and prepared for the next word: the request he would never be able to dismiss.

"Please."

Chapter 13

Evainne stared into his bi-colored eyes, and her resolve teetered at the pain and anguish reflected back. Dark circles ringed his orbs of fuchsia-and-jade; ghosts she hadn't seen before must have returned to haunt him during her absence. Her hand trembled as she placed her palm against his stubbled cheek. As sexy as she found his five o'clock shadow, she hated the reason for his haggard appearance.

His lids shuttered while he cupped her fingers, leaning into her timid touch. "I have missed you, *ziat'xahn.*" His harsh whisper stroked the softer places in her heart and she wanted nothing more than to fall into his embrace. Yet her brain was unwilling to give up control. "I am sorry if my actions spoke otherwise."

Choking back her tender emotions, Evainne sat back on her heels. "I guess I was expecting a warmer reception." She offered up a weak smile. "I … I don't think I've ever heard you so scared."

Kahlym turned his face toward her palm and pressed a hot kiss directly in the center of her shaking hand. "I must apologize if I frightened you. I fear I needed to act quickly before things … escalated."

She bit back a heavy sigh, pinching her bottom lip between her teeth. "We can sort out who's sorry for what later. I need to know what I almost did, so I can make sure not to do it again."

Silence descended, and for a minute, she thought she would need to brandish the magic word once again. Her lips parted, but he beat her to the punch.

"When the Seventh Quadrant was young," he said, "many of the inhabitants did not understand the powers of the Divines." Evainne closed her eyes, images jumping into her mind as he filled her in on ancient history. "On more primitive worlds, their abilities were seen as evil, and those who possessed them were 'sacrificed' to drive away famine or pestilence or any other plagues. Thousands were lost to ignorance and fear. It was said these special few were able to speak across the stars to those like them."

In the dark behind her lids, she pictured women, men, and creatures tortured on horrific devices, screaming out in agony, while on her mental split-screen, another being halfway across the universe would jerk in response, their setting completely different from those in pain.

"Eons would pass before the emperor gathered all the Divines on Rimma, yet it is said, in times of high emotional distress, Divines can possibly hear the cries of each other."

"Is … is that what I was doing? Which is why you kept telling me to calm down." Defeat had resonated in her simple words, and her head hung heavy. She recalled R'uan's mental shielding lesson, perhaps a bit too late. She'd been in such a damned hurry to get back and not once had she given a thought to the huge differences between her old home and her new one. "I am so sorry. Are you sure nothing got through? I mean, what if—"

A gentle touch on her lips halted any further lame apology. "Do not worry, *ziat'xahn*. Ontaxa is truly a strong and secure safehold for us. The planet is blanketed by thick vegetation, which makes signals going both in and out nearly impossible…"

Something missing in his punctuation chilled her blood. Steeling her nerves, Evainne opened her eyes and attempted to catch Kahlym's wandering gaze. "But?" She captured his chin, guided his face back to her. "What aren't you telling me?"

Emotions flickered on and off in the tourmaline depths, answers appearing and disappearing with each passing heartbeat.

He still doesn't trust me.

Frustrated, she twisted away, inches short of escape, when his hands gripped her waist. "Please, Evainne. You… It is not that I do not trust you." Frowning, she glared over her shoulder, encouraging him to continue. "I … I honestly do not have the answers you seek. I know your rage did not reach beyond these walls, but … I also know you are much more than an ordinary, or weak, Divine."

She refused to divert her gaze as she settled back onto his lap. "What do you mean?"

A strained smile touched his lips. "Have you yet to guess? There are five Divines, each one able to control only one of the five elements."

Her breathing ratcheted up a notch. "Yeah, I remember. There's one for, um, body, soul, time, space and, um…"

"The fifth controls destiny: The Divine Fury." Kahlym dragged his rough knuckles against her jaw and her brain spun in dizzying spirals, unwilling to grasp his implied conclusion.

The movement started out small, but grew quickly—a head shake so vigorous, her vision blurred. She blinked rapidly but refused to agree with her sexy captain. "No. Uh-uh. No way. What … Kahlym? How can you… I mean, c'mon. You're joking, right? There is no way…" Evainne sputtered until only nonsensical sounds fell from her lips. *This is crazy.*

"Is it truly crazy?" His hands cradled her face, forcing her vision to focus. "You have proven your skills as a Healer." He glanced over her shoulder, indicating her first miracle when she'd mended her back without any effort. As his gaze returned to her, adoration radiated from his expression. "On more than one occasion, actually." Kahlym paused once again, and Evainne's mind was thrust into that med bay, when she'd pulled Brel out of death's clutches.

He placed a soft kiss on the tip of her nose, bringing her out of her darker thoughts. "I have seen your fighting skills, marking you also as an Adept. You found your way back here, alone. That solidifies your abilities as a Traveler. Can it be—"

"No, wait a minute." She laid her fingertips across his lips to get him to stop talking. With too much information pouring into her mind, she was close the breaking point, her mental shelves beginning to buckle under the strain. "Xandar did the return trip."

His warm breath tickled her palm while the hint of a smile warmed his bi-colored eyes. "He might bear the facial markings of a cleric, but he couldn't have been capable of the journey himself. He confided this to me." After pressing kisses against the pads of her fingers, he slipped her hand into his. "You are more than any Divine Fury in the history of the Dantaran galaxy."

Divine Fury.

She breathed out an airy, mirthless laugh. "Does that mean I get more pissed off than your normal Divine Fury?" Blood-cooling dread had kicked her sarcasm into overdrive. How long would her charade of feigned strength fool everyone? Judging by Kahlym not letting go of her hand, she didn't have him convinced in the slightest.

"There is nothing wrong with being scared. Were our situations reversed, I would be terrified, as well."

Defeated, Evainne dropped her shoulders, collapsing under the heavy weight of realization. "Yeah," she said, "but at least you know the rules. I'd call that one hell of an advantage." Needing space, she slid backwards off of his thighs to pace around the quaint room. The living walls cocooned them in comforting silence. She strode closer to touch the vibrant vines, and to her surprise, the texture was rougher than she'd expected; branches intertwined, creating a cool, solid surface. Cracks and seams between the leaves were perfect hiding holes for her frantic mind, and the longer she stared into the in-between spaces, the more she wished she could vanish into the slender dark.

She sensed Kahlym's silent approach, the heat of his presence warming her skin an instant before his fingers grazed her bare arms. Dampness flooded her core, and she swallowed back a needy moan. "I only know of legends and fables, Evainne. You, *ziat'xahn* … you have surpassed all other Divines who have ever been. The ancient tomes spoke of one who'll control all of the elements; one who could unite Healer, Adept, Traveler, Seer, and Fury. A Paramount Divine. They live only in myth, as none have ever been seen in the life of our universe." Evainne shivered as Kahlym slid one hand from shoulder to shoulder while other his fingers gripped her hipbone, pinning her against the hard planes of his chiseled body. "I… You may yet be more than even the prophecy foretold."

The switch mid-thought caught her attention and she clutched his wrists, signaling her next move. Shuffling her feet, she spun about to face him, and her nose bumped into his solid pecs. God, he smelled good. She fought the urge to lick her way up to his strong jaw. *Down would work just as well.* Mentally smacked her rising libido, Evainne bit the inside of her cheek to remain focused. She was still mad at him; jumping his bones would definitely send a mixed message.

"You stopped yourself. What were you going to say?" she asked, and he dipped his chin even as he refused to meet her gaze. Sighing, she leaned back, needing a little perspective. "Kahlym, please. I'm tired. I'm hungry. I haven't really slept in God only knows how long, and I really don't want to play these guessing games." He flinched, and she grabbed his bulging biceps. "And no. I wasn't suggesting a break. Please, just tell me what you were going to say."

His jaw muscles bunched and flexed while the faint tap of rain filled the ensuing silence. "I…" He cleared his throat and raised his gaze. So many conflicting emotions had raced across his face, she almost lost her resolve. Then a sad smile tugged at the corners of his lips, stirring the dormant butterflies in her gut. "I know you deserve far more than I can ever give to you," he said at last. "Yet, I harbor hope that I have not lost you."

The fluttering wings in her stomach kicked into overdrive. *Damn him and his pigheaded nobility.* But, opting for a more neutral response, Evainne cupped his cheek. "Kahlym," she said, "I am far from lost to you." Grief shimmered in his tourmaline eyes, and her vision blurred. She sniffled back the press of tears. "I don't know if I'm ready to forgive you just yet, though. I … I still need to know you won't ditch me in a closet at the first hint of danger."

A stubborn frown wrinkled his brow, and she resisted the urge to kiss away his bullheadedness. "What kind of mate would I be if I did not protect you?"

Her jaw swung open, her heart blurting out an answer before her brain could censor the words. "The kind who sees his mate as an equal."

"I see you as—" Her determined stare convinced him to change his tune and he sighed. "You are right," he said, defeat coloring his voice.

"GAH!" She squirmed out of his arms and stormed over to the bed, hoping distance would cool her rising desires. "Dammit, Kahl. This isn't about who's right or wrong, here. This is about trust. This is about opening up and letting … well, dammit. It's about both of us letting the other one know things. Hell, I'm not completely innocent in this, either. I know there are things I've kept from you." She plopped down, head heavy as she stared at the floor. "But it's only because I don't think telling you about the time I broke my leg riding my bike down a flight of stone stairs when I was ten is going to be of any importance. You, on the other hand, have answers to questions I don't even know I should be asking."

"Sorry if we're interrupting anything," Brel's voice filtered in, shattering the tension. Evainne raised her head, concerned by the direct tone. R'uan and Falka followed a stride behind and she thought she spied Xandar's shadow hovering beyond the threshold. "But I'm afraid we've got news that simply won't keep."

Evainne shifted her gaze to Kahlym. Anguish bled from her lover, his eyes swiveling between his brother and her, and the selfish drive to tell Brel to screw off was so tempting. But the last remaining rational brain cell reminded her she was back and there would be plenty of time to deal with the elephant in the room.

With a deep breath, she rose and crossed over to Kahlym. Her mind flashed back to another memory: A chrome-and-white tiled room filled with pinging machinery, and in this surreal scene, Kahlym stood proud and regal, one shoulder resting against the open doorway. Confidence had oozed from his relaxed stance. Now, doubt clung to his shoulders, shrouding her hero in a thick blanket of indecision.

Was this her fault?

She pressed her palm against the warm flesh of his chest. Beneath her outstretched fingers, his heart beat strong and steady, its rhythm calling out to her and she stared entranced at the artful interplay of pale against exotic bronze. Tingles trailed along her arm as her slender fingers were swallowed by his massive mitt, and a weak smile touched her lips as she popped up onto her toes, brushing a tender kiss on his cheek.

Time was of the essence, and more important issues needed everyone's attention.

"You tend to your captainy duties, hon. We can talk later." Her simple words hit their target, and she spied a glimmer of her fearless warrior through his intoxicating tourmaline eyes. He replied with a slight dip of his chin, releasing her hand after one parting squeeze. Her eyes followed him as the group moved out of the chamber and disappeared down the corridor. Before she gave chase, she shook her head, grumbling to herself, then moved toward the silent sentinel guarding from a safe distance.

She felt the weight of Xandar's sidelong gaze following her, yet he made no attempt to stop her. Evainne frowned, curious at his nonchalance. As she closed the final distance, he locked eyes with her, tilting his head toward the opposite hallway, and vanished into the shadows. Trying not to trip over her trailing skirts, she dashed after him.

Six strides into her impromptu sprint, she jerked to a halt after slamming into Xandar's chest.

Backpedaling, she rubbed at her nose, then popped him on the arm. "Hey. Next time, use your brake lights. Why aren't you joining the party?"

Xandar shook his head. "I have no interest in the machinations of my father, not even as an outsider." Sadness and determination rang clear in his tone, telling her the topic was closed to further discussion. "How are things progressing between you and my brother?"

With a heavy sigh, Evainne wrapped her arms about herself to rub away the imagined cold. "Not too good." She studied the floor and shuffled along an interesting weaving path of deep green vines. "He's just so damned stubborn. No matter what I say, he continues to see me as someone, or something, that needs protecting." She spun about, snapping her gaze up. "Do I look weak or timid to you?"

Xandar tilted his head, the muted light shimmering off of his faded facial tattoos. "Let me ask you this: Have you considered why?"

"Why?" She blinked, waiting for the rest of the question. But silence dragged on and her impatience ground to a halt. "Why what?" she said. "What am I supposed to be considering?"

"He knows you are not weak. He has seen you in battle. Yet he still protects you. Why?"

She tossed up her hands, giving in to her exasperation. "Because he's a man! A stubborn, misogynistic, pigheaded…" She sputtered to a halt when words failed her.

"Product of a society built on the centuries-old premise that any Divine is to be revered beyond life itself and is to be untouched by any but another Divine."

Her jaw dropped. His statement had been soft yet effective.

The hint of a tender smile touched his stern mouth. "Once again, *hoc sinh*, you have not seen beyond your own emotions. You believe Kahlym is refusing to see you as more than merely a woman, but you do not realize the truth of your request. In the Dantaran galaxy, it has been known since time immemorial the Divines are god-like beings, born to be worshipped and placed on the highest marbled pedestals. They are unattainable to mere mortal creatures like us." He gestured grandly toward the distant circle of friends she now considered to be family. "What you are asking is for him to go against everything that has been drilled into him since he drew first breath; to go against a religiously held conviction where transgressions were punished by death; to betray his ingrained beliefs, simply because you wish not to be seen as what you are."

Air rushed out of her lungs as her stomach settled at her knees. How could she have been so blind? Her legs buckled, and a chair materialized beneath her ass before she crumpled into an undignified heap.

"Listen to my voice and breathe." The familiar directions from her teacher started to ground her, and she willingly followed his simple command. With each stuttered inhale, she forced her mind to replay every demand she'd made and each argument that had followed. *Blind? No—how could I be so dense?* She'd assumed nothing more than a normal testosterone overload had been guiding Kahlym's protective side. Never once did she ask him anything. Instead, she'd bulldozed through everything, handling situations with as much grace as a dump truck, then had gotten her panties in a twist when things hadn't gone her way.

She weakly raised her gaze from the floor. Her teacher had crouched down, his face eye level with her.

"Xandar, how could I ... I mean, why..."

"You were not raised in a universe where laws and beliefs that have spanned millennia still hold power and sway over its people." His logic and understanding, unfortunately, did little to soothe her aching conscience. "On your homeworld, nations follow different religious paths, believe in different ideologies. Some are rooted in history, while others are only decades old. Even when two nations disagree, neither side will truly acquiesce their core beliefs. Here, there is no corner of the galaxy, not even in the most isolated realms, where the Divines and their power are unknown. For Kahlym to risk his very soul to touch you, to be with you, speaks volumes of the depth of his love for you."

Evainne focused on the air rushing in and out of her lungs, while her mind processed this new information. Her parents had never placed faith in anything beyond the almighty dollar and the opinions of the elite. She herself didn't believe in much, only what she needed to survive to see the next day with her self-respect intact. While she saw Kahlym as a man—an incredibly sexy space man, at that—she'd neglected to consider any part of his history before he'd slid onto the scene, guns blazing, to save her life.

A light squeeze to her shoulder pulled her back to the present. Embarrassment heated her cheeks, and she raised her gaze, meeting the pair of insightful, lapis eyes.

The hint of a smile tilted the edges of his mouth. "Perhaps you could … cut him some slack?"

Her sharp laugh snuck out ahead of her tears. Between sniffles and coughs, she dashed her hand across her leaking eyes. "You really need to stick to the formal language, Toa. Slang sounds too weird coming from you." Then, exhaling with a loud huff, she banished her useless self-loathing and squared her shoulders. "I guess I have a lot to learn, too. I … I'm just having a hard time simply letting this go. I know you're right, but…" She trailed off, her thoughts racing in too many different directions.

"This doesn't completely let him off the hook, though," she stated, putting her foot down. "He could've told me about all of this. Let's say he's moved from the doghouse onto the porch."

Xandar pinned her with a serious stare, his enigmatic expression encouraging her to reconsider. Without another word, he took to his feet, pulling her up to stand at his side, and together, in a strangely comforting silence, they walked along the hall that led in the same direction Kahlym and his crew had traversed earlier.

After they'd entered the vast chamber, Xandar tipped his chin toward the grave trio huddled in quiet conversation on the other side of the room. Kahlym frowned at nothing in particular, stroking his bearded chin. An angry crease had cut a deep furrow across his forehead, and the filtered sunlight painted his tourmaline eyes with sparkling lights and dangerous shadows. Tantalizing tingles tiptoed across her bare arms, tangible memories of his warm caresses, and the butterflies in her gut fluttered to life.

"Are you certain he's only on the porch, *learom-xahn?*"

As the presence at her side slipped away, she swore she heard an uncharacteristic chuckle from her stoic mentor.

All right, so maybe he's in the house. But was she ready to have him in her bed?

Chapter 14

"So, what do we do, Captain?"

Kahlym gnawed on several responses, deciding which voice to use to answer Falka's simple question. He had wondered how long it would be before Qaen once again emerged as a thorn in his side. It was sheer luck Falka had stumbled across the latest imperial decree on the broadnet, calling for Kahlym's head as well as the return of the kidnapped Divine, and had recognized Qaen's mark, accepting the job. Disgust and anger ran neck and neck, while reason came in dead last. "You mean, besides castrate the bastard as soon as I get the chance?"

R'uan scoffed, his arms folded across his chest. "Get in line, Kahl. I think you might need to fight both your brother and your mate for that right."

He did have a point. As much as his hatred had grown for his devious former navigator, it paled in comparison to Brel's rage. When Qaen had betrayed his crew and turned them over to the Rimmarian Thrall back on Skirnahn Waystation, they'd barely escaped with their lives. In truth, if not for the newly discovered Divine healing skills of his beautiful Evainne, their numbers would have been one shy after a devastating blast had nearly claimed his brother's life.

Kahlym slyly slid his gaze toward Brel, whose normally bright citrine eyes were haunted, veiled by shadows while he absentmindedly rubbed the faint scar in the center of his chest.

"At this point, I don't care who gets the first strike," Kahlym said. "I'm certain everyone will have the chance to cause some damage." He locked eyes with R'uan. "In your honest opinion, what's the probability of Qaen locating us here?"

R'uan tapped his chin, a pensive frown wrinkling his brow. "I know I have never invited the ass over for a meal, and he and Dhaer have always knocked heads, even at the best of times. Besides, even if he were to pass beyond the canopy, none of our people would give information to an outsider."

"Falka," Kahlym said, shifting the focus away while he formulated the best course of action. "Is there a way to attune the long-range sensors on board the ship to let us know if anyone unfriendly is in the area, as well as scan the Thrall communications for necessary news?"

His tech stood silent, deep in thought. A long furrow cut into her forehead, and she set two of her hands on her narrow hips while the fingers on her third limb rubbed the back of her long neck. "I don't think it would be impossible to do. A pain in my ass, of course, but not the worst thing you've asked me to accomplish in the thousands of favors over the years."

Kahlym nodded and clasped on to her slender shoulder. "Any additional eyes might give us a couple of extra seconds to react. I'm sure if Evainne were here, she would add her thanks to ours."

A rare blush hit Falka's cheek and she hastily ducked her head to hide it. Without another word, Falka turned on her heel and headed out of the open chamber. Kahlym was well aware of the impact his words had on his grouchy tech. While she was more than content to complain about any new task, if it was made known it would benefit his angel in any way, Falka responded with reverent devotion and a minimal amount of grousing. A wistful grin touched his lips. Did Evainne realize exactly how miraculous she was? Given how easily she had gained the bristly and pragmatic Shee Va'an as an ally, it gave him hope for similar success within the other homeworlds of the Seventh Quadrant. Perhaps even he stood a chance to once again stand in the light of her presence.

"Now, don't get me wrong, here," Brel said, interrupting Kahlym's stray thoughts, "this place is a fortress, so I'm gonna say we are safe for a while." He folded his arms across his chest as he glanced around the room. "But how long are we going to, well … hide here?"

Kahlym stared at the verdant wall, his brother's words echoing his own silent query. News of the attack on the missing prize of the Rimmarian Emperor had spread like fire through the Dantaran galaxy, enraging sympathetic homeworlds, yet dwindling the number of potential safe havens. Leave it to the political machine to spin a kidnapping attempt as a rescue operation.

Was he looking to hide?

Why hide? He was in possession of the most formidable Divine to be born in a thousand lifetimes. With Evainne by his side, no one would dare stand against the Stria. Rumor had it, the stranglehold of the once-formidable Thrall was weakening, as stories of Evainne and her compassion filtered through the Seventh Quadrant, filling the inhabitants with hope. The balance would shift. It must. His people had been too long living under the yoke of Rimmarian Emperor and his greed.

"Hide?" Kahlym parroted back Brel's question, hoping to kick-start a sensible response. "I don't think this is exactly hiding. But we do need to regroup and plan our next steps. Up until now, we've been blessed, and I don't know how much longer our luck is going to last. We cannot afford to take any undue risks, and—"

"Who are our strongest allies?"

All heads swiveled as one toward the surprise speaker, and Evainne strode out of the shadows. Confident, she held her head high even as she plucked her way with the flowing skirts hiked near her waist. Memories of her strong, bare legs wrapped around his body drove away Kahlym's ability to think, quicker than smoke on a windy day. With each of her approaching strides, blood drained below his belt line, though pride swelled in his chest, the powerful emotion beginning to squash his deeply entrenched guilt. He had made his choice, and he promised himself he would live with the consequences.

<*Be careful, kherdes. You're drooling a little there.*> Kahlym elbowed Brel in the ribs as his angel joined the group. Then he fumbled for words as his brain picked apart her question.

"Uh, allies?" he stammered out. "We have our strongest bases here, on Raedyn Originae and on Outer T'chan, Lozzan's home-world. There are several secure outposts on every planet, and most of the Achtillian sector is unhappy under the Thrall's command but have yet to stand up and declare their allegiance to us."

A serious furrow creased her forehead as she tapped her chin thoughtfully. "Okay, but that doesn't tell me a whole hell of a lot. Is there a map or something? I need to see this to get a better idea of what you mean."

"There is a galaxy terminal in the loran room, just a little way down the hall," R'uan announced, leaving his statement unfinished. "But first off, I think it would be best if we all sat down for a meal. We can take some time and put all our heads together." He glanced around the room, and Kahlym's eyes followed the same path. Dhaerin nodded emphatically, and Xandar lifted a shoulder, his long-missed stoic patience centering the group.

"That's the first smart thing anyone's said," Dhaerin said, slapping his hands together and then rubbing them with childlike glee. "Give me two minutes and we'll be feasting like kings." Without another word, the Ontaxian bounded out of the chamber and disappeared down the hall.

R'uan groaned, dropping his face into his open hand. "I should've known better than to mention food in the presence of the walking garbage pit." With a tired gesture, he pointed toward the path his denmate had followed. "We'd better get going or there will be nothing left. Trust me on this one. I swear the reason he is the last sibling is because he nearly ate us out of house and home."

Kahlym chuckled and stood aside as the rest of his crew filed out. Xandar caught his gaze before joining the exiting group, then glanced behind to their silent Divine. Kahlym dipped his chin, understanding the subtle message, and his brother slipped out. Once again alone with Evainne, he pondered his appropriate response. She remained a few feet away, her fingers twisting around each other, entangling the rich olive green gossamer fabric between her fidgeting hands. His heart flip-flopped.

"If you would like, I can have some food brought to you here," he suggested, hoping to break the tension. Cautious, he edged closer to her, carefully gauging her reactions. Her gaze drifted around the room as she worried the corner of her bottom lip between her teeth. "If you prefer some … privacy."

Standing directly in front of his angel, he reached out, capturing one finger then another, until he cradled her hands in his. His thoughts slingshot into the past, calling up the images of a pristine white-and-chrome med bay. Evainne had just awoken into his world, injured and distraught. With his only concern focused on her, he had crawled onto the narrow cot and pulled her into his arms to soothe her. Her skin was like heaven, her hair a thick curtain of bloodwine silk hiding her sweet face from his sight. He had only intended to caress her cheek when she intercepted his hand. With delicate and innocently erotic inquiry, she had traced her fingertips along every inch of his hand. In that moment, with that one open gesture, he was lost, her name branded forever on his heart.

He returned the favor to her, studying the hands that held his life and his happiness. Faint scars marked her knuckles, evidence of her strength and her willingness to wade into battle to protect herself. He stroked her short nails with the pad of his thumb, her pale skin like ribbons of moonlight against his coppery bronze.

Fascinated, he entwined his fingers with hers, giving her hand a gentle squeeze before he placed both of her palms against his chest.

"Evainne." He breathed her name in reverent awe and wrapped his arms about her tense shoulders. "Forgive me, *ziat'xahn*."

He rested his cheek against her fragrant curls, drinking in the calming serenity only his angel could bring. Yet, as he snaked his hands down her back, her head shook from side to side.

"No, Kahlym," she said, leaning away from his embrace. Fear cooled his blood and he forced his lungs to drag in the next breath. She tilted her head back and met his eyes. Her deep chocolate pools were lined with unshed tears.

Dear Ishtanti, what have I done?

Evainne wiggled one hand free and Kahlym prepared for the impending slap. Instead, she cradled his stubbled cheek tenderly. "I'm the one who should be asking for your forgiveness. Begging is more like it," she continued, her chin quivering as a weak smile touched the corner of her mouth. "I was so stupid and convinced I was so right about everything, and I never once ... thought about what I expected you to do ... for me, and—"

He brushed his lips against hers to halt her self-loathing speech, cupping his fingers around her hand. She whimpered softly and he deepened the kiss, pouring all the love and understanding in his heart into her. She melted into his embrace, tightening her grip on the front of his loose tunic and nearly crawling into his clothes with him. Savoring the taste of her once again on his tongue banished the emptiness of the past several days. The prophetic words from his fevered dream tapped on the back of his mind, but now was not the time to take them out for study.

Kahlym drew in a long, slow breath, breaking the seal of their kiss. Unwilling to completely part, he took a couple of small sips from her lips before releasing her from the shelter of his arms. He swallowed hard, dismissing the doubt still gripping his spirit. With his Evainne back once again, he felt whole. Trailing his hands across the slick fabric covering her back, he inhaled deeply. She responded in kind, and his eyelids slipped down while he enjoyed the simple joy of her breath against his skin.

<I'm so sorry, Kahl.> Her voice filled his heart, giving him the strength he thought he had lost. He held her closer, resting his cheek atop her head.

"Shh, *ziat'xahn.* You have nothing for which I need to forgive." He nuzzled his face into the silken tumble of curls and smiled. "I have you again in my arms and by my side." He paused, brushing his knuckles under her chin to raise her eyes to him. Even her red-rimmed eyes could not detract from her beauty. He wiped away the silvery tracks on her cheek with the pad of his thumb. "And I will do all I can to keep you exactly where you are, and where you are meant to be." A slow smile pulled up the corners of his mouth, and soon, she returned the gesture. The room brightened, and in that perfect moment, Kahlym thanked the Goddess for her blessing.

"Are you two ever gonna come up for air?"

Brel's voice had echoed down the hall, reminding Kahlym of their current setting. He opened his mouth, preparing a witty comeback, but his angel beat him to the punch.

"I'm a friggin' Divine and I can do whatever the hell I want, so piss off, Brel."

Laughter rang out from every corner, moving away from their open room, and Kahlym glanced down at his smirking mate. "Well said, my beloved." He placed a kiss on the tip of her pert nose. "But I need to make sure you have food. You will need your energy for the apology I have in store."

Her eyes flared wide and a wicked twinkle lit up the deep brown pools. "Oh, don't throw me into that briar patch, sweetie."

His brows tugged together at her strange phrase and he filed it away for further consideration later. Instead, he released her from his embrace and interlaced his fingers with hers. "If that means anything like I am hoping it does, we'd better get food soon. I do not intend to let you out of my bed until both of us have been fully … forgiven."

Chapter 15

Qaen stared out into the nothingness that was the Great Black. Kahlym couldn't have just vanished into thin air. *I don't care if the bastard's fucking a Divine.* No way did she have that much power.

The problem was time, and he was running out of it. Two cycles back, he'd promised the emperor he'd deliver Kahlym, his crew, and the entire Stria leadership caste, cementing his seat on the Praxxiran council. Since then, he'd wormed his way into the good graces of the Strian captain, learning trade secrets and forging his own alliances along the way. Things were going perfect. So he should've known. That was usually when shit went sideways.

He'd just gotten his final contact orders, the where and the when of the hand-off for the entire crew of *Tiamat's Revenge,* when that damned girl had to show up and screw the whole plan.

"So, what's plan B?"

Qaen sneered, focused on the galaxy of lights and numbers visible only to him. Images shimmered as he tried to delve deeper. His annoying copilot appeared as a gray blob, clouding his vision and shattering his calm. His concentration broken, the stars winked out, and he glared up at Panza's sour puss.

"You know, you have absolute shit for timing," Qaen grumbled and climbed out of the suspended nav chair. He grabbed on to the steady metal frame while his legs remembered how to support him, and his stomach clenched, empty and neglected. He swallowed a mouthful of saliva, coughing when the scant liquid went down the wrong tube. "How long have I been dark?"

Panza M'Uubair, son of the Rimmarian Emperor, stepped back and folded his arms across his chest. "Two moon-risings. I've been trying to get your attention for the past five hours."

Rolling through his shoulders, Qaen offered his prickly passenger a one-fingered salute while he worked out the kinks from such an extended dive. He dragged a hand along his cheek, stubble scratching his palm, and he slapped his face to wake up his drowsy body.

"I can help with that if you need," Panza offered.

Narrowing his eyes, Qaen leveled his unamused gaze at him. "Like I've been telling you, mate: I don't do boys." He added a sickeningly sweet grin to seal the deal, and Panza recoiled, stalking away. Pleased his barb had struck true, Qaen dared a couple of steps. His muscles ached from disuse, but he managed to finally get his legs beneath him. Certain he would remain vertical, Qaen limped over to the personal, inset cold cabinet, vaguely aware of Panza prattling on behind him. He fished out a drink, ignoring the rambling reprimand. Qaen had mastered the ability to cut out any unwanted interruptions, including voices, while surfing the Black, and without sound, his companion looked like a broken puppet, limbs flailing as he paced the confines of the navigator's loft. Qaen cracked open the bottle of strong alcohol and sipped at its heavy contents as he enjoyed the entertainment.

Far too quickly, he tilted back an empty container. Time to end this current distraction.

"Are you planning to get to the point sometime in my lifetime?"

Panza froze and snapped his wild, jade green eyes in Qaen's direction. The slender mustache hugging the man's thin upper lip twitched in an angry dance. "Are you planning to find the fucker sometime in *my* lifetime?"

Qaen whistled faintly and shook his head. "Such strong language. Not getting perturbed now, are we?" He quickly raised his hand to dismiss any further sputtering. "Do you know anything about the Stria?"

Panza scoffed. "I know enough. One should know about one's enemy."

"Then you know about the hundreds of little hamlets on any of a dozen planets loyal to them, right?" Qaen waited, intrigued by the emotions chasing across his passenger's face, and when defeat cycled around, he continued. "Yeah, now you're figuring it out. Literally thousands of backwater places are willing to harbor him. I have an idea, however; a different strategy, if you'd like."

Seconds ticked off in silence before Panza leaned away, gesturing for him to finish. Qaen had taken the opportunity to fish out another drink. "It involves that girl of his."

"You mean the Divine?"

Divine. He scoffed at the thought. "Yeah, that's the one." In their initial meeting, Qaen hadn't seen her as anything other than a female to fuck; she had a decent rack from what he could tell, given that she'd practically been wearing that bastard Kahlym as a coat. But she'd managed to escape from the hanger bay on Skirnahn Waystation, even after scrapping with his assassin lover, Kaxxahn. Still, he wasn't entirely convinced of her elevated status. It would take more than luck and rumors to make him a believer.

A knock against his shoulder yanked him back to the present and, blinking to clear his head, Qaen glared and shoved Panza away from him. "Back off," he snarled as he distanced himself. Last thing he needed was an additional price on his ass for kicking the shit out of the Thrall leader's only son.

"How can the girl help us? That reject sent her away."

"But how far?" Qaen had been pondering this as soon as he'd heard about the botched takedown on Raedyn Primus. Every news wave under the Thrall's thumb had reported it as a Strian attempt to assassinate members of the High Council. Too bad other rumors had spilled out of the Jhuen household first, all mentioning the kindness and beauty of a mysterious Divine with power unlike anything witnessed.

"My gut's telling me she's closer than we think," he continued as he opened the second bottle. "All we need to do is listen. Someone will talk; someone always does."

Panza narrowed his beady eyes. "So whose line do we tap?"

Qaen heaved a long sigh, giving a sidelong glance at the recently vacated nav chair. "All of them."

A buzz from the sensor array grabbed Panza's attention. "What's that?"

"Company."

"Company?" Panza parroted back, folding his arms across his narrow chest. "I was not aware we were expecting… That's Kaxxahn's ship."

Qaen quickly tapped out the coordinates for a waystation on the nearby moon, a cruel grin tugging up his lips at Panza's nervous tone. "Don't worry, mate. She's been on the same mission as us. Figured it was time to get another set of eyes to point out something we've missed. Besides," he added, steering their ship toward the approaching rendezvous location, "I think we're gonna need some additional firepower soon."

The rocky surface zoomed closer as Qaen's thoughts wandered. *You can't run forever, Kahlym. Sooner or later, I will find you and finish what we'd started.*

Chapter 16

With great effort, Evainne peeled her eyes open to peer into the surrounding darkness. True to his word, she and Kahlym had spent the rest of the day lost in each other's arms. Words had been few and far between, their actions speaking for them. After their delicious meal, and ignoring the conversations surrounding them, Kahlym had escorted her back to their borrowed room and stripped her bare in record time. She'd returned the favor, her lips devouring his as she clawed at his cocooning gearsuit. Then, with his hands gripping her waist, he'd lifted her off the floor and released the fly of his gearsuit. She'd wrapped her legs around him, unwilling to break their kiss, and had welcomed him into her body with a heavy moan.

They'd made love standing inside the room, using the wall as a back rest. The first round was hot and fast, their frenetic hunger pushing her to a sudden peak. Once she'd caught her breath, Kahlym slipped out of the rest of his clothes and, sweeping her into his arms, moved her onto the private balcony. She vaguely recalled him saying something about Ontaxians enjoying sex in the rain, and as the sultry night air caressed her drenched bare skin, she completely understood the allure. The sweet drops poured down, funneled by giant leaves, adding to the erotic friction between their bodies.

Finally, they'd made their way to the massive bed. There, he'd slowed their furious pace. He was thorough and tender, kissing and massaging her knotted muscles from head to toe, and her eyes rolled back into her head as he took special care with her sensitive core. Time slipped by in an orgasmic haze; all the while, Kahlym whispered loving words into her ear and onto her skin, branding every inch of her, and she couldn't have been happier. And so, exhausted and drained, Evainne had collapsed in a limp heap upon his chest, sweat-drenched and blissfully out of breath. She'd counted each beat of his heart beneath her ear, the strong and steady lullaby sending her to sleep within seconds.

Now, groaning softly, she rounded her spine, stretching her aching muscles. A pair of strong arms coiled around her, keeping her solidly pinned against a warm wall of flesh.

"Whatever it is, *ziat'xahn*," Kahlym murmured, pressing a kiss onto the back of her neck, "it can wait."

The corners of her lips curled up into a lazy grin, and she snuggled deeper into his embrace. "But the universe needs you."

"Screw the universe," he growled hungrily, then dragged his tongue up the column of her throat as he ground his throbbing shaft against her ass. "I need you."

Evainne sucked in a sharp breath between her teeth, arching her back as dampness flooded her core. "You've had me so many times, I lost count." She dug her nails into the meat of his forearms, gasping as he eased his cock inside for another round. "God, Kahl, at this rate, I'm not gonna be able to walk right for a week."

His laugh, deep and sensual, poured down her bare skin, pitching her over the edge in record time. "I like the sound of that," he said. Languid and careful, he sank into her, before inching out and driving in once again.

"I'm, ah … not surprised by … oh, God … by that at …

Kahlym!" She held on to the arms encircling her as she again surrendered to ecstasy. So much still needed to be said between them, and as soon as she stopped orgasming, she'd get right on that. For now, words and air tangled on her tongue, sounds struggling to escape while oxygen vied for entrance. Her heart pounded in time with his, proof of their unbreakable link and unyielding love, and warmth, comfort, and joy flooded her spirit. Within Kahlym's loving embrace, Evainne had found a home she was willing to fight to protect.

She cried out, the soul-shaking realization bringing her to dizzying peaks, and she clung on to Kahlym, riding wave after crashing wave of pleasure. He tensed at her back, her name a strangled growl that he purred into her ear as he joined her in their personal heaven.

<My beautiful angel.> Upon hearing her lover's voice echoing inside her head, sheer contentment flowed through her veins, and she croaked out a weak laugh between free-flowing tears.

"I've missed you so much," she said. So what if she sounded pathetic. Time to stop hiding behind her self-righteousness and get to the truth of the matter. "Kahlym, I—"

"Shh," he whispered into her ear. Carefully, he eased himself out of her, then readjusted her rubbery arms so she lay draped over his chest. "My brother was right, *ziat'xahn.* I was a fool to send you away." His voice had rumbled across her skin, and she nestled deeper into his protective hold. "I ... I couldn't chance your life against the depths of cruelty of which I knew my father was capable, though."

Evainne shivered at the memory of his father's lecherous looks. Only by using her wits and wiles had she managed to outfox the man who'd stolen her from her only friends with desires to sell her to the Thrall Emperor as a baby factory for the next generation of Divine puppets.

Kahlym must have sensed her shift in temperature, and he trailed his fingertips along her bare arms, encouraging her blood to fire up. She returned the favor, drawing lazy circles on his sweat-damp skin.

"Fear controlled my actions, Evainne."

His hand stilled in the silence.

He was holding something back. She knew it with every fiber of her being.

Evainne scooted out of his hold and rose up to rest on her hip, her legs tucked in close. She used the discarded sheet as a shield, tucking it beneath her armpits. The soft fabric rubbed against her sensitive nipples and the extra length pooled in Kahlym's crotch. *Good thing, too.* If she caught sight of his growing interest, nothing of any value would be said. Instead, she focused on his entrancing tourmaline eyes, determined to banish the lingering shadows still darkening the exotic pools.

"And anger controlled mine," she said. "You're not the only guilty party here, sweetie." She pressed a finger to his parting lips and shook her head. "Please, Kahl. I'm no saint. I can get my panties in a bunch just like the next person." An adorable, confused frown tugged his thick brows together, and she winked. "Meaning I can get upset by little things as much as anyone. And when you…" She swallowed hard, forcing down her wounded pride. "When you sent me away, I was furious, thinking you didn't trust I could protect myself. I jumped to the conclusion you believed I was weak and feeble and—"

"Evainne, I know all too well how strong and fierce you are," he said, his voice soothing as he brushed away her cascading tears. She leaned into his broad palm, wrapping her fingers around his wrist.

"Even when I'm bawling like a baby?" she squeaked out between sobs.

Through the blur of her tears, she recognized the smile that had first captured her heart. "Even then, *ziat'xahn.* You are my heart, and never again shall I fear, for you will always be at my side."

Laughter caught in her throat, then finally sneaked past the waning sobs. "Good, 'cuz I don't like being mad at you."

Kahlym chuckled and gathered her back into his embrace. "The feeling is mutual. And you didn't have to contend with a pissed-off crew, as well."

Evainne sniffled back the waterworks and again counted the strong and steady rhythmic beats beneath her ear while Kahlym took in a deep and stuttered breath, and her actions mirrored his. She pondered briefly on the idea of who led whom, but in her heart, she knew the truth: both, and neither of them. They were now one spirit living in two bodies. R'uan had called it a "soul-bond," and she was beginning to understand the truth of its connection.

Voices rising and falling grew closer to the door, with one new speaker emphatically making their point. Evainne glanced up to Kahlym's face. "I have a feeling we're gonna have visitors sooner than we wanted."

Kahlym's gaze slipped toward the barrier, a curious grin on his lush lips. "I think you may be right, and judging by the—"

"I heard what you said, Dhaer," interrupted a determined feminine voice, "but I don't think Kahl will mind if I pop in and—"

The door slid open, and Evainne swiveled her head toward their guest. A young Amazonian woman bounded in, dressed in a bright green flowing tunic over a pair of loose, olive pants, two high, rainbow-striped pigtails trailing to her shoulders. Her feline features were more delicate than Dhaerin's or R'uan's, but there was no denying the familial resemblance. Peridot green eyes peered out from the slick midnight black fur, and a fleeting smile morphed into a panicked "O" as her gaze bounced between Evainne and Kahlym.

"Uh, hi?" Evainne lifted a hand and waved. *<Should we do something?>*

<Wait for it, my angel...> A mischievous snicker filtered through their link, and she rolled over in his arms, pinning him with a curious smirk.

Confused, Evainne opened her mouth, when a strange squeak filled the room, followed by a heavy thump.

Not again.

"A ... a th-th-thousand p-p-pardons, D-D-Divine," stammered a voice from the floor.

"Oh, fuck me sideways," Evainne groaned as she flopped over onto her back and draped her arm over her eyes, while laughter filled the room from both within and without. "Can't I catch a break?"

———————————

Chapter 17

———————————

Kahlym glanced at the faces of those gathered around the open atrium. Muted sunlight streamed in, bathing the room in a golden glow, melting away his apprehension. His angel sat beside him, her long fingers laced between his as she listened intently to R'uan's current events report. After peeling Zybella off of the floor, more than once, and after a lengthy shower with Evainne, he'd rejoined the rest of his crew to prepare an arduous plan of attack. Remnants of the lavish spread lay strewn around the table, small empty plates scattered and piled up in front of all gathered.

Save one.

Zybella's gaze never moved from Evainne, no matter the amount of teasing she received from her brothers. Yet each time his angel shifted her own gaze, Zybella found something of interest on the ground.

"Zy," whined Dhaerin for the umpteenth time as he tossed up his hands, "would you stop?"

Evainne rested her hand on the pilot's shoulder, settling the agitated Ontaxian back into his seat. "Let me try," she said. Kahlym

117

sank farther into his chair, curious as to his fiery mate's proposed solution. As graceful as a dream, Evainne rose, then knelt down beside the silent Ontaxian female.

"Let me guess. I'm not quite what you expected, huh?" She spoke calmly and softly, her direct words aimed at the heart of the matter as always, and a proud smile touched Kahlym's mouth. He shifted his gaze to his crew, who all watched with baited curiosity. Somehow, some way, this particular interaction was pivotal. He returned to his quiet observation as Zybella's cracked whisper broke the silence.

"It-it is forbi—"

"Not any longer," Evainne stated, and Zybella lifted her chin, her shocked peridot eyes focused solely on Evainne. "See, I've never been big on following rules, especially ones telling me who I can talk to." His angel slid her gaze over until she locked eyes with Kahlym. "Or who I can love."

Kahlym's heart soared at her open declaration, as if the words spoken aloud further solidified their soulbond. She gave him a playful wink before returning her focus to Dhaerin's frozen sister.

"It's time for some serious changes," she continued, gripping Zybella's shoulders and guiding her to her feet. Even though the other woman towered over his angel by nearly a head and a half, Evainne's powerful presence alone dominated the room. "And the first one is: My friends don't grovel. To me, to anyone. Ever."

The cooling winds outside stilled; the forested world held its breath in anticipation. Zybella trembled for a moment before throwing her arms around Evainne tightly and wailed "Thank you" amid sobs.

Relieved laughter filled in the spaces, and Kahlym rose with the rest of his crew. Smiling, he placed his hand on Evainne's shoulder.

"Well," she said, "that's one way of doing it, I guess."

"Group hug!" Dhaerin bellowed, scooping up whoever was within arm's reach as he bounded across the room, then added Evainne and Zybella into the pile of limbs. Groans and complaints melded with the growing chuckles, giving some much needed release.

Xandar managed to stay on the outskirts of the circle, until Brel extended one big hand and dragged him in. "C'mon, *kherdes-xahn*, bring it in."

Kahlym shrugged, offering his older brother half a grin. "You didn't think you were going to get away again, did you?"

"For a minute, I had hope." The bland barb failed to hit its mark, and Kahlym enjoyed the momentary peace. The only family who mattered was right here in this room with him. Perhaps he could hope for better times to come.

A hand frantically thumped against his chest, breaking into his serenity.

"Can't … breathe…"

Kahlym threw back his head, raucous laughter pouring out as he peeled the group away from Evainne. She clung to his arm and dragged in deep, giggling gulps of air.

"First I can't get anyone to give me hug. Then you try to smother me." Her smile echoed in her voice, and Kahlym joined the mirth as he led her back to her chair. "Boy, when you guys change your minds, you *really* change your minds."

"You never asked me for a hug," Dhaerin chimed in, then thrust out his bottom lip. The childish pout looked ridiculous on his mammoth leonine features, but it did draw a smile from his still-sniveling sister.

Evainne patted his hand gently. "I'm sorry, hon. Next time, I'll know better."

With the mood lighter, Kahlym refocused the group to the difficult task ahead. "Somehow, I don't think the Thrall will collapse if we just throw our arms around each other."

"True," added Xandar. "But the small steps are perhaps the best ones to take."

Brel shook his head vigorously. "No, we need to hit big and hit hard. Now, when they're not expecting it, and while they believe Evainne has been lost to all. We need to—"

"Strike the match."

All eyes swiveled to Evainne and a puzzled frown tugged Kahlym's brows together. "A-a what?"

"A match, a match," she repeated, excitement and frustration coloring her voice, giving a frantic edge to her fidgeting gestures. Her pleading gaze swung to Xandar. "Help me out here, Toa."

Kahlym followed her eyes, studying his brother's calm expression.

"A sparkan," Xandar said.

"Seriously?" Dhaerin screwed up his face, confusion in his deep topaz eyes. "How the hell is that gonna do any good?"

"Don't you see?" Evainne jumped to her feet. "All we need to do is light the candle. Plant the seed and let, well … let nature take its course."

Even as connected as he was to his angel's every thought and emotion, Kahlym was having trouble following her line of logic. "I'm not sure I understand what you mean, *ziat'xahn*."

"When I was a kid, I'd heard the story about the three princes," she began, spinning her chair about. She rested her forearms on the curved back. "Their father, the king, wanted to test them to see who would take over his kingdom when he died. So, he gave each of them a thousand gold pieces. With the money, they each were instructed to buy enough of anything they wanted to fill one of the chambers in the castle. He gave them three days to find what they needed."

Kahlym studied his crew's faces; all were engrossed in the tale she wove. In his mind, he pictured every detail: the three boys, and the palace, as well. He wasn't able to bring the compassionate father figure to life as easily. As she continued in her telling, he closed his eyes and listened.

"After three days, the king called his sons to him. First, they went to the chamber of the first son. The oldest son had spent all of his money on bricks, and the pile went halfway up the wall. The king was impressed, but said nothing. So he went to the chamber of his second son. The middle son had spent all of his money on feathers, and his pile surpassed the bricks. The king was impressed, but still said nothing."

"That sounds like our father," Brel mumbled. "Never satisfied with anything."

Kahlym snorted his derisive agreement, the faceless male in the story now wearing the mask of Anaxar. He held his tongue.

"Trust me, I know that feeling," Evainne said, sympathy and understanding shifting her voice.

"What about the youngest?" Zybella asked, bringing a smile to Kahlym's face. While the question was barely above a whisper, he was grateful she was willing to join in.

"When the king went to the chamber of his third son," Evainne said, "the room was empty, and the youngest son had only two things in his hands: a candle and a match. His brothers laughed, mocking him for his foolishness, saying, 'How much money did you spend?' The third brother shrugged, telling them he had only spent pennies. 'How can you expect to win this contest?' they asked. Saying nothing more, the youngest son stepped into the dark room, then struck the match and lit the candle. The glow filled the entire room and spilled out into the hall. The king placed a hand on his youngest son's shoulder, declaring him the winner, and his rightful heir."

"Strike the match," R'uan said, awe and understanding filling his voice.

"And ignite a rebellion," Kahlym added as he opened his eyes, scanning the faces of his crew. Evainne's story had stirred something in each of them: hope. She'd inspired them, and Kahlym could only sit and watch, humbled by the ease at which she'd raised everyone's spirits. Even an unaccustomed smile sat on Falka's usually stoic face. He hadn't realized his tech could show any such joyful emotions.

"But," Brel broke through the peaceful haze, "exactly how do we do that?"

R'uan rose and stood beside Evainne. "You have all seen how one minor act of kindness helped to dismiss nearly a lifetime of ingrained religious doctrine. If we can get the word out that a Divine stands alongside the Stria…"

Another deep silence filled the room.

Evainne placed a gentle hand on Kahlym's shoulder, and he dragged his gaze up to her angelic face. "Do you want to tell them, since you've got the better words for it?" she asked.

Kahlym felt the heat of every stare leveled at him, while he lost himself in the warm, brown eyes of his loving female. He reached up, lacing his fingers with hers, gathering strength from her faith and her love.

"Tell us what, *kherdes*?"

"Seems, kiddies," Evainne started, an impish smirk curling her lush lips, "I'm more than meets the eye. So to speak."

Kahlym brushed a light kiss across her knuckles, then he rose and, taking a deep breath to sort out his thoughts, turned his gaze to his friends. No, not friends. Family, both by blood and by bond. He draped his arms protectively around his angel.

"I believe Evainne is not only a Divine, but she is the one foretold at the beginning of our recorded histories." Kahlym scanned the room, pensive expressions giving way to awed whispers. "I believe our Lady Evainne … is a Paramount Divine."

Chapter 18

Emperor Gha'jahn M'Uubair curled his long fingers into tight fists, squeezing harder the longer he stared at the words flickering across the vid screen. Nearly twenty moon-risings had passed since his promised Divine had once again slipped through his hands. He had even taken the precautionary steps of gathering viable seed from the three ancient Divines in case their search took longer than any of them had left. At first, he imagined her to be lost for all time. Yet, across his entire empire, word of her filtered in—tales of miracles and of her beauty, as she mingled with the common people, poured in from every corner of the Dantaran galaxy.

"How is that bitch getting everywhere?" he growled, narrowing his gaze at his High Council advisers. Not one of the males was brave enough to meet his eyes. The three remaining Divines sat apart, their heads bowed, while hushed arguments tickled his ears. His jaw clenched as the useless silence droned on.

One female. She was just one damned female. How difficult was it to capture a helpless woman far from her own home? When Divine Seer Hollix had discovered the uniquely necessary genetic signature halfway across the known universe, it was simple enough to lock the biotransport on to it and pull her here. A standard journey; no fuss, no muss. Instead, she winds up on a prison transport, then gets spirited away during a bloody breakout. And, thanks to the ineptitude of his underlings, he had gotten only glimpses and blurry video feed images of her. The assassin who had accepted the contract had fought her during another escape and had claimed she was nothing special. Yet this nothing, slip-of-a-girl continued to evade every hit squad since her arrival nearly thirty moon-risings ago.

"What is she?" he roared, slamming his hand down hard enough to leave a dent in the shimmering chrome. His rage cut off the blabbering representative from Raedyn Primus. If Anaxar Jhuen had come through with his part of the bargain, a more intelligent and cunning man would be at the table. Instead, he was stuck with the sniveling bureaucrat, and the patriarch of one of the oldest families in the Dantaran galaxy could only wait out in the hall like a servant.

"Well, um, sire … it seems that … um, she is—"

"Enough." The one word and his sharp look stopped any further fumbled excuses. Then he snapped his fingers and gestured to his guards. "Get me Jhuen."

Councilor Xhineer stuttered out a protest, his chair scraping against the tiled floor as he clambered to his feet. "Your eminence, he is—"

"Exactly who I should be listening to, as he is the only person in this palace who has even seen her, you simpering louse." He was the emperor, and the Goddess be damned if a cowardly sycophant was going to dictate with whom he could or could not consult on matters of the realm. The longer he waited for his men to follow his command, the more he realized Xhineer would have to go.

Gha'jahn motioned his personal sentry nearer. He said nothing of importance for the banks of tiny electronic eyes recording every movement, muttering something about bringing in food and drink.

His private message was much darker, and traveled over unobserved wavelengths. *<Be sure Xhineer meets with an accident by this time tomorrow.>*

"Very good, sire." With a slight bow, orders received and understood, the man backed away, his footfalls soon disappearing toward the hall leading to the kitchens. As his captain turned the corner, Jhuen and a retinue of Thrall guards entered the room.

"Ah, Sub-Confidant Jhuen." Gha'jahn tipped his chin to the approaching group. "So kind of you to join us." He studied the man as he drew closer. Eyes like fire rubies seared sidelong glances at the men once his equals, now his overseers. Still, years of staunch military training kept his back ramrod straight and his long strides confident and measured. Jhuen was known for his viciousness and aggression in battle and tactics. Perhaps he could focus those skills on the problem at hand.

Anaxar inclined his head. Not one hair was out of place in his severe martial cut, his salt-and-pepper beard and mustache neatly trimmed to frame a pair of cruel lips. "You called for me, sire."

Thinly veiled contempt had melted through his voice, and a devious smile spread across Gha'jahn's face. "We did. We were wondering if you could enlighten us regarding this missing Divine."

A tic began at the edge of Anaxar's mouth, causing his mustache to jump in an aggravated beat. *Curious*, Gha'jahn mused. What had the girl done to warrant such loathing?

"She is intelligent," Anaxar said, "I will give the little bitch that." Gasps and outraged whispers hissed amongst the gathered ministers. "Do not underestimate her. As to her powers, I know nothing. She neglected to show any abilities in my presence."

"How dare you speak—"

Gha'jahn lifted a hand to silence the offended Divine Traveler. "You had your chance to bring her to us, Haseunn. Your failure has created a problem that may destroy our way of life. However," he continued before the other Divines could chime in, turning back to the Sub-Confidant, "I would suggest, Jhuen, you keep a civil tongue if you plan to keep it attached to your person."

Anaxar splayed his fingers across his chest and offered a reverent bow. "A thousand apologies for letting my temper get the better of me, sire."

The emperor hid his appreciative smile with his hand. The man had balls; he'd give him that. This kind of Ruling Hand would get results. But elevating to the High Council the father of a known Stria sympathizer might be tricky.

"You are certain she is gifted?"

Gha'jahn shifted his gaze, gauging the temperature of the room. All eyes were riveted on Jhuen, with several councilors licking their lips in anticipation of the word that could alter the course of the current regime.

Anaxar dragged air into his lungs, then exhaled slowly, as if drawing strength from the atmosphere around him.

"Absolutely," he said at last.

At this, voices rose and fell, all vying for supremacy, in the vast chamber. Gha'jahn steepled his fingers and stared at both everything and nothing.

And so it begins.

Chapter 19

"Evainne? Evainne!"

"What? I'm up, I'm up." Evainne's head jerked up as Xandar's hand jostled her shoulder. Fully awake for the moment, she rubbed at her heavy eyelids and scooted back into a seated position.

Xandar glared, his narrowed lapis blue eyes regarding her from beneath thick, black brows. "You are not. You are a breath away from collapsing. Don't bother trying to deny it."

Damn. Her bright idea to spread the word in a grassroots fashion was coming back to bite her on the ass. Days had blurred together as she traveled to distant villages all over the Seventh Quadrant to meet with key players in the Stria hierarchy. She'd lost count of the number of times she had to drag people up off of their knees, some up off of the actual floor. Granted, it didn't help that, even though he'd stayed back on Ontaxa, Yhan'tu had insisted she go everywhere in a damned regal robe. And both Xandar and Kahlym had taken his side.

At the thought of her semi-traitorous lover, she slid her gaze toward the ship's cockpit, where Brel and Kahlym focused on the banks of panels as stars zoomed by. Their current transport, borrowed courtesy of the Rimmarian imperial fleet, needed fewer crew members than had her normal ride, and the cozier quarters made for fewer secrets. Kahlym had opted to relinquish the captain duties to Brel and Xandar, claiming it would interfere with his ability to protect Evainne. She knew his chivalrous words were a lie. A thinly concealed lie, but a lie nonetheless. There was nothing Kahlym couldn't do if he set his mind to it.

At first, she'd been afraid her lover was still caught up in his self-imposed web of self-doubt. She'd opened her mouth, prepared to protest, but when Kahlym had met her gaze, her words had dried up on her tongue. The haunting shadows in his intoxicating bi-colored orbs were gone, and the fierce warrior who'd swooped in to risk all to rescue her was back. But Brel had demanded he sit in the navigator's chair, and with the brothers' tag-team manning the helm, Evainne believed nothing could stop them.

Except me. They traveled at such breakneck speeds, and with great haste, and it was seriously wearing her out.

<Ziat'xahn, do you have need of me?>

Kahlym's calm voice soothed her troubled mind, though it did nothing to banish her exhaustion. Swallowing hard, she looked up and caught his stare reflected in the thick, curved glass. Once, she'd asked him to let her be his strength. Now, she feared she was becoming everyone's weakness.

Images in her field of vision blurred, but not before she spied movement in his general direction. By the time his arms had wrapped around her shoulders, her waterworks was in full force. She clung as uncontrolled sobs wracked her. *<Xandar's right, Kahl. I can't do this.>*

"Bullshit." Brel had broken the tension with one of his new favorite words, and Evainne choked out a giggle. Apparently, she'd forgotten to shield her mind again. Hearing many of her go-to profanities from all of the guys on *Tiamat's Revenge* always made her smile, though. The only real exceptions were Yhan'tu, who probably wouldn't say the word "shit," even if his mouth was full of it. And Xandar.

As she composed herself in Kahlym's embrace, she flipped through her memories, recalling only a handful of times she'd heard her former teacher swear, and in each instance, the colorful language had served its purpose, shocking her out of her dangerous mood at the time.

"Evainne, you have proven to everyone there is nothing you can't do," Brel continued. "You talked about lighting a match, and you have. By now, that asshat on the throne has gotta be scared out of his wits. You don't have anything to be ashamed of."

"With all that said," Xandar pointed out, "I believe a rest has been more than earned."

"No," she said, "I can—"

Luckily for her, the brothers knew the lie before it fell from her lips. The ship veered into the nearest hyperlane and took off like a shot. She wished she could have lodged a stronger protest, but Kahlym's fingers tracing soothing circles onto her back stole the fire from her stubborn streak. Opting for shelter instead, Evainne closed her eyes and pressed her ear against Kahlym's chest; the steady beat combined with his rhythmic inhale and exhale made for the perfect lullaby. A floating sensation followed, and after her short levitation act, her bed magically appeared beneath her.

On instinct, she reached out for Kahlym before he could escape. "Please, stay," she mumbled as her fingers twirled around the sleeve of his gearsuit. One thing she hated about the ziplocs: no loose fabric to grab. She would be sound asleep in seconds, but she didn't want to be alone right now.

The air thrummed, a sign that Kahlym was chatting offline with his brothers, and soon, the mattress dipped behind her. "Thank you," she said and, smiling, she nestled back. Kahlym draped an arm around her.

"I cannot deny such a tempting request," he purred into her ear. Even exhausted beyond all comprehension, his voice had still snapped her body into sensual overdrive—her legs scissored together as she arched her back, grinding her ass into his groin. "Not so tired now, *ziat'xahn?*"

The rumbling growl pouring down her spine ramped up her desires another notch. "Don't blame me, *kerriad.* You started this all."

It had taken some digging, but Evainne had found the right word to sum up the depth of her feelings toward Kahlym: fierce lover. He was that, and more. Her world spun until she was facing Kahlym. Just the right amount of stubble dusted his once-smooth cheek; not so much to hide his chiseled jawline, yet enough to tantalize her skin when he nuzzled her neck.

She traced the edge of his full lips with her fingertip, following the upward tilt. "And you seem more than willing to make sure I hold up my end of this," he replied. She trailed her gaze up until she reached his tourmaline eyes, recalling the first time she'd looked into his unusual and disarming stare. Not in her wildest imagining could she have envisioned a spaceship with the cast of characters she now considered family.

He placed a kiss on the tip of her nose, then cradled her face in the palm of his hand. "There will be time enough for passions after you have rested."

Frustrated, her eyebrows pulled together, giving him her best glare, but judging by the smile warming his eyes, it might have read more like a pout. With the pad of his thumb, he wiped away the furrow across her forehead, and her eyelids fluttered down.

<*Now who's not playing fair?*>

Kahlym's laugh echoed through her mind as sleep claimed her.

KLAXONS BLARED an instant before the ship shook violently, the jolt throwing Kahlym out of bed and onto the floor. Darkness flooded the interior as he climbed to his knees.

"What the hell was that?" he said. The emergency lights kicked in, and he glimpsed his drowsy angel in the reddish hue. Only a matter of time until the Thrall caught up with them. He was surprised their visits had gone undetected for as long as they had. Now, a return to their safe haven on Ontaxa, with their precious cargo intact, was crucial.

"Stay here." Kahlym jumped to his feet, but not before Evainne grabbed a hold of his arm. Spinning, he placed a fiery kiss on her lips, branding her onto his soul, then broke the seal of their mouths and pressed his forehead to hers. "Please," he said, "do not argue with me on this."

Without waiting for her response, he dashed out and ran the short distance toward the cockpit. Sparks flew from a smoking panel off to his left and he yanked open the searing-hot metal door. With a wince, he carefully disconnected the smoldering wires, swearing under his breath, and patted at the flickering flames.

"Who hit us?" he yelled over the sirens, the words aimed at the wall while he focused on reengaging the navigation system. The short fire had done no sustained damage, and he secured the control panel. "Brel? Xandar? Talk to me."

"They didn't exactly leave a note, Kahl," Brel roared in response, and his brother's anger kicked Kahlym's legs into action. Three running strides later, he skidded to a halt and surveyed the scene for himself. The hyperlanes had vanished, but stars still sped by as the ship dipped and zigged in random vectors. Another blast rocked the hull, and Kahlym grabbed on to the doorframe to stay on his feet.

"Dammit," Brel grumbled as he yanked on the ship's controls, fighting to keep them stable. "Kahl, get on that damned nav console and see if you can find out who the fuck is out there."

Kahlym nodded sharply and sidled into the tucked-in seat. He hated using the nav gear; the all-encompassing surrender to the Great Black necessary for specific details always left him with searing headaches and the urge to vomit. Forcing down his rising bile, he closed his eyes and slipped the goggles over his head, then steadied himself with a deep breath and willed his eyes and his mind open. His stomach lurched as the vast Dantaran galaxy appeared before him and he turned his head smoothly, deliberately, searching for signs of their unknown opponent. A flash of white off to his right, followed by a black-and-chrome streak, drew his attention.

"Crap! It's one of ours."

The discussion over which ship to use on this mission had taken nearly half a day. After exhausting all reasons, they'd decided upon an enemy ship. While it made the planet inhabitants standoffish at first, it did make travel between their stopping points easier.

Until now.

"Ours?" Brel and Xandar asked in perfect harmony.

"What do you mean 'ours'?" Xandar demanded. "How could the Thrall have discovered us?"

Kahlym shook his head, and the universe spun out of control before his eyes. He slapped his hands across his mouth to hold back the meager contents of his empty stomach. A couple of swallows later he trusted his voice enough to speak. "No, not us." He gestured toward the ship. "Us. It's the Stria. I think it's Galassan's ship."

The sleek fighter bore the faceted, cobalt blue teardrop emblem of the Stria, and as it whizzed past, Kahlym spied the unique insignia of his friend and ally, Levar Galassan. Frantic, he shouted over his shoulder. "Someone tell him he's about to destroy our only hope of defeating the Thrall, or we're dead!"

Sounds of buttons flicking and knobs twisting filled the cramped cabin while Xandar and Brel attempted to contact the vessel outside while Kahlym stared on in terror. *Come on, Lev. Listen to your damned radio.*

"What is our frequency? I can't find the right signal!"

Closing his eyes, he mumbled a quiet prayer to Ishtanti, and added a private plea to Evainne, as he braced for the impending impact. He should be with Evainne at this time. *I'm sorry, ziat'xahn.*

Silence descended, thick and heavy. Yet no explosion split the seconds ticking by.

Kahlym cracked open his lids to peer out into the vast space beyond their ship. Galassan's craft hovered off their starboard side, frozen against the starry backdrop.

"Thank the Goddess," Kahlym sighed in relief. "Tell him we owe him a drink."

"I didn't get through."

Confused by Brel's statement, Kahlym removed the shielded goggles. The reappearing consoles swam in his vision. He dug his thumbs into his temples, hoping to drive away the jarring ache. "Xandar?"

"It wasn't me."

"So, I guess the frequency you need is, um, epsilon mark ten."

Kahlym swung his heavy head toward Evainne's voice, though his roiling gut was not pleased with the sharp action, and again he slammed his palm over his mouth as his eyes squeezed shut. Soft fingertips brushed across his forehead, and the nausea vanished.

"You okay there, sweetie?"

He captured her hand and placed a kiss in the center of it, then raised his gaze to his angel attired once again in a gearsuit. He'd wondered how long it would take before she ditched the regal gowns. She was beautiful in everything she wore, though he preferred her in nothing at all. A smile touched his lips as he forced his mind back to the present. "I am now."

"Kahl? Is … is that really you guys in there?"

"It's us, Lev," Brel answered while Kahlym climbed out of the navigator's seat. A frown tugged his brows together. Evainne had yet to meet his eyes, and an eerie glow haloed her body. With her hand in his, he led her into his embrace, and she shuffled closer, her movements wooden and stilted. During their excursions to the various Stria strongholds, Evainne was reticent to tap into her Divine abilities. In truth, she hadn't needed to. Word of who she was had reached many of the outposts ahead of them, giving

Kahlym the opportunity to discuss strategies with key leaders, so this was the first time since leaving Ontaxa she had displayed any of her skills.

Fear. He'd recognized the dangerous emotion coloring her aura as he drew broad, slow circles across her back with his hand. She'd nearly lost control in a fit of anger after her return, and now, it appeared she was afraid she would jeopardize them should she use her powers in any way.

"You are safe, *ziat'xahn*," Kahlym whispered into her ear before resting his cheek on her soft bloodwine tresses. "And you saved us all." At this, a fraction of the tension in her shoulders slipped away, and she mumbled something unintelligible into his chest. He held her closer.

A hand gripped his shoulder and he glanced up. Xandar stood at his side, concern reflected in his lapis blue eyes. "Lev wants us to follow him to his ship. Apparently, he feels remorse for damaging our vessel and wishes to help us with the needed repairs."

<Is she okay, kherdes?>

Kahlym nodded, answering both questions with the same answer. "Tell him we would appreciate the aid."

"In the meantime," Xandar stated, "I think it is time for Evainne to return to her training."

The urge to tell his older brother to screw himself was tempting, but in his heart, Kahlym knew Xandar was right. If Evainne was the Paramount Divine spoken of only in hushed whispers, then she would need to learn to trust herself and her awakening skills.

His knuckles light under her chin, Kahlym nudged his angel to lift her gaze to his. Streaks of gold flashed in her deep brown eyes while unshed tears clung to her lush lashes. *So beautiful.* A hint of pink warmed her pale cheeks, and he cradled her face, brushing away the lingering drops with the pads of his thumbs.

"Are you ready, *ziat'xahn*?"

The lightning storm in her eyes gradually faded, and a shy smile touched her lips. "Yeah." She sighed, the single sound washing away any doubt. "I gotta get my head in the game, and to do that, I guess I'm gonna need some help."

Xandar clasped both of their shoulders. "Good. Because we just docked on Lev's cruiser, and he's quite eager to meet with the one strong enough to disrupt his communications array from ten klicks."

Kahlym arched a brow, then shifted his gaze down to his angel. "Evainne?"

She shrugged sheepishly, gnawing on her plump lower lip. "I had to get their attention somehow."

He placed a tender kiss on the crown of her head, weakly trying to hold back his grin. "Remind me to always listen when you call, *ziat'xahn.*"

Chapter 20

After having spent the past two decades on Earth, setting everything about his past into memory, Xandar had discovered some things would never truly be forgotten. Namely, the deep connection between himself and his brothers. Brel was still quick with a smile and a joke. Apparently, time had softened his sibling's mercurial temper, just as the years apart had altered his younger brother.

He rubbed at the ache in the center of his chest. When he'd set out to test his theory of space travel all those moons ago, he'd had no intention of abandoning the people who'd relied on him. Kahlym had second-guessed every step he'd taken, and the constant hatred and hounding from his parents had only made matters worse.

"You coming or what?"

Xandar smirked and set aside his trip along memory lane as he hoisted his bag onto his shoulder. "Are you in a hurry?" He glanced over at Brel waiting in the narrow corridor.

"I'm tired of stooping all bloody day," his brother groused, rubbing at his neck. "I'm more than ready to stretch my legs out in something other than this infernal death trap."

"I can't argue with you on that, *cal-kherdes*."

Brel grinned. "It is good to have you back, Xan."

Xandar kept his back to his brother until his smile reached a believable level. Yet once he turned about, his mouth drooped. He'd missed so much, had left both of his siblings to face his parents alone. "I never should have—"

"Have what?" Brel shook his head, halting the apology a long time coming. "Never should have started that shuttle engine? I've been watching you since you dropped back in, and you act like you need to make up for things."

"Don't I?"

Brel led the way toward the loading ramp. "If you told me you wanted to escape before you married the emperor's daughter, I would've helped. Hell, I would've booked passage for you on the next freighter heading to Bashir, or anywhere else you wanted to go. I definitely couldn't blame you for not wanting that headache." Stride for stride, they strolled out onto the tarmac. Kahlym and Evainne had taken off with their host moments after their ship had landed. They were as safe as possible, given the situation.

"But you didn't plan for what happened. Plus," his brother added, "if you hadn't landed on Terra—"

"Earth," Xandar corrected.

"Fine. If you hadn't landed on Earth..." Xandar chuckled at his sibling's exaggerated emphasis. "Then you wouldn't have been there for Evainne. You wouldn't have prepared her as you did. She still would've been dragged here, but she would've been unable to fight or protect herself. And maybe—just maybe—no one would have been around to save her."

Those same points had been running through his mind ever since Evainne had pounded on his front door all those days ago. "But what if she was tagged by the emperor *because* of those trainings I'd given her? What if those skills had somehow triggered her Divine abilities?"

Brel shook his head, his mouth forming a perfect straight line as he grabbed Xandar's arm, halting their forward progress. "No. I can't and won't believe that. You know the stories as well as I, *kherdes.* The skills of the Divines are innate; it is what they are born into. She would have been found. I feel it in my bones."

When Xandar had begun training her, the purpose had been simple: focus. So much chaos had surrounded her, allowing anger and fear to guide her. The unfounded hatred her parents had aimed toward her had reminded him of the unwarranted cruelty his younger brother was forced to endure. So, desperate to make a positive difference, he had started her with basic meditations and centering exercises. The fighting, she had taken to much quicker than he had anticipated, and with greater skill than he had expected. During those early days, he had leaned heavily on the advice of Bao, the Sumo wrestler who'd adopted Evainne as his surrogate little sister. Together, they'd taught her to balance her highs and lows.

Now, he had the daunting task of training a Paramount Divine.

"That may be true," he sighed, resigned to his brother's words, "but now, a difficult job still lies ahead."

Brel shrugged and nodded toward the approaching entourage. "Yeah, but this time, you don't have to do it alone." On cue, Evainne appeared from behind one of the uniformed guards. The once skinny, angry young girl had grown up, and she now strode, strong and fierce, in the midst of the gathered warriors.

A swelling of pride filled Xandar's chest as their two groups converged. Kahlym followed close behind, standing off to her left, appearing like nothing more than her personal protector, and the words of Shezheer's prophecy slipped into his mind. Even after so many years, he'd never forget the old woman's vacant and rheumy emerald eyes, the Seer's trance deep and profound as she sealed the rocky path of Kahlym's life.

"Eyes unmatched shall witness untold sorrow;
Through the lost traveler's heart shall infinite sadness be shattered.
Winterborn will control the Fates;
As one shall great tasks be carried.
Grief will prevail lest love and fury unite the divided."

"Why didn't I see it …?"

"See what?" Brel asked. "Did I miss something?" Xandar hadn't realized he'd spoken aloud and, stunned by his own obliviousness, he dropped his face into his open palm.

"No, I did. The prophecy," Xandar mumbled, shaking his head. "All that time and not once did I think of that damned prophecy."

"Hang on." Evainne's no-nonsense tone had cut like a knife through his wandering thoughts. "All those birthday parties where Bao teased me about being dropped off by Santa instead of the stork, and you didn't think of that friggin' prophecy? Now I know this thing wasn't a fix."

"Fix? Was something broken?"

Xandar chuckled and raised his gaze to Kahlym. "Nothing except my mind, *kherdes-xahn*. Had I remembered the old priestess' words, I might have spent more time working on Evainne's temper and less time on her martial skills."

"Careful there, Xan," Brel warned, resting a bent elbow on Xandar's shoulder. "I've seen her fight, and I wouldn't take her on."

Evainne rolled her eyes with an exaggerated groan. "I'll have you know, I'm doing much better with my anger management issues."

A strange silence hung heavy in the landing bay, and Xandar arched a brow as Evainne kicked at the ground. "Well … I haven't put my fist through any walls lately."

"When you face the emperor—and you will—he will use every trick in his vast arsenal to rile you into making a false move." Xandar shifted his gaze to their impromptu host. "Galassan, it is good to see you."

Levar Galassan, captain of *Devil's Armada*, extended his hand

and clasped Xandar's forearm. "By all the stars in the sky. I never thought I would see you again in my lifetime." Rich laughter bellowed from the boisterous, good-natured Achtillian as he nearly yanked Xandar off his feet to pull him into a rib-crushing hug. Lev was the first flight instructor Xandar had had as a young man, and age did not appear to have slowed Lev down. A few more lines now creased his high forehead and a couple of extra pounds hung on his lanky frame, but for the most part, he was exactly as Xandar remembered him. "I didn't believe Kahl here," Lev went on, pointing his thumb over his shoulder, "when he said you had returned from the grave."

"Shall we say the rumors of my demise were a bit premature." Xandar inclined his head, the rigid gesture earning another round of belly laughs from their host.

"Come," Lev boomed. "This is cause for celebration." He wrapped one long arm around Xandar's neck, while he gestured toward Evainne with the other. "An old friend *and* a Divine on my ship. This is truly a sign of great changes on the horizon."

A strange, whispered murmur of one single word darted through the landing bay: Divine. Brow furrowed, Xandar glanced around in rapt curiosity. Within seconds, every crew member in the immediate area had taken a knee, heads bowed in reverence.

"Fan-fucking-tastic," Evainne grumbled, tossing her arms toward the heavens. "Great way to blow my cover. Now I have to start all over again."

Xandar shrugged as he met her perturbed stare. "At least we can spar in peace." He offered her a sly grin and tipped his head toward the groveling masses. "No one would dare cross paths with an angry Divine."

"Fine," she groused. "As long as I can catch some Z's first. All this night around me has totally screwed up my body's sleep cycle."

Xandar drew his brows together, but nodded. "Until tomorrow." He watched from beneath his own drooping lids as Evainne and his younger brother trailed after Lev. After mulling over her logical rationalization, he sighed and hefted his pack across his shoulders. *How much longer will she dismiss all the signs?* he wondered as he caught up with the departing group.

Chapter 21

Evainne slapped the ground with her palms as the world tumbled once again. Apparently, she was out of practice with her judo throws. She windmilled her legs and popped back to her feet in a low crouch. Air raced in and out of her lungs, and it felt good. She missed fighting, with its energy coursing through her as she prepared for the next attack. It had been far too long since had she been in a knockdown, drag-out battle and it would take time to get her edge back. Case in point— the current training session. Sweat poured from her body, the gear-suit a sorry alternative for her old *gi*. Easy enough to ditch the boots and work barefooted, although she had to justify the rationale to all except Xandar. Bao had talked about a needed connection with the earth, and she was beginning to put some stock into the silly concept.

She raised her hands into a loose guard, countering Xandar's sidestep with her own. Determined to keep distance and not get her ass handed to her again, she slid her feet along the soft surface and kept her gaze fixed on her teacher. Xandar had always been an unrelenting sparring partner, never accepting anything but her A-game in every match. But that was when nothing more than a trophy or a ribbon were at stake.

Now, things were different. Lives were on the line, and not only hers: her lover, his brothers, all the crazy aliens living on board the massive ship, all depended on her. Faces of the thousands of people she'd met in their recent excursion through the universe, swam up into her vision. Young and old—all of their hushed words of thanks and praise still echoed in her ears. Even now, she sensed Kahlym in the room, the distant sound of his heartbeat always present in her head. It had taken some doing, but after the second day of sparring, she'd convinced him he didn't need to rush in and rescue her whenever a punch landed. The more she thought about Kahlym, the more she lost focus and her breathing ratcheted higher.

Something akin to a freight train barreled into her, knocking her flat onto her ass, while arms like steel wrapped around her midsection. She flailed around, frantic to catch her bare toes on the padded mat to gain a measure of traction. Ducking her chin, she drove her shoulder toward the floor and rolled with the generated momentum, and once the ground was again beneath her knees, she kicked out hard, twisting within the unrelenting hold. Her feeble escape failed, and her cheek kissed the slick floor.

"Get your damned head in the game."

Xandar growled his disappointment, and she snapped her teeth together, holding in her building anger. Opting for a different tactic, Evainne rotated her extended right arm then drove her elbow back toward her opponent's head. The blow wasn't strong enough to do any real damage, but as Xandar leaned away, she freed her trapped arm and seized the minute opportunity to push off the floor, knocking Xandar off-balance and giving her space to escape. Quickly, she scrambled to regain her feet, but Xandar's hand latched around her ankle and dragged her backwards. She fell onto her face, then, gritting her teeth, she spun onto her back.

She realized her mistake too late. Xandar pulled hard on her leg and drove his knee toward her chest. Evainne jerked up her arms, locking her elbows together to protect her ribs. She knew her teacher would never intentionally hurt her, but she'd earned her fair share of bruises during their bouts before she ended up in another galaxy. As his leg descended, she flicked out her wrists and dug her fingers into the meat of his thigh. Her arms ached and trembled as she struggled against his weight levering down onto her. She squeezed her eyes shut, frustration reaching a tipping point and, roaring out, she shoved with all her might, then scooted onto her side. No longer pinned to the ground, she slammed her open palms against Xandar's shoulders … and sent him soaring across the room.

"Oh, shit." Terrified, she scuttled over to where Xandar had landed in a heap. "Shit, I'm sorry. I'm so sorry."

Xandar groaned as he gingerly eased into a seated position. He rubbed at the back of his head and pinned her with an admonishing stare.

"Is that how you are managing your anger, *hoc sinh*?" he said. Evainne sat back on her haunches, arms leaden as they hung at her sides. He was right. "By using your newly discovered skills in attack?"

"I was—"

With a flick of his wrist, Evainne shut her mouth as he wiped away the blood from the corner of his lips, then sighed loudly. "I know what you were, Evainne." He climbed to his feet, wincing, and she slunk beside him. "You were frustrated, and you lost your temper. This is not the first time I have heard the same excuse from you."

"Yeah," she scoffed, "but before if I blew my top, I was usually the one ending up on her ass." Then hindsight kicked her hard, and she cringed.

"So this is what, your idea of payback for my trying to help focus your aggression?" Xandar asked, pinpointing her thoughts, and he grabbed on to her arm, but embarrassment kept her gaze locked on to the floor. "I need your eyes. Evainne, look at me."

Evainne, clenching her jaw to keep her treacherous tongue in line, lifted her eyes. A weeping cut on the apple of his right cheek sat beneath his swollen purple eyelid. But nothing could hide the spirit-crushing disappointment in the one remaining lapis blue orb boring into her. "Even after all these years, you still cannot see the truth."

That did it.

"What fucking truth?" she railed, aching fingers curling into dangerous fists.

"That until you believe in who you are, you will never become what you are destined to be."

Evainne barked out a bitter laugh, wrenched her arm free, and stalked away, shaking out her clenched fingers. "Not this fortune cookie bullshit again, Toa. You fed me the same line when I was young and stupid enough to listen."

"No." His single, calm word slammed the brakes on her tantrum, and she froze in mid-stride, then turned to face him. "Evainne, if there is one thing in your life you have never been, it's stupid. Reckless, headstrong, stubborn … those I will give you." Blood trickled from the hairline cut slicing through his bottom lip.

I did that, she thought. The bruises, the gashes, the black eye. All of that was her doing. In an instant, she was transported back to that cramped dojo.

Her lungs burned and her limp arms refused to hold their guarding positions. Sweat, tears, and blood created a sticky veil, blurring her wavering vision. Toa paced around the circle just beyond her reach, his ever-present wraparound shades glaring at her with imagined disappointment.

"Why do you hesitate?"

She shifted her gaze toward her teacher. Her opponent, Mitch, a boy a few years older than her, jumped on her lapse in concentration and rushed in, tackling her around the waist. Swearing under her breath, she backpedaled, heels sliding across the slick pad. Air whooshed out of her lungs and her brain fired on over-drive. As her feet left the ground, she dug her fingers into the red belt around his midsection, then pulled with all her might. Her partner had too much momentum and her feeble attempt at a counterattack only managed to throw him off-balance. Together, they crashed onto the worn-out mat, and pain shot up her leg, ankle pinned beneath the bigger foe.

Instead of crying out, she elbowed Mitch in the gut. Once freed, she wrapped her legs around his shoulders and neck, locking her ankles until he slapped the mat in submission. She released her legs with a gasp, then rolled onto her back. She had only a moment to enjoy her victory before a hand dragged her up to her feet.

"You do everything the hard way. Why?" Toa's long legs ate up the ground and she was powerless to do anything more than hop alongside him. "You could have taken him with that move before you got hurt. Why do you hesitate?" He spun her about and, with a clatter, her ass landed on the cold seat of the metal folding chair.

"Because … Because I don't know!" she yelled, frustration and agony blending into a volatile concoction that was becoming her go-to emotional response. "Because he pissed me off! Because you distracted me. Because—"

"No." His sharp retort stopped her excuses in her tracks, and his expression was stern, unreadable, and confused the hell out of her while he examined her swelling ankle. "You blame your failings on everything around you, yet the truth is, you do not believe you can do a thing." She flinched and hissed out, his probing fingers finding each tender spot. "You second-guess each move, even when victory is within your grip. Doubt and uncertainty keep you weak."

"I'm not weak," she whined out. Tears ran hot down her cheeks, but she blamed them on the pain. She angrily dashed the back of her wrapped hand against her watery eyes. Toa cupped her aching ankle, his massive mitts swallowing up her size-five foot. A strange cooling sensation seemed to emanate from his gentle touch, spreading a much-needed sense of calm into her angered spirit.

"I did not say you were weak; your doubt is holding you back from becoming what you are meant to be."

The same hands that had made the pain vanish all those years ago now rested on her shoulder, and Evainne choked down the rising emotional tide.

"Yet you are also fierce, compassionate, and determined, *hoc sinh*," he went on, pulling her back to the present, "and those are the skills you need to hone and refine."

"But all these people—everyone—looking to me to save them? Hell, I can't even save myself." Drifting lost in a turbulent sea of responsibilities, she was buckling, and she just wanted to hand over the controls, even for a moment. "I know I'm fucking things up left and right, and this was my bright idea to go on this idiotic mission. Each time I think I'm closer to getting a handle on my anger, the slightest breeze sets me off. Toa, what do I do?" The prior name of her old teacher had fallen from her lips before she could switch it.

Xandar squeezed her tense muscles, and Evainne blinked back the tears refusing to slow as she studied the ground beneath her feet. "Get off the cross," he said.

A strangled laugh slipped past Evainne's clenched jaw, tension seeping out of her confined stance, and she met Xandar's understanding expression.

"Someone else needs the wood," they responded harmoniously. He smirked, and she shook her head slowly, the light chuckle dismissing any remaining stress.

"Evainne, can I ask you a question?" Xandar said, and she nodded, wiping her sniffly nose against her sleeve. "You've been edgier than normal, and you seem to be experiencing mood swings more frequently. Am I right?"

She drew her brows together, searching for his true question as well as for her answer. Given the current reality, Evainne figured she was entitled to her fair share of mental meltdowns. But was it more than normal?

"What about eating?" he continued. She gnawed on her bottom lip as her forehead ached with the ever-deepening frown. "You're having trouble keeping things down at breakfast, aren't you?"

A familiar, comforting presence stepped in behind her; Kahlym wrapped his arms around her shoulders, pulled her back to rest against his chest. She reached up to grip his supportive forearm, her chin resting on her knuckles as her brain struggled to dismiss the evidence Xandar presented.

"She has little in the mornings, and even the blandest foods make her queasy."

Evainne swung her head from side to side, pieces refusing to settle into a believable image. "I'm kinda under a lot of stress," she said. "So … no. I mean, how can that be that … I … I'm…"

With a gentle touch on her chin, Xandar guided her gaze upward. Their eyes locked, and a knowing grin tilted up his lips. "Yes, Evainne," he said. "You're pregnant."

Chapter 22

The converted cargo hold's contents snapped into crystal clarity as Kahlym picked apart Xandar's words. In his waking eyes, the ghostly visage of Shezheer shimmered in the distance, her head inclining to him before the vision dissolved.

Evainne was with child. *His* child.

Torn between elation and the desire to throw up, Kahlym stood frozen. The final piece of the prophecy had fallen into place. Then … why couldn't he celebrate?

Perhaps because of the trembling angel in his arms. She mumbled something, words slipping out in rapid fire, and Kahlym struggled to make sense of it all. Her short nails clawed at his arm, and he massaged her shoulder, hoping to ease her rising panic. Frowning, he met eyes with his brother standing across from him.

<Be patient with her, kherdes-xahn.> Xandar nodded and backed away, leaving them to absorb the news together. When he reached the threshold, he looked over his shoulder, smiling warmly. *<And congratulations to you both.>*

The metal door sealed them in silence, and Kahlym gently turned Evainne about. Her bound bloodwine tresses whipped from side to side, her fear flooding the chamber. "Evainne?" he whispered to gain her attention.

Her hands gripped his wrists as her head drooped. "I … I can't … This is wrong. He's gotta be wrong. He has to—"

Kahlym fought against his rising agony at her hollow words. "Why do you say that?" he croaked out. Did she not wish to have his child?

She choked out a mirthless laugh. "We're in the middle of a revolution, Kahl. Now is not the time for me to be … I need to be at full strength to face the emperor."

"Wait, what?" Confused, he shuffled a step back and tipped up her face to better read her eyes. "Face the emperor?"

Expression vacant, strange shadows darkened her brown orbs. "I started," she said, then paused, giving his wrists a squeeze before continuing. "*We* started on this road. The ball is rolling; the match had been struck. And I'm … I'm not about to slow down because … because…" Seconds ticked by before her mask slipped away and her eyes welled up. "Omigod, Kahlym. I…We…"

Kahlym's lips parted as he prepared his heartbreaking apology, but Evainne stunned him with a bone-cracking embrace, her arms flung around his neck. "Kahlym, we're gonna have a baby!" Relief coursed through his veins, and he gathered her close, nuzzling into the hollow of her throat. Her joyful laughter intermixed with her falling tears, and soon, he responded in kind. He spun about with his angel held to his chest, savoring her rich laughter as they twirled. He placed her feet back onto the ground.

"You—" He hesitated a moment. "You're not upset?"

Her plaited hair whipped about as she shook her head, and she leaned back to look up into his eyes, beaming. "You just have to promise to still love me when I get as big as a house."

Cradling her damp cheeks, he plundered her mouth, savoring the sweet happiness mingling with the salty tears. How had he become so blessed? Had the Goddess decided he'd suffered enough, or was this to be the cruelest punishment yet?

Determined to banish the hateful thought, Kahlym returned his attention to the gift in his arms. He would protect his angel and his child with his dying breath, and calm washed over him as he gently broke the seal of their lips.

"There will simply be more of you to love."

She sniffed back her tears, her smile reaching to her eyes, and farther. "Gonna hold you to that, sweetie." Stepping back, Evainne eased out of his embrace, then dried her face with her fingertips. "I may be feeling a lot of things right now, but upset isn't one of them."

"Feeling things, such as…?" Certain she was finished composing herself, he interlaced their fingers and strolled toward the bench along the wall.

"God, where do I start?" She gave her head a slow shake as she sat beside him. "It's a tie between exhilaration and abject terror. You know I didn't have the best role models on how to raise a kid, right? What if … what if I turn out to be like them, or even worse?"

Kahlym lifted her hand and, with her fingers splayed, pressed her palm flat against his chest. "*Ziat'xahn*, you are the most kind and loving person I have known in the whole of my life. You are going to be the strongest, most compassionate mother to our son."

"Son?" Evainne chuckled, cupping his cheek with her free hand. "What if it's a girl?"

He turned his face to kiss the protective wrappings concealing her skin, though his lips only managed to brush the pads of her knuckles. "Then I will be doubly blessed to watch our daughter follow in her mother's footsteps."

"This is really happening, isn't it?"

Kahlym swiveled his gaze back to his angel. As she'd said, a myriad of emotions chased across her face and swirled through their link—good and bad, positive and negative, hope and fear, all ebbing and flowing with each breath. Yet through it all glimmered joy, and this gave him courage. He merely nodded, unable to contain his jubilant smile.

"I love you, Kahlym."

To hear the simple declaration in his own language falling from the tongue of his Evainne filled him with an all-consuming inner peace. He held her gaze and, issuing a silent thank you to Ishtanti, placed his hand over her heart.

"You are my very soul, Evainne. I will love you until death and beyond."

Her deep brown eyes sparkled, and he fell into the rich depths. Until a stray thought melted the smile off of her face. Concerned, he tugged his brows together. "What is it?"

"We can't let people know," she said. "Hell, if Yhan'tu finds out, he'll never let me do anything at all." While he wanted nothing more than to shout the news from the highest hill, she was right, and though her lighthearted tone buoyed his spirit, something darker had brought on this choice. "If the emperor finds out … he will not only triple his efforts to find me, he'll probably kill you and, and…"

Her hand slipped from his and covered her belly instinctively. She began to curl in upon herself, and Kahlym leapt into action. With a gentle grip on her shoulders, he guided her to sit tall. "Do not let your mind give in to this, *ziat'xahn.*" He struggled to find the words, so he closed his eyes and spoke from his heart. "I would give my life to keep you safe," he said. "We will protect our … our child. We will only tell those we can trust." He touched his forehead to hers. "I will never be able to say how happy you have made me, my beautiful angel."

His words faded until only their paired breathing whispered through the silent space. All too soon, the world would crash down, as it always had. But for now, Kahlym sat quietly, fingers weaving through her loosely braided hair, and held Evainne, his savior. His Divine.

"Hey, there you are! Time to eat and—"

Kahlym opened his eyes to Brel, who'd flung open the door and poked his head in past the threshold. His easy smile melted into concerned frown. "Did I miss something? You two all right?"

"Not two," Evainne answered, raising her gaze to him. With a playful wink, she directed her words toward Brel while shifting to hold Kahlym's gaze. "Three."

Evainne stood up and stepped past Brel, confusion screwing up his features as she disappeared down the corridor. Kahlym kept his focus on his brother while mentally counting down: *Five ... four ... three...* He was almost at two, when realization dawned on Brel, and as Brel's enthusiastic hug nearly took him to the ground, he thought, *I probably should've snuck out after Evainne.*

Chapter 23

Pregnant.

The single word spun in Evainne's mind as she strolled down the corridor leading to the galley. In her heart, she couldn't bring herself to be surprised. She and Kahlym had been screwing like bunnies, after all, since that night in the reflecting pool.

She skidded to a halt. Not once had she even thought about any kind of protection. Before she'd stepped through the universe's joke door, she wouldn't have even kissed a guy unless she had a condom in her pocket, just in case.

Then she met Kahlym. From the moment she'd looked into his exotic, tourmaline eyes, she had fallen—hard. Perhaps part of her didn't think she could get knocked up by an alien. Now, she carried his child. Did this make things easier, or more complicated?

"Greetings to you, Blessed Divine."

An unexpected voice had snapped her back into her immediate surroundings, and with barely a thought, she locked up her mind tighter than Fort Knox as she tipped her chin toward the speaker. She only saw the top of his bowed head as she approached. She assumed it was a him; she'd only spied a few other females on board, and since the speaker wasn't wearing a gown, she figured she'd go with the male supposition. Though she'd worked hard to get their host's crew to stop groveling whenever she breathed, most continued to insist on her honorific title. *Well, at least I didn't have to peel him up off the floor,* she mused. Baby steps.

With the man's gaze glued to his feet, she was certain he hadn't seen her nod. "Uh, yeah. Hi."

"I—"

She stopped, caught by the fragmented vocalization. "What's up?" she asked, and the rounded shoulders began to tremble. Evainne picked up an odd vibration in the air and, throwing decorum out the window, she grabbed on to him before he shook himself apart. "What?" she demanded, harsh and abrupt.

He jerked his head up. His robin's egg blue eyes took up nearly half of his face. "It is not safe for you here." His small, lip-less mouth had barely moved, and the whispered words had chilled her blood.

"Why do you say that?" she inquired, her own voice hushed. Evainne focused on the crew member in front of her to read the colorful halo encompassing his body. Oddly enough, she hadn't required much training on that front; she'd always been able to tell if someone was lying to her. Though she did have trouble figuring out those who were convinced their fucked-up version of things was the truth.

The light surrounding the being in front of her was pure white; nearly sparkling, it was so pristine. "Please, Blessed Divine. You … you have been so kind to my tribe, and it would dishonor my ancestors if you were harmed and I did nothing to stop it."

Unsure if he'd clam up as soon as Kahlym came around the corner, Evainne opted to keep this private. <*I think we might have trouble here. Hang tight for a second.*> Waves of loving concern washed over her, and she bit down on the inside of her cheek to hide her smile.

She relaxed her death grip on the crew member's arm and

dialed down her empathetic panic. "That sounds really noble," she said, "but I need to know why you think I'm not safe here."

His slender arms shook like twigs in a twister as he reached for her hands. "It is apparent you have already done battle to remain safe, Blessed Divine." Heart-wrenching grief contorted his smooth face, an odd, pale green tear sliding down his pearlescent cheek as he gently raised her blood-splattered knuckles up as evidence. "You must leave this ship. You must be kept safe."

<*False alarm.*> Evainne heaved a sigh, and the knotted tension in her shoulders relaxed. "What's your name?" she asked, adding an easy smile to her request.

"My … my name?" Her impromptu savior quirked his head, his large eyes regarding her curiously.

Evainne chuckled and closed her fingers around the long, four-digited hands. "Yes, your name. I can't go around saying 'Hey, you' when I want to get your attention."

"I-I-I am called Myclen." The poor guy looked like he was going to burst apart.

Then Mike it is.

After giving his fingers a squeeze, Evainne unwound the protective wrappings from her hands. "Myclen, thanks for your concern, but I promise, I am unharmed. Where I'm from, this is how I make sure I *don't* get hurt." Two pairs of boot heels echoed in the hallway behind her, and she covertly waved off the approaching brothers. "But if you happen to discover anything that might cause harm to me, or any on board this ship, please tell me."

"Everything okay here, *learom-xahn*?" Brel's deliberate use of the familial term appeared to have eased her new buddy, his large oval eyes still focused on her.

"Just making new friends, bro." She tossed a smirk and a wink over her shoulder. "Looks like my sparring might be freaking out the natives."

Brel chuckled, bumping his shoulder against hers as he passed by. "Don't worry," he said, clasping Myclen on the arm, "she is more than capable of taking care of herself. But that doesn't mean the rest of us cannot be as vigilant."

Myclen nodded, his large head bobbing as his stare darted to each person gathered. "Oh, yes. Yes, I completely agree."

She liked the guy. It had taken a lot of courage for him to break with his ingrained beliefs and talk to her in the first place. Perhaps she was making more than baby-step progress.

Kahlym closed the distance behind her, hovering at her left-hand side. She immediately recognized his show of possessive power, his dominant hand free should he need to reach for his holstered weapon.

Brel steered the man down the hall, but Myclen stopped and, spinning back to face Evainne, he cupped her hands. With a reverent bow, he touched the backs of them to his high forehead.

"My life, I pledge to you, Blessed Divine."

The sincerity in Myclen's voice, coupled with his aura's shimmer, brought a smile to her face. Brel rolled his eyes and once again took a hold of her new friend to guide him down the corridor. She caught snippets of Brel's words as the pair headed farther away, the bulk of the fading commentary about how to get in touch with any of them if Myclen heard anything.

A devious thought crossed her mind. With a light jab of her elbow, she caught Kahlym's attention. "Looks like you're being replaced, sweetie." Biting down on the inside of her cheek to keep a straight face, she glanced up to read his response. "You win some, you lose some."

She shrugged and managed to side step before his fingertips skittered along her sides. Tickling? She squeaked out a surprised giggle, then spun about to face him.

"Replaced, am I?" he growled playfully, his wiggling fingers inching closer.

Laughing hard, she batted at his encroaching attack, shuffling backwards to stay out of range. "Well, a girl's gotta have options, you know."

Kahlym swooped in and, without missing a beat, hoisted her over his shoulder. She yipped out, uncontrollable laughter pouring free as he marched down the hallway, heading to who knew where. They would be earning some strange looks from anyone passing by, but Evainne didn't care. At this moment, she wasn't the Paramount Divine, set to save the universe. Right now, she was only a woman sharing a silly moment of joy with the man she loved with all her heart.

Chapter 24

Qaen rolled through the knots in his shoulders, twisting his neck from side to side, working out the kinks as he took to his feet. After seventeen moon-risings, he needed a serious break. The brief respite with Kaxxahn had provided little information, and he wasn't sure if it was comforting or not that the assassin had had just as much luck trying to ferret out the location of that bastard, Jhuen, and his band of merry misfits. After a few hours of dalliances, his fuck toy had left to pursue her own leads.

Since then, he'd been stuck with the useless princeling as his only company. Panza was shit for conversation. Plus, the man didn't have the right plumbing for his current needs. Yawning, he elbowed the comm link on the wall.

"We're stopping for supplies."

He didn't care if the bastard responded, or even agreed to the layover. He needed to stretch his legs and get some, no matter what the emperor's son thought. While Kaxxahn had taken the edge off of his hunger, he'd need another partner soon. As he contemplated other options, his mind swirled back to his last visit to Raedyn Septicon. Between Khundyl's legs, he'd learned that Kahlym and his bitch had stopped there looking for replacement crew members. He'd pressed her for information as he teased her body. Yes, the girl was a Divine. No, they had not gotten new recruits. However, the most important piece of intel he'd discovered was that his secret remained safe; she hadn't leaked word of his betrayal to the rest of the Stria.

Always good to have allies whose moral compass was just as skewed as his.

After climbing out of the nav chair, Qaen stumbled along the narrow corridor leading to the main cockpit. Already Panza was heading in his direction, obviously about to start some shit about the call to dock, but before the fucker could get a word out, Qaen flipped him off and shouldered past. "I saw *Devil's Armada* in our sector. She's about eighty klicks out. I'll simply drop in to see if Lev's heard anything about Jhuen and his crew."

"I will be slaughtered if I'm spotted," Panza sputtered, his silvery skin turning sickly green while his brows rocketed toward his hairline.

Qaen flashed him a shit-eating grin. "Then I guess you'd better hide good, dearie—and now." He focused on the display panel in front of him as angry mutters trailed down the hall. Qaen snorted in mirthless relief.

"Incoming vessel, identify yourself."

Qaen slipped on the headset as he slid into the pilot's seat. "Marauder XJ-Beta. Transport from *Tiamat's Revenge* looking for refueling."

"What if they don't believe you?" the annoying prince called out in an overly loud whisper.

Qaen snapped his head about, glaring down the corridor. "Would you shut the fuck up? Damn, grow a pair." Grumbling, he turned back to the starscape. The titanium hull of the Stria cruiser grew larger as he waited for confirmation. Maybe he should ditch the sniveling asshole and be done with him; tell the emperor his son had died valiantly, or some other load of crap. As tempting as that prospect was, his fate was tied to bringing everyone back to M'Uubair alive, including the heir to the Rimmarian Thrall.

Seconds ticked by, and a cautious frown tugged Qaen's brows together. "Contact the nearest battalion forces," he said. "How long before they can rendezvous with us at this location?"

"Proceed to the aft landing bay, Marauder XJ-Beta."

Qaen nodded as the line went dead.

"They can arrive in under ten minutes," the answer came, echoing along the metal interior. "Do I send the order?"

Scenarios raced through Qaen's mind as he maneuvered the ship onto the correct approach vector. Was it a trap? Had he been outed? He flicked a switch and deployed the landing gear. He tightened his grip on the control stick, his arm trembling as he guided his craft to the tarmac. They were among his supposed friends, but better to be safe than dead.

"Get them within seconds," he answered, powering down the engines. "We might need to get out of here quick." Once everything had been secured, Qaen yanked off the comm set and climbed out of the cockpit. He leveled his gaze at Panza. "Stay out of sight and wait for my signal."

"Which will be what, exactly?" The officer folded his arms across his chest.

Gnashing his teeth, Qaen grabbed the front of Panza's jacket and nearly pulled the man off of his feet dragging him closer. "Well, if I return and we take off, then we won't need additional firepower, will we?"

Panza tore Qaen's hand away from his throat. "That much I figured out myself."

"Good," Qaen grumbled while he retrieved his blaster and armed up. "Then you'll be smart enough to know if we're about to be fucked." And before he could do something he'd regret, Qaen punched the gangplank release, chuckling darkly as Panza scrambled for cover. "Just keep an ear to the comm."

He disembarked, dismissing the receding profanities at his back. Two sentries headed his direction, and he painted on his friendliest smile. If he could play nice with the Rimmarian princeling, he could easily fake a grin or two with his once-allies. After exchanging basic pleasantries, Qaen got down to the business of pleasure.

"Say, do you guys know if Fallicia is still on board?" Though he preferred his romp partners with less meat on their bones, the plump Ontaxian would slake his appetite for the moment.

One soldier elbowed the other with a knowing grin, and as if on cue, the cargo off-loader in question strolled around from the back of his ship.

"Well, Qaen'Deenkarra, as I live and breathe." Fallicia winked and wiped her dusty hands down the front of her coveralls. "To what do I owe this honor?"

Qaen opened his mouth, preparing for the full seduction, when she shook her head. "Fuck it. I don't care." She grabbed his belt and dragged him away from prying eyes. The sooner he got his rocks off, the sooner he could speak to Lev. *And the sooner I can be rid of that bastard.* As he bent his willing partner over the nearest stack of crates in their secluded corner, Qaen realized the term "bastard" applied to both his traveling companion and his quarry.

As the hunger for payback fueled his body, he slammed his cock into Fallicia, mercilessly and relentlessly.

Chapter 25

"I know it's a lot to take in," Kahlym said, eyes trained on Lev as the half-eaten plates of food lay strewn across the curved table. He'd done his best to give the necessary information to his ally, while holding back delicate details such as the true depths of his connection with Evainne. She obviously showed him favor, but he'd been successful in his guise of personal guard; he always remained one step behind her in public, his hand never far from his weapon. In truth, the defensive position had become more of a habit, now that she carried his child.

And each time that fact crept into his mind, his spirit sought out hers, while his fingers inched closer to the butt of his gun. Their secret must remain hidden; he couldn't risk the wrath of the devoted members on Lev's ship should news of her condition spread.

Lev rested his fisted hand against the corner of his mouth, a furrow of deep concentration cutting across his smooth forehead, while Kahlym fought the urge to reach for Evainne's fingers beneath the table. Only a handful of their host's crew remained; direct members of the flight and navigation units, he assumed, but did not ask. He had placed his trust in his comrade. Time would tell if his judgment was correct.

Lev let out a long stream of air, breath whistling over his knuckles. "That's putting it mildly. I thought seeing him again"—he tilted his head toward Xandar—"would be the high point on the insanity scale."

Evainne scoffed. "Oh, trust me on this one, sweet cheeks; I don't think that fucker has peaked yet."

Gasps and mumbles filtered through the air, driven by the officers on the other side of the table. Lev, on the other hand, threw back his head and barked out a sharp laugh. "Dear Evainne, you are definitely unlike any Divine in Rimmarian control."

A crooked smile tilted her full lips, and Kahlym groaned, the crotch of his gearsuit shrinking as the blood raced from his brain to his aching cock. "Well," she added, "I've never been a big one for following anyone's control."

Brel and Xandar raised their hands in unison. "I can attest to that," Xandar commented, while Brel nodded and muttered his agreement.

Like magic, Evainne had both cut to the heart of the matter and diffused the growing tension, with ease, and Kahlym wanted nothing more than to lose himself in her loving embrace. His desire would have to wait, though, until they returned to their quarters.

Her rich laughter was a balm to his soul as she waved off Brel's continued braying. "Yeah, yeah. Laugh it up, fuzzball." She turned back toward Lev to return the group on point. "So, can we count on your help?"

Lev glanced around at his present crew members, meeting each set of eyes and waiting for a response. Chins dipped, and some thumped fisted hands across their hearts. With every affirmation, Kahlym sent a prayer to Ishtanti, and his smile broadened.

<*Damn, kherdes.*> Brel's voice rang out in his head. <*She's one hell of a negotiator.*>

He nodded in silent reply as he sifted through memories of their earlier excursions. As they'd traveled to the far edges of the Seventh Quadrant, stopping at small Stria outposts, Evainne had been quiet and demure. Dressed in the flowing robes becoming of her status, she'd spoken little to the leadership or the religious caste; instead, she'd spent most of her time with the common people, sharing her food with children brave enough to approach her, her comforting smile warming her beautiful face. She'd intended to light the darkness holding his world in fear; instead, she'd blasted the universe with illumination and renewed faith.

Lev took to his feet, pulling Kahlym out of his daydream, and he rose to join his host.

With a proud grin, Lev clasped Kahlym on the shoulder, gesturing to those still gathered at the table. "It is my pleasure, and my supreme honor, to offer any assistance you may require," he said. "I will have two men return with you to take over the duties of navigator and ship's assistant engineer. I am certain I could find others who would wish to join you in your task, as well." Then Lev shifted his gaze to Evainne. With great reverence, he placed his open hand against his chest, fingers curling in as he bowed his head. "And to you, Blessed Divine, I pledge my loyalty. My life is yours to command."

Similar words had fallen from Kahlym's own lips as he long-ago cradled her in his lap in the med bay of his ship. She'd been frightened, in a strange place and surrounded by hostile enemies. Yet without even seeing his face, she'd taken a chance and saved him. Now, she held more than his life in her hands. Today, she held the future for all. He shifted his gaze to her, drinking in the natural beauty of her creamy skin as she slid her own gaze in his direction.

Love you.

With all heads bowed, she'd mouthed the words for him and him alone.

Kahlym smiled and returned the sentiment, imagining his knuckles brushing along her jaw. A timid blush painted her cheek, and that sexy, crooked grin curled her lush lips. He swallowed back his primal growl, eager, as his gearsuit put a stranglehold on his throbbing erection.

"Uh … thanks," she replied, her nervous laugh drawing Lev's eyes up. "But how about I leave the life-commanding to the owner? I've got enough trouble with my own shit."

"And this is why you're the perfect champion for the Stria, *learom-xahn*." Kahlym glanced sidelong at Brel, his odd statement drawing the attention of all. "You understand the importance of taking responsibility for one's own actions and decisions."

"Yeah," she countered, "even when you don't have a choice in the matter."

Lev nodded. "Well said. Come." He jabbed Kahlym in the ribs with his elbow, grinning. "I will find your new crew members. The repairs to your ship should be close to completion. We have a regime to overthrow." Their host's laughter followed him down the corridor as he departed.

Kahlym chuckled, rubbing his side. "Why does he make that sound like fun?" he asked as he leveled his gaze at his brother while their group took their leave one by one, returning to their duties.

"Different strokes, *kherdes*," Brel answered with a noncommittal shrug. "But he does have a point."

Kahlym bobbed his head in agreement. "That he does. Let's see if the ship is ready." Spirits high, he fell into step behind Evainne, with Xandar taking point and Brel covering the rear. His fingers itched, desperate to touch her. *Soon,* he mused, tamping back his rising libido. If their ship had been prepped, they could be on their way back to Ontaxa. If not, he'd return to his assigned living quarters and plunder her to his heart's content.

"Watch it, bucko," she murmured, "or we might end up giving these people a show they'd never forget."

"Would you two please stop?" Brel whined in hushed tones. "By the Goddess, it's bad enough to know my little brother is having sex, but do I have to hear all the gory details?"

Ahead of them, Xandar groaned and dropped his face into his

palm. "Thank you, Brel. I could have done without that added imagery."

The four of them laughed as they continued on to the landing dock, where neat rows of sleek fighters guarded the long walls, cockpits open and awaiting pilots when needed. Theirs was the only vessel in the repair bay, and it appeared to be fully operational. Workers carried crates of provisions into the ship, coming out with hands empty, prepared for the next load. This was good.

"Hey, Kahlym. What are you doing here?"

Kahlym glanced at the approaching figure, and recognition sparked as the Ontaxian neared. "Fallicia." He grinned as the friendly female wrapped her burly arms around his shoulders. "It is good to see you."

She slapped his back, then released him, a toothy grin on her pale tawny face. "I should've known I'd run into you sometime. Just saw your nav."

Ice raced through Kahlym's veins, and his stomach dropped into his boot heels. "What did you say?"

Confusion tugged her brows together as she thumbed over her shoulder. "Yeah. I left Qaen a second ago and—"

Kahlym grabbed her shoulders, a panicked retort poised on his tongue, when alarms screeched out. He jerked his gaze toward the convex window off to his right, where Thrall ships zipped out of the hyperlanes to fire on the heavy cruiser.

"Fuck."

The single word had fallen from everyone's lips in scary synchronicity, and Fallicia jolted out of Kahlym's grip, dashing toward one of the ion guns.

"Don't trust Qaen!" Kahlym called after her.

She spun about, jogging backwards, shouting back, "I don't! I just fuck him!"

Kahlym blinked, too stunned to respond as she turned and continued on her initial trajectory.

"At least she has her priorities straight," Xandar remarked, knocking his shoulder against Kahlym's to encourage their own escape. "Come. We have no time to waste." Taking the lead, he ran for their vessel. Kahlym laced his fingers through Evainne's, and he started to race after him. But Evainne dug in her heels, pulling against his lead.

"Wait, we have to help Lev."

Sirens wailed as, one by one, the light fighters of *Devil's Armada* launched into the fray. Kahlym pointed toward the exiting ships. "Lev is more than able to handle himself. But if Qaen discovers you here…" No more words passed his lips; the reality was too brutal for him to give it voice.

"You better tell me you're getting out of here, Kahl," Lev's voice poured out of the comm link on Kahlym's wrist. *"There should be a couple new recruits waiting on board. Until peace reigns, my brother."*

He raised the link to his mouth, eyes never leaving Evainne. "May Ishtanti keep watch over you, my brother." Hand in hand, they covered the scant distance to their ship. Once she was safely inside, Kahlym slapped the ramp retrieval, and the craft lifted off the ground.

"All in," he yelled toward the cockpit. "Let's get outta here." Kahlym bounced off of the walls, staggering to keep his feet as Xandar maneuvered the vessel's nose toward the exit. Evainne wobbled ahead of him, and he gripped her waist to help steady her, placing his faith in his brother's skills as a pilot while he guided his angel into a safe seat.

After grabbing on to the rounded frame, Evainne fell into the suspended chair. As she turned to face him, Kahlym was reminded of a similar image, the scenario nearly mirroring the present: the race to escape; her beautiful brown eyes gazing up at him. His own eyes drifted shut, lost in the memory as he leaned down to press his forehead against hers. She trailed her fingers upward along his jaw until she dragged her short nails against his scalp. He dug his talons into the metal back support to remain standing. If he were to die now, in the arms of his Evainne, he would regret nothing.

"Nobody's dying here today," Brel roared in defiance as their ship sped through the chaos of the surrounding fire fight. A blast at the aft side jerked the vessel, but no alarms sounded. "Two more seconds and…"

Kahlym held his breath, sending out a quiet prayer as the silence of the hyperlanes blotted out the battle. Once certain they were out of immediate harm, he peeled open his eyes. Evainne's thick lashes painted dark crescents on her porcelain cheeks, and he slanted his mouth toward hers, intent on savoring the heaven he knew waited on her lips.

"B-b-b-blessed D-D-D-Divine?"

"Are you kidding me?" Kahlym sighed out, releasing his death grip on the innocent seat and turning to face the timid speaker.

In the corner, limbs outstretched and bracing him awkwardly against the wall, cowered the Achtillian who'd swooped in, intent on saving Evainne after her sparring match with Xandar.

Evainne chuckled lightly, her escaping breath hot against Kahlym's throat, and he groaned in frustration.

"Hey, Myclen," she quipped. "Welcome to the party."

Chapter 26

"Blessed Divine? Your meal has been prepared."

Kahlym groaned, mood ruined once again. With a heavy sigh, Evainne wrapped her arms around her lover and called out over his shoulder.

"Uh, thanks, Myclen. I'm, um … I'm kinda in the middle of something here. I'll eat later."

Two days had passed since they'd slipped clear from the sudden attack on their host's craft. After they'd landed safely back on Ontaxa, Kahlym was able to contact Lev. Apparently, one of the officers present during their meal briefing had recognized Qaen strolling along a corridor and had signaled for the traitor to be arrested. Nothing more than crappy timing, but the little snake hadn't been found among the bodies, and knowing that psycho was still on the loose had only heightened the level of tension in her newly adopted family.

At least the addition of the replacement crew members from Lev's ship had given them a full contingent should *Tiamat's Revenge* hit the friendly skies again soon. All of the new guys were working out.

Except for one.

Since being discovered doing his imitation of a cornered spider, Evainne's new protector had done nothing but get under foot. He insisted on preparing every meal for her—and only her. At first, it was charming. But right now she was horny, and her overly clingy chaperone was doing his damnedest to keep her celibate.

"Would anyone notice if I threw him off the top of the canopy?" Kahlym growled, frustrated, into her ear, his rough voice sending lightning through her veins.

A needy moan slipped from her lips as she hooked her ankles around his legs, her body aching. "He means well," she replied.

He dragged his tongue along the column of her throat, ending with a nibble at her lobe as he languidly rolled his hips, inching deeper inside her. Crackling static hummed in the air, and Evainne tugged her brows together, opened her mouth to question the interruption, when Brel's voice bled through the closed door. After a brief conversation, the speakers drifted into the distance. She chuckled and slid her hand up to cup Kahlym's face.

"That's cheating," she admonished, tone teasing and playful.

Still buried inside her, Kahlym levered onto locked elbows and pinned her with an impish grin. "You wouldn't let me blast him out of the airlock on the way back." His swirling tourmaline pools darkened as he shifted his eyes along the length of her body. Both heat and chills trailed across her skin, her nipples hardening the longer he stared. "By the Goddess, Evainne. You are so beautiful."

Her head-to-toe blush encouraged him and, balancing on one hand, he palmed her ass. With a solid grip on her thigh, Kahlym inched deeper until his hip bone knocked against her throbbing core. Groaning heavily, Evainne arched her body, eyes rolling back as pleasure coursed through her veins. Beyond the green, growing walls, the night's rising storm set the pace for each stroke and thrust. Words took too long to form. During these starkly intimate moments, Evainne simply opened her mind to Kahlym, just as she opened her body to his. Now, desperate for release, she rocked her hips and reached up for his shoulders.

Kahlym dropped his chin, his heated, bi-colored gaze better than any aphrodisiac. Evainne threaded her fingers into his thick tangle of obsidian waves, pulled him toward her, and devoured his lips. His hungry growl poured into her mouth and she answered with her own aching sigh. Oxygen was overrated; only the feel of his skin against hers and their building ecstasy mattered.

Kahlym slid his mouth from hers, allowing her to refill her starving lungs while he kissed and licked his way along her jawline. Fire coursed through her, intensifying, inching her closer to the delicious precipice.

Sweat dripped between her breasts, trailing down to pool in her belly button and adding to the slippery friction. His rough hands caressed her slick body and his strong legs entwined with hers as he drove his thick shaft into her molten core, and Evainne's eyes drifted shut, lost in the sea of sensations.

Aware of her impending peak, Kahlym increased his thrusts, then pinched her sensitive earlobe between his teeth. The erotic combination pushed her to an explosive orgasm and, squeezing her eyes shut, she cried out as her quivering sheath milked his pulsing member. Soon, his back bowed as he joined her in the perfect moment....

Exhausted, sated, Evainne gasped for air, savoring the weight of his body keeping her grounded. She traced swirls along his damp back with her nails, allowing him to take the lead in breathing. Never in her wildest imagination could she have believed sex would be such a deep connection.

"How long can … can we…"

The corners of her lips drew up at his curiously innocent question. "I think we have to stop once labor starts." He stilled in her arms, and she struggled to contain her giggles. "But I'm pretty sure we're safe until then."

To her surprise, he dragged his fingertips lightly against her sides, and with a strangled squeak, she tensed up. Since he'd learned of her ticklish spots, Kahlym had reveled in watching her squirm while peals of uncontrollable laughter poured out of her until she couldn't breathe. He wasn't completely impervious to her counterattacks, but his target areas were tougher for her to locate. So they tangled and tousled on the sweat-slick sheets, laughing as the tickle war raged on.

"Okay, okay, okay," she conceded, her bare ass bumping against the wall as she grabbed his long, slender fingers. "Uncle, uncle." She wiped at the joyful tears sliding down her cheeks, then gathered up the discarded sheet beneath her armpit and leaned over to brush a soft kiss on his stubbled jaw. "I'll let you win," she whispered. "This round."

Turning away, she managed one step from the bed before Kahlym had wrapped one steely arm around her midriff and pulled her back. She glanced over her shoulder. Her lover had crawled up onto his knees, his bare, coppery bronze skin still glistening from their long, intense lovemaking. And judging by his growing erection, he was ready for more.

"Exactly where do you think you're going?" he said, and heat pooled in her gut as she basked in the passionate fire of his hungry gaze. He cradled her face, slanting his mouth over hers, and the warmth of his breath fanned the embers smoldering just beneath her skin. Her eyelids fluttered shut and her lips parted in rapt anticipation.

"I do hate to interrupt," Xandar's voice crept in from beyond the closed door, "but I've got some news I think you'll want to hear."

This time, Evainne groaned, thumping her forehead lightly against Kahlym's. "Can't we catch a break?"

"The universe calls," Kahlym murmured. He brushed his lips against her furrowed brow. "My Blessed Divine."

"Yeah, yeah." Evainne wanted nothing more than to crawl back into his lap. *I also want a Ferrari in my driveway.* But, determined to meet her fate with her big girl pants on, she steeled her spine and stepped out of the comfort of her lover's embrace. "We'll be right out," she called.

After grabbing one of the ziplocs off of the stack, she trudged into the narrow bathroom shower to quickly clean up. Apparently, no one in this part of the universe understood the simple pleasure of showering together. However, the time alone did give her a moment to sort through her scattered thoughts, and as her fingers tapped the appearing buttons on the wall console, she unpacked and organized her life.

She'd joked about a break, but in truth, her brain had yet to fully process her current reality. Not only was she tagged to be some supreme leader, but she was also about to become a mother, and as the water jets pounded at her aching muscles, she splayed her fingers across her belly.

Could Xandar have been wrong? Maybe he'd simply been guessing. Yet, the longer she weighed the evidence, the more she believed it was the only logical explanation. How far along was she? Would this pregnancy be the standard nine months? She was, after all, carrying the child of her alien lover, though she dimly recalled Yhan'tu stating that their two races had diverged from the same family tree. *Damn*, she mused, *I should've paid more attention in science.* What if she wasn't able to have the child? What if she turned into something even worse than her own mother? What if…?

<Ziat'xahn?> Kahlym's soft voice broke into her frantic questions. As she shook her head, cementing her into the here and now, she realized her human car wash cycle had actually ended. Her body, working on automatic pilot, had taken charge of the memorized habits, while her brain had remained on hiatus. Even her hair rested along one shoulder, her fingers finishing off the final twist of her long braid.

<Sorry, sweetie. I'll be right out.> Determined to stay alert, Evainne focused on the task of dressing. She was getting quicker with the correct order of operations with the gearsuits, and she discovered

closing the back seam before stepping in was the most important rule. She stalled, though, as she zipped up the front seam. At some point, the truth of her condition would be obvious in the shape-hugging outfit.

She gave her brain another rattle and thumbed the final closure shut. *Well, that'll keep Yhan'tu off my back about wearing those friggin' gowns, at least.*

Evainne yanked up the top of her left boot, then elbowed the door open. "All yours—Well, hey, Xandar," she said, shifting gears suddenly as she realized she had other company. "Guess it couldn't wait."

Kahlym must have used a shower stall in someone else's room; her lover was already dressed, his damp hair still dripping down the front of his loose, black tunic. Gone was her playful mate, though, and in his stead stood the brooding, haunted warrior once again.

She followed his lead and put on her game face. "What's up?"

"How are you feeling, Evainne?" Xandar's superficial query stirred nervous snakes in her gut.

"Toa, you suck at stalling." She crossed to the guys standing beside the vid wall, folding her arms on her journey. "Spit it out."

Xandar held her gaze, and she struggled to sort through the myriad of emotions swirling in the lapis blue depths. After a heavy sigh, he turned toward the screen and, with a wave of his hand, horrific images sprang to life.

Across the alien landscapes, buildings smoldered and bodies lay strewn. Evainne raised her trembling fingers to her lips, and as the grisly scenes continued to flash by, the serpents in her stomach picked up their wriggling pace. She began to recognize the burnt out remains of homes, and when the camera panned to a small, disfigured body with a shock of bright yellow hair, she raced to the small bin beside the bed and lost what little food she had left from last night's meal.

Law'tan. He'd had the most infectious laugh, and when he smiled, his dimples had nearly pierced through his cheeks, they were so deep. He had just turned five, and his amethyst eyes had twinkled with joy when he talked about his new baby sister.

A broad palm stroked gentle circles over her back, and the tears refused to stop after her stomach had cramped up.

"I'm so sorry, Evainne."

"He ... he ... was ... *innocent!*" Anger and grief melded into a toxic fire that ate through her heart. "How can this ... this monster have kept power as long as he has?"

"Because this monster will make whatever sacrifices he deems necessary to ferret out his enemies." The dark voice had echoed through the room, and all warmth seeped from her blood. Leaning on Kahlym's arm, Evainne climbed to her feet. *"You may still be hidden from me for the moment, my Divine, but soon—oh, so soon…. Your friends cannot protect you forever."*

"And neither can your goose-stepping goons keep your ass safe from my wrath," she fired back, aiming her words at the high ceiling. "By slaughtering those people, the only thing you've done is to further seal your fate. You just pissed off the wrong bitch."

Chapter 27

"How the hell did he get through?"

"Has the canopy been breached?"

"Why didn't the alarms sound?"

Voices shot out rapid-fire questions all vying for attention as more crew members spilled into Evainne's sleeping chamber. R'uan dashed in with Dhaerin hot on his heels, the Ontaxian denmates adding their confused concerns into the mix. While Kahlym had no answers for anyone, he did his best to keep track of who wanted to know what. At the forefront of his mind, however, was his eerily silent angel. To the gathering masses, she appeared calm. But he knew her. Her arms hanging by her sides vibrated while rage oozed from her pulsing aura.

"He's gone," she said, tone flat. "He never was here. The message was attached to the video. Fucker is still holed up in his damned fortress on Rimma."

"*Dym Char'ann?*" Yhan'tu stammered out, his large body quivering as he struggled between bowing and standing tall.

Evainne flicked her wrist, halting any other inquiries. "Wait… There's… He's—"

With an agonizing howl, Evainne grabbed her head and dropped to her knees. Panicked, Kahlym rushed to her side, yet before he could comfort her, a blast of energy threw him halfway across the room.

"The bastard's using the Divines under his control to attack her," Xandar growled and, acting quickly, he motioned R'uan closer. Kahlym scrambled to his feet, but the same force that had flung him like a child's toy remained firmly in place, keeping Evainne terrifyingly out of reach. Refusing to give up, Kahlym pounded against the invisible barrier in determined anger.

"Evainne!" he roared, helpless to comfort her as she writhed. Tears flowed down her pale cheeks, and her eyes remained squeezed shut. "Dammit! Someone do something!"

"R'uan!" Xandar called out, hands spread wide as he pushed against the shimmering barricade. "They're trying to get her to use her Divine Cry so they can locate her."

Kahlym doubled his efforts, knuckles bleeding and aching. *<Listen to me, ziat'xahn. Help is on the way.>* Though his loving words were met with heart-wrenching cries, he continued to shower her spirit with waves of strength.

Separated from Evainne, Kahlym watched Xandar and R'uan kneel beside her, their smooth, deliberate movements allowing them to inch closer. Following their lead, he pressed his own shoulder against the solid nothing that caged him. Sweat dripped off of his chin while his efforts gained him no ground, and Evainne curled into a tiny ball, her body trembling as her wails filled the room. Prayers to the Goddess fell from his lips, and he sent any remaining ounce of his mental power out to Xandar and R'uan.

The temperature in the room climbed steadily as the battle for his angel raged on. Brel dug his fingers into Xandar's shoulder; Dhaerin gripped R'uan's forearm. "Kahlym," R'uan yelled, "grab on to Brel and Dhaer. You *have* to get through to Evainne."

"What do you think I've been trying to do?" His arms felt like they were going to shatter, and she was far across the room.

"She's locked us all out," his brother said, the words driving into Kahlym's heart like daggers, "and I don't know how much longer she can fight without help."

I need to know I'm your strength and not your weakness. As her gentle plea from the past echoed through his heart, Kahlym stopped his struggle and instead, with a calming exhale, extended his fingers toward his brothers. Sparks danced along his skin, yet he refused to balk. He could only imagine the agony his angel was enduring; he would bear this minor suffering to save her. He managed to clasp Brel's thumb and Dhaerin's wrist, closing the loop.

<*Ziat'xahn. Hear me now. You are my strength, my angel.*> The screaming, yowling cries in her head bled into his soul, but he could not give in. <*Do you remember my touch?*> Direct contact would be the best way to calm her, but their current situation called for a switch in tactics. In his mind's eye, he traced his fingers along her quivering arms. <*Let it center you. Our soulbond is true, and you are my heart. Can you hear my breath calling to you?*>

With a long, slow inhale, he reached along their link, encouraging her body to respond in kind. Brel joined in, even as he torqued his arm about to get a more solid grip on Kahlym's hand. The barrier before him wavered, and he was vaguely aware of Xandar's encouraging words. <*Let it guide you to those who love you and are here to help you.*>

"C'mon, R'uan. Reach." Dhaerin's strained voice had grabbed his attention, but Kahlym dared not open his eyes lest the distraction break his concentration. Sweat poured off of his skin in a thin, steady stream as the room slowly turned into an inferno. The confused, frantic energy emanating from his angel began to take shape, and his blood froze as he realized she wasn't alone. Another Divine had been sealed inside the invisible cage with her.

"Xandar," he called out, still focused on the ethereal struggle, "somehow she's trapped that damned fool, Haseunn, with her when she slammed down her shields to keep us all safe."

Through the strange mist, he stared on in shock as Evainne

battled the much more experienced Divine. The Thrall's Traveler had appeared within the dimension slightly off-center from real, but as a much younger man, and his hands were wrapped about her throat. Kahlym knew his fear would do her no good. She was stronger than she realized, and she had skills the emperor knew nothing of. The truth of his belief in her lifted Kahlym's spirit, and it soon became the prayer on his lips.

<Evainne, my beloved. Can you sense the beat of my heart?> Electricity jolted through his body from fingertip to fingertip, Xandar and R'uan closing the circle. *<It beats only for you. Let it bring you back to me.>* Surrounded by family and connected by direct contact, Kahlym widened his link to allow Evainne to feel the presence of his brothers of blood and destiny. She'd touched all of their lives, and through their love for her, the barrier keeping them at arm's length pulsed in time with his heartbeat.

"Whatever you're doing, Kahl," R'uan remarked, "I think it's starting to work."

Buoyed, Kahlym peered deeper into the swirling abyss, determined to offer whatever aid he could, and his breathing ratcheted up, his beautiful angel needing to pull in extra air from his lungs. He'd willingly give his last breath for her. *<Haseunn is a Traveler, ziat'xahn, not an Adept. Play upon your strength and his weakness.>*

Message received, Evainne dipped her chin and switched tactics, and Kahlym struggled to keep track of her movements, her limbs like liquid lightning as she took control of the fight. With two sharp strikes, she had the ancient Divine pinned to the ground, her arms trembling as they locked around his neck. As the temperature gradually leveled out, the visage morphed back into the old man he was. Evainne threw her head back, crying out, and Haseunn vanished in a puff of brilliant lavender smoke.

Kahlym landed in a tangle of limbs, along with the rest of his brothers. Ignoring his aching arms, he scurried on his hands and knees over to his angel, who'd collapsed in a heap, her back rising and falling in time with her thundering heartbeat.

"Evainne? Evainne! *Ziat'xahn?*" He gathered her into his lap and held her against his chest as relief coursed through him, and he forced his body to drag in deep, healing lungfuls of air. Chaotic emotions tainted her heady, familiar scent. Whispering soothing prayers, Kahlym rested his cheek against her damp tresses, rubbed his hands against her icy cold arms. The temperature of the room, as well as her skin, gradually returned to normal.

"When he ... I mean ... when that..." Her stuttered words tugged at his heart, and he gently tightened his embrace. "I-I remembered what happened before and I-I had to do something to keep everyone safe."

"And you did, *Dym Char'ann.*" Hearing the honorific come from Xandar was odd, but the reverent title truly seemed to fit her at this moment. Kahlym glanced up as Xandar clasped both his shoulder and Evainne's. "You did that, and so much more."

"But next time you get jumped by invisible assholes"—Brel wiped the back of his hand against his slick brow—"how 'bout you let us arm up first?"

"It's a deal," she conceded, voice barely above a whisper.

Soothing laughter filled the chamber, and Kahlym returned his focus to his silent angel. Leaning away, he carefully placed his knuckles beneath her chin, and his stomach dropped at the reddened, finger-shaped welts that stood out on her ivory throat. She lifted her face to him, and an icy ire sludged through his veins. One beautiful eye was purple and swollen shut, while an ugly cut still wept on the apple of her cheek. A timid, crooked smile curved her split lips, and she winced as she spun about in his lap.

"Yeah," she said, "but you should see the other guy." Her feigned levity brought tears of guilt to his eyes. "I've had worse, haven't I, Toa?"

"I do wish you would stop trying to make getting the crap beat out of you a regular habit, *hoc sinh.*" Xandar's sardonic tone had echoed the sentiment in Kahlym's heart, and tenderly, Kahlym brushed the pad of his thumb against the sticky trail of red at the corner of her mouth.

"I am so sorry, *ziat'xahn*. Are you…" He paused. How should he ask the question swirling in his mind? He lowered his arm, splaying his fingers on her belly. "Are you all right?"

Her soft, warm smile and slow nod melted away his earlier apprehension. "Yeah, I'm good. Guess they didn't want to take a chance on damaging the baby factory, so the asshole avoided any punches below the belt." She covered his hand with hers, her gentle touch centering his soul, and he cupped the back of her head with his free hand, touching his forehead to hers, savoring the peace only her presence could bring. Voices rose and fell, but he didn't care. At this moment, all that mattered in the universe was his angel, and he was going to savor this serene embrace.

"Are … are you serious?"

Dhaerin's unusually hushed tone finally got the better of him. Kahlym opened his eyes to look up at his gawking pilot, whose bright orange eyes flitted in rapid succession from the placement of Kahlym's hand and up to his face, the ticking movement taking on an almost comical pace.

"Is the cat out of the bag?"

Kahlym frowned at Evainne's strange, muttered question. He shifted his gaze back to her, but his brother provided the answer before the words fell from his own tongue.

"Yes, *learom*," Xandar said with a heavy sigh. "I'm afraid your secret is not so secret any longer."

Something in the surrounding silence caught Kahlym's attention and he climbed to his feet with Evainne cradled in his arms, unwilling to let her go for even a second. He was prepared for her to fight against his protective hold, but when she leaned in, winding her arms around his neck, he sighed in relief. He met the eyes of his brothers and his adopted Ontaxian denmates. Shock, pride, and joy flowed from the strong males, and happiness filled his heart.

R'uan stepped in, placing one hand each on both Kahlym's and

Evainne's shoulders. "If by my life or my death I can protect you, I will pledge all that I am."

Dhaerin flung open his arms and squeezed as many into his broad embrace as his reach would allow. And just when Kahlym thought he could grab a breath, Brel matched the tight hug from the other side.

"We're gonna have a family," Dhaerin whispered, his infectious excitement bringing a needed smile to Kahlym's face.

"No, Dhaerin," Xandar chimed in, "we *are* a family. Now we're going to be adding another member." All eyes dropped down to the precious cargo held against Kahlym's chest.

Evainne scoffed. "But I swear … I will castrate the first person who leaks this to Yhan'tu. I don't plan to sit on the sidelines for the big boss battle."

Chapter 28

"**N**o!" Gha'jahn roared out, jumping to his feet as Haseunn vanished before his eyes. The two remaining Divines gasped and huddled together to avoid the raining ash from one of the most powerful Travelers in a life's age.

The trap had been easy enough to bait; his men had simply rooted out strongholds loyal to the rebellious Stria faction to wipe the traitors off of the map. The live feed of the policing had been sent to every corner of the Seventh Quadrant, though his message had been for only one pair of ears, and because the net had been cast so wide, he'd tasked all of the Divines to search for response from the elusive female. Haseunn had calmly stated he'd heard her and had sent his mind out to retrieve her.

But the longer the seconds ticked away, the more Gha'jahn's confidence had begun to wane. "Does it usually take this long?"

Qi'tan, the ancient Healer, adjusted his thick spectacles higher on his crooked nose and shrugged. "Traveling is not within my realm, sire, but her original voyage here did take more time than anticipated."

Narrowing his gaze, he glared at the flippant old man before returning his attention to the boring statue imitation of the Divine Traveler until, irritated, he waved over a servant and requested his glass to be refilled. No sense in watching this engaging entertainment parched.

But the first drops had barely passed his lips when the impossible had occurred. Haseunn's eyes had flown open, his jaw agape, and in the next breath, he was no longer there. A dissipating plume of pale purple smoke lingered in the space where the Divine had once stood.

Glass fragments had tinkled on the stone floor and Gha'jahn's arm had vibrated as a vague pain registered in his mind. Though the remnants of the crystal goblet lay scattered at his feet, the jagged stem slicing into his palm had done nothing to cut through his shocked rage.

"What. Just. Happened?" he bit out as he leveled his fiery gaze toward the cowering fools.

"This is not possible, it simply is not possible," Divine Seer Hollix muttered as he shook his head and began to pace in ever-shrinking circles.

Laying hands upon a Divine was forbidden, even for the emperor, but the urge to slap some sense into the man was so tempting. Instead, Gha'jahn crossed to the fireplace and tossed away the remains of the broken drinking vessel, flicking beads of his blood into the crackling flames. The fiery tendrils hungrily devoured his offerings, and he continued to feed the greedy monster one life-giving drop at a time. A light touch to his shoulder halted the trail of crimson, as well as the nagging sting from the now-healed gash.

"What is not possible?" Gha'jahn snapped, and before the Healer could steal away his anger, he shrugged out of the weak hold and stormed across the chamber. He might not have been able to give the blathering Seer the shake he craved to administer; however, he could place himself directly into the man's meandering path. Hollix bounced harmlessly off the emperor's chest, stalling the man's momentum. A pair of rheumy onyx eyes lifted to lock with his, confusion muddling the Divine's wizened expression.

"There has never been a record of a Divine being slain in this manner."

Gha'jahn grit his teeth as his fingers balled into dangerous fists. "Well, obviously the records need to be updated," he said. "Could she have used a standard weapon? Because as far as I know, Divines are still mortal creatures and subject to killing by old-fashioned means." So what if his thinly veiled sarcastic tone bordered on blasphemous? With one of the last living Divines under his control dead, if he didn't find this elusive female soon, replacing the fold would be difficult to say the least.

Hollix shook his head, wisps of white hair flinging about, and he waved off the emperor with a dismissive hand. "His physical body was here. Mortal weapons would have done no damage to his ethereal form."

"Could she be…?"

Gha'jahn shifted his gaze to the Healer, who shuffled closer, his unfinished question hanging like a primed grenade. Drawing his brows together, Gha'jahn stared as the two old men locked eyes and mumbled rapidly, their conversation clipped and nonsensical.

"How could that—"

"Not this far from the central planets—"

"And a female? That's—"

"We must consult the Tablet."

Without another word, the two Divines ambled out of the emperor's presence.

Gha'jahn stared slack-jawed and stunned by the impudence as the pair slipped into the hallway leading down to the royal repository. A heartbeat passed while he contemplated his response: Wait or follow? They'd left his chamber without so much as a "by your leave," as if protocols had vanished along with their brother. If they discovered anything in their search, though, they were duty bound to report it to him immediately.

But curiosity currently outweighed his need to stand on ceremony and, grumbling under his breath, he stomped after the visionaries, tossing a parting glance over his shoulder to the spot where Haseunn had once stood. A glimmer of settling dust filtered through the blue moonlit rays streaming down through the spherical vaulted ceiling. *This female will pay for this loss.* And his mouth watered greedily as he fantasized the hours of punishment he would heap upon her body before handing her over to the other Divines.

Determined, he spun about and ducked into the steep stairwell.

"And that bastard son of Anaxar's will watch it all, right before I rip his heart from his chest."

Chapter 29

"I think I'd kill for a hot tub right about now."

Evainne didn't think her grumbled whine would travel far enough for anyone to hear, but the perplexed look on Zybella's face told a much different story. Embarrassed, Evainne tilted her head and gave a half-hearted shrug. "Well," she said, "not literally."

Before she'd landed in her own version of Oz, a long soak had served as an escape from the weight of everyday life. At this moment, she was desperate to get away from her mind's play-by-play of the fight with the now-dead Divine Traveler. She shifted her gaze, staring off into the distance as the rerun began anew. The original jolt of pain had taken her by surprise, and on instinct, she'd slammed down her shields to protect her mind. She'd never intended to trap herself in with the very cause of her agony.

"You have been hiding from us," said the surprisingly young man. "We are only here to help you transition into what you are meant to be."

Evainne kept her eyes focused on her ethereal opponent. "Yeah. I think your idea and mine of what I'm meant to be are not even in the same area code." She countered his lazy, circling steps, using the time to study him. His tangerine eyes betrayed his age; years of entitlement and power corrupted those milky pools.

Was this what the man had looked like in his youth? Too tall and too slender, he reminded her of a constipated scarecrow, and his long face and drooping mustache only added to his comical appearance. Did he think she would fall for this?

She blinked, and he stood directly before her. Swearing, she jumped backwards, heels skidding across the ground as she landed on her ass. "I would prefer if you would simply return with me," he said. "Please, make this easier on yourself, and perhaps those who have been sheltering you will be allowed to live."

That did it. Locking her jaw, she kicked out, sweeping his long legs out from underneath him. He windmilled his arms, limbs flailing as he fought to remain upright, and she used the distraction to pop to her feet, arms settling into a comfortable, loose guard.

"Bring it, bitch."

The horse face twisted and contorted in rage, and with an unearthly howl, he launched himself toward her, arms outstretched. She sidestepped his obvious attack, grabbing on to his forearms and, following the momentum, snapped her right elbow up. The bone-on-bone collision sent a tingling down to her fingertips, but the blow only pissed him off more. When he swung his eyes back to her, his disguise slipped, and she caught a glimpse behind the curtain. The sneak peek had lasted only a second. Without hesitation, he flicked his wrist, and two forceful imaginary fists battered her head with a combination of crosses and jabs. Stars exploded in the surrounding darkness, and she staggered to regain her balance.

"You cannot win here, child."

She drew her knee up, then pistoned her leg out with bone-shattering force, driving her heel into his gut. Instead of crumbling to the ground, though, he latched on to her extended ankle with both hands and twisted his shoulders. She tucked her elbows in tight, then kicked off the floor and, using the spiraling energy her opponent had generated, spun in mid-air. Her unexpected counterattack yanked him off of his feet and he released her leg as he collapsed. She pulled her chin in to her chest to soften her rough landing, but the ache in her shoulder told a much different story.

In the distance, she could almost make out Kahlym's voice calling to her. She sat up, tilting her head toward the sound, straining to make out his words through the strange silence. The bastard caged with her inside this weirdness jumped on her loss of focus and wrapped his fingers tightly around her throat. Evainne scratched and clawed at his face, nails tearing at the mask and, slash by slash, she revealed the truth of him. Pale gray skin clung weakly to the bony skull, yet a demonic fury in his shimmering orange eyes bored straight into her soul. Panic fueled her body and she tried to buck her back up off the ground.

<Our soulbond is true and you are my heart.>

She gasped for air, struggled to draw her legs in closer. For an old man, he was stronger than a friggin' ox. Realization dawned: If she passed out, he'd be able to walk off with her and she would be lost. This encouraged her to fight harder.

"Kahlym!" she cried out in desperation.

<Evainne, my beloved. Can you sense the beat of my heart?> The steady rhythm called to her blood. <It beats only for you. Let it bring you back to me. Haseunn is a Traveler, ziat'xahn; not an Adept. Play upon your strength and his weakness.>

His words slammed the brakes on her fear. Stupidly, she'd been going about this all wrong. With a resolute nod, Evainne took in a sharp inhale, then threaded her hands between the bony arms pinning her to the ground. The apparition frowned and leaned in, playing right into her trap. Her fingers wound around the wisps of silver hair and she yanked him down as she snapped her head up. Her forehead slammed into the center of his sour face, bits of bone and gore spraying in all directions. Yowling, he toppled to the floor, and Evainne coughed, sucking in much-needed oxygen as she crawled toward her fleeing foe.

"Where do you think you're going?" she croaked out as she captured his leg. Energy from beyond the confines of her bubble coursed through her veins, carrying along with it the warmth of Kahlym's touch and love. One final scramble and she locked her arm around the Traveler's neck.

He wheezed. "You ... cannot escape your..."

Flexing her bicep, Evainne wrapped her fingers around her fisted hand and leaned in to the strangling hold. "Fuck you," she hissed out, sweat dripping into her eyes as her arms trembled. "And fuck your fate."

With a primal roar, she threw her head back and squeezed with all her might. In the next heartbeat, her deadly foe exploded in a shower of dingy purple ash, and she was surrounded by waves of love, back once again with her family.

A full day had passed since the battle with the Traveler, and her entire body still ached. While her new healing skills had made short work of the damage from her metaphysical smackdown, it'd done nothing to relieve the fatigue from the process itself. Sleep was elusive. Each time she closed her eyes, the twisted faces of the tortured souls and the once-joyful smile of a now-dead five-year-old child swarmed into her mind. Even the comfort of her lover's embrace could not completely banish the heart-wrenching scenes she'd witnessed.

Since rest was nothing but a pipe dream, she opted to spend her time trying to figure out the next steps. Kahlym and his crew had contacted the other Stria strongholds they'd visited, determining how best to keep them safe should the Thrall Emperor decide to pull his stunt again. Nearby warriors and ship captains ferried survivors to planets with stronger defenses. Their allies were as safe as they could be, given the volatile nature of the universe.

Evainne's hand drifted toward her middle, but she quickly jerked her betraying body part up to massage her throbbing temples. News of her condition was under tight wraps, but each time she passed R'uan or Xandar, a shining twinkle in their eyes made her bite the inside of her cheek to hold back a goofy grin. And it hadn't slipped her notice that each of her "adopted" brothers seemed to find some reason to "be in the neighborhood." Easy enough to explain the practically hourly guests, given that she was sleeping with their captain and had apparently done something thought to be miraculous. Yhan'tu had returned to his subservient self, bowing as he trailed along in her wake, and if her nerves weren't on edge already, she'd have smacked some sense back into him. When her jaw clenched to the point of pain, an invisible hand would stroke her cheek while a distant heartbeat called to hers, calming her.

Xandar told her she needed to work on her patience. Time to seriously put her mind to that task.

"Hot … tub?" Zybella quizzically rephrased Evainne's odd desire. Certain members of their circle, including Zybella, knew nothing of her pregnancy. The less who knew about it, the better her chances were of keeping that bomb out of their enemy's hands. She trusted the gentle Ontaxian, but she didn't want to put her in harm's way so she could have another female to talk to.

Evainne chuckled, nodding her head. "Yeah. It's basically like a big bathtub with really hot water and jets of bubbles."

"Then perhaps, *learom-xahn*, you would enjoy the meditation springs of Bashir."

Evainne turned to R'uan, who'd joined the conversation. The gentle giant smiled as he stepped next to his sister. Whereas R'uan brought to mind the white tigers she'd seen in magazines, Zybella was more like a sleek panther. Never in her wildest imagination could Evainne have thought she would be friends with seven-foot-tall humanoid cats. Then again, her fantasies also hadn't included a sexy space pirate with tourmaline eyes, and who had the heart of a warrior and the soul of a poet. Each time her mind drifted toward Kahlym, the butterflies in her gut took flight. Love, fear, apprehension, and even guilt, churned inside her, the precarious mix of emotions fogging her sense of purpose and dividing her mental energy.

"Meditation springs, huh?" she pondered aloud. "Sounds like I could kill two birds with one stone there."

R'uan blinked rapidly, and his brushy brows pulled together. "Beg your pardon?" His pleasant expression generally reserved for small children or frightened animals brightened Evainne's muddied thoughts.

With a crooked grin, she wrapped her fingers around his massive bicep. "One of these days, I'm gonna have to teach all of you guys about the wonders of idioms." She gave his arm a final pat. "Basically, it means I can get my hot tub and, well, maybe I can do some mental work to boot."

The corners of his smile drooped a fraction, and she groaned in reply. "Yeah," she said, "I'm still having trouble with the whole clear-headed thing."

"Evainne." R'uan draped an arm around her shoulders. "How much of the elemental emotions have you learned?"

Elemental emotions? She drew her brows together as she pondered the odd phrase. She tapped her chin and flipped through the Rolodex in her mind. "Uh, I think I might vaguely recall hearing that…" But no matter how she dragged out the words, no solid idea popped into her brain. "Nope, I got nothing."

"Did I hear we're going to Bashir?" Dhaerin had poked his head into the hallway, Brel and Kahlym behind him. "Damn, I haven't been there since I was a kit."

Evainne swiveled her gaze to the gathered faces—some eager, some laced with concern, while one in particular watched with cautious optimism. "Well," she said, "it looks like we're going on a field trip." Dhaerin and Brel hooted in gleeful delight, then disappeared toward parts unknown. She heaved a deep sigh and leveled her eyes to Kahlym. "Might as well get Xandar in on this. No sense in leaving anyone out."

"I believe the springs will do all of us some good," Xandar chimed in as he rounded the corner, the sly smile telling of his running into the overly enthusiastic giants heading in the opposite direction. "And R'uan, you may be right about the elemental emotions. Now would be a good time for such study."

"Great," Evainne grumbled as she stalked toward her chamber. "Just what I need—more homework."

Chapter 30

"So what's the deal with these … these elemental emotions?"

Kahlym blinked at Evainne's blunt segue. She had been oddly silent during their take off. The healing waters on the nearby moon of Bashir would be reached within a couple of hours, but it had begun to feel like an eternity sitting one seat apart from his angel. Because they'd been joined by a handful of Ontaxian soldiers, not to mention Evainne's self-appointed personal guard/annoying shadow, Myclen, Kahlym had been forced to maintain proper distance. The Stria troops were well aware of their connection, but he dared not reveal the exact nature, nor the true depth, of their relationship. Until the day of their victory, their love, their soulbond, and especially their child, must be kept out of the light of day.

But the night would be theirs, and Kahlym vowed to make up for the day's formalities when again he held Evainne in his arms.

"The elemental emotions," Myclen said, nearly leaping up in his eagerness to be of use, "are Fire, Water, Air, and Land. They represent the standard base emotions of anger, calm, joy, and trust, respectively. Nearly all beings are governed by one elemental emotion, and this is used to determine the life path at an early age." Evainne nodded slowly, her brows tugging together as her impromptu instructor blathered on. Kahlym clenched his teeth and stifled a perturbed groan, digging his talons into the palm of his fisted hand.

Without warning, Myclen launched himself from his seat to squeeze into the scant space separating Kahlym from his angel and continued to parrot the sacred teachings, oblivious. "Those ruled by Fire are placed in military service; Water and Air children find their homes among the clerics. Some have also crossed into research, like me," he said with a dash of feigned humility and a slight incline of his large head. "While infants of the Land study interplanetary relations and politics. It is more than common knowledge in all home-worlds of the Dantaran galaxy. But how can this be that you did not know of this, Blessed Divine? Did your training not include the most basic teachings?"

Xandar's unaccustomed growl blended harmoniously with R'uan's disgusted scoff. Kahlym lifted his hand to his mouth to cover the faked cough hiding his chuckle, and a low whistle from Dhaerin in the pilot's chair added to the confined tension.

<Now I understand why you want to strangle him.> Kahlym nodded discreetly at Xandar's frustrated mental response.

Evainne waved off the grumblings of her adopted brothers and navigated the sticky situation with grace and ease. "Kid, I am just beginning to figure all this crap out, so this is a shit ton of trial by fire. Where I'm from, people sorta … figure out what they want to do. Sometimes it's right, and sometimes it's not. But nothing is set from birth. So, yeah. We don't have the same belief systems you guys have here. Hell, the only thing the people on my planet all believe is that their god is better than everyone else's and are willing to kill for it at any given moment."

"Kill?" R'uan asked. "In the name of a deity?"

Evainne shrugged. "Well, that, plus money and power." Kahlym added his gaze to the collective group completely focused on Evainne. She swiveled her narrowed stare around the interior of the ship. "You guys are kidding, right? Hell, what is all this fighting about if it's not religion, money, or power?"

"Power is always the main focus here, Divine," said Ma'avi, a crew member who'd joined from *Devil's Armada*. The reserved Praxxiran was highly intuitive, which made him the best navigator Kahlym could have asked for, even better than his previous nav. He was unsure if Lev was bereft over losing such a talented set of eyes, but he was definitely grateful for the addition. "Most of the homeworlds within the Dantaran galaxy have been under Thrall rule for so many centuries, they are no longer able to govern themselves. It has made them timid and weak."

"Fear can be a strong motivator," Xandar added, voice heavy. Kahlym used to look up to his older brother as a force of nature; Xandar had been the bravest male he'd known. Yet, something in his tone now belied the shadows of the past that still haunted him.

Evainne shook her head. "No. Fear is a conformity. It's an excuse to let things stay as they are." She shifted her gaze to each face, lingering until moving on to the next. "Don't rock the boat. Don't change the status quo. Those in charge tell us all of these things because they don't want to lose their grip on their control."

"She's right." Brel rose to his feet. "For far too long, we have allowed the Thrall to treat us like misbehaving children. Now is the time to strike."

Grumblings both for and against immediate action filled the cabin and began to spill out into the corridors. One by one, the others jumped up, and soon, everyone stood nose to nose with one another as arguments ensued. Those wanting to attack now defended their position against those in favor of a more gentle, thoughtful approach, and Kahlym stepped between Brel and one of the Ontaxian guards when things became more heated.

A shrill whistle split the air.

Silence fell in its wake.

Evainne tossed her arms over her head, then casually stood up, and Kahlym felt the edges of his lips curve up as his angel drew all eyes to her.

"How about this?" she said. "How 'bout everyone stick it back in their pants and start using the big head instead of the little one, huh?"

Myclen dropped to the floor, arms outstretched in reverence as the rest of the males muttered embarrassed apologies. The new crew members took a knee, while Brel rubbed the back of his neck in delayed remorse.

<*I had almost forgotten how blunt she can be.*> Xandar's thought mirrored Kahlym's own, and the urge to pull her into his arms and kiss her was overwhelming, the angry frown creasing her forehead only stoking his building fire. Instead, he stepped in behind her, standing off her left-hand shoulder—his proper place as her personal sentry.

"Dhaer?" Evainne called out. "Please tell me we're almost there. I've got a bunch of people in need of cooling off, and one of them is me."

"*Don't worry, learom,*" Dhaerin's voice echoed back through the comm speakers. "*We're on final approach now. No sign of any other ships in the area. Just sit back and we'll be there in no time.*"

Kahlym brushed his fingertips across her back, the touch light, his movement unseen by anyone, and through their tender connection, he took in a slow and calming inhale, guiding her body to follow suit.

"Good," she said. "The sooner I get out of this flying sardine can, the better."

"And that right there," Xandar stated plainly, "is your Fire."

Kahlym wished he could close the scant distance separating them. Her frustration was becoming a palpable entity, and the temperature had dipped a fraction of a degree.

"Great." Evainne folded her arms beneath her breasts. "So being pissed off is part of the Fire elemental emotion?"

Xandar shrugged. "In a manner of speaking."

The ship's engines whirred to a soft whine before cutting out, the slight sensation of weightlessness vanishing with a slight bounce. Dhaerin triggered the hatch release and daylight spilled in almost as quickly as the gathered passengers piled out. Myclen lingered by the opening, hands folded subserviently in front of his tilted waistline. Kahlym's withering stare did nothing; a flick of his angel's wrist sent Myclen along his way. Once the dust amid the hasty departures had settled, only Xandar and R'uan remained in the galley with them.

Evainne heaved a heavy sigh and rolled her knotted shoulders back. "Wow, glad to know I still can clear a room like a fart in an elevator."

Free to relax his tense stance, Kahlym wrapped his arms protectively around her and pulled her in to rest against his chest. He ignored Xandar's sharp laugh at her strange phrase, needing to surround himself with his angel's calming presence and, resting his cheek against her soft, fragrant tresses, he dared a tender kiss on the crown of her head. A certain part of his anatomy wished for much more, though, and strained against his form-fitting gearsuit.

"Do not be angry with them, *learom-xahn*," R'uan said, a comforting grin warming his face. "They are soldiers, and since birth they have been taught that Divines are not as they themselves are. Your brethren have been placed on pedestals and worshipped for nearly ten thousand cycles, and for them to see not only one in the flesh, but to also watch her struggle with the same troubles and frustrations, this can be … how should I put it?"

"Scary," Evainne said, finishing the statement with precision. "Yeah, I guess it would be." Kahlym hugged her close, and she wrapped her fingers around his forearms. Her touch seemed more for his benefit than hers; her grip was light, yet her energy weighed heavily on his spirit. "So how does my anger fit into all of this?"

"*Ziat'xahn.*" Kahlym pressed his lips near her ear. "Come. We have arrived at the springs and we can continue this conversation in a more relaxing venue."

With a broad grin, Brel poked his head back through the ship's open hatch. "You guys coming out or what? I think Zybella has already staked out the best pool, so you might need to arm wrestle her for it." He vanished, then ducked inside once more. "Nope, false alarm. She's actually holding it for you. Looks like you found another loyal protector, Blessed Divine."

His laughter filled the cramped chamber with needed joy, and Kahlym joined in. "Friends we definitely need, and strong allies are even better." In his heart, he wanted nothing more than to sweep his angel into his arms and carry her off to the bubbling spring. So, with the devious seed planted, Kahlym opted on another manner of transport: he spun her in his embrace, crouched down, and tossed her over his shoulder.

"Hey!" she cried. "What the...?" Evainne sputtered in surprise, smacked at his back, but without missing a step, Kahlym stalked toward the open hatch. The crook of her knees held his arm nicely and her current location put her shapely ass within nibbling distance. She squeaked, kicking against his hold as he playfully swatted her lush backside. "Is this any way to treat a deity?"

Kahlym chuckled, enjoying the press of her bouncing breasts against his shoulder blades. "Oh, so *now* you want to be a deity?" he quipped.

His strides ate up the sandy path leading to the cascading pools that dotted the amber hills of Bashir. The blue sun hung low; soon, night would cloak the entire valley. Smiling in the moment of peace, he slid her down the length of his body, and a hungry growl slipped through his clenched teeth as her core brushed against his groin. "I will worship you night and day, and with relish, my beautiful angel." At his words, her deep brown eyes darkened at the prospect, her cheeks taking on a delicious blush. Kahlym shifted his gaze, tipped his chin toward the distant horizon. "But I thought you might like to see this for yourself."

Her astonished intake of breath stoked the fire in his gut, and he pulled her back to rest against his chest. Words were not needed. Soon enough, the universe's demands would be heaped upon their plates. But for now, he simply savored the feel of her body pressed against his.

Chapter 31

Evainne blinked back a push of tears as she stared out at the unusual, breathtaking sunset. In her brownstone in Boston, she'd never had a good view nor an exotic locale for watching picture-perfect sunsets or sunrises. Her norm? The sky melting from a dark gray to a duller version in the winter and for most of the spring, while summers shifted from black to bright. She did love the colors of autumn the best, though none of those experiences held a candle to the purples and fuchsias currently painting swirls on the distant horizon. The sinking sun's neon blue glow sent tendrils of fading light into the encroaching night, slowly pulling a blanket of stars over its head before vanishing beneath the rocky surface.

Overcome, she reached behind for Kahlym and, walking her fingers along his arms, lifted his hands to wrap herself in his embrace. His warm breath along the back of her neck sent anticipatory chills along her skin, and she leaned back, savoring the quiet moment.

"Are all the planets in your galaxy this beautiful?" she asked, voice cracking, awe stealing her breath.

Kahlym trailed his fingertips lightly along her exposed throat. "Each of the Seventh Quadrant's homeworlds has its own charm. Bashir is a sanctuary moon, pristine and pure. Here, there is no technology other than what is brought by those who visit."

"Sanctuary?" she pondered. "But I thought Dhaerin said he'd come before." *Why would anyone ever leave here?* she mused as the remaining light melted from the sky. Expecting darkness, Evainne watched as a soft amber glow began to emanate from the towering columns of rock, their strange highlights shining down onto the vast array of pools dotting the landscape and climbing up the nearby hillside. Hints of hidden flowers perfumed the air, blending with the waters' slightly salty aroma. Is this what a tropical paradise would be like? *Minus the near-death experiences and the three-armed aliens, that is.*

"He did," Kahlym replied. He stepped around her, and she dragged her gaze away from the landscape, up to him. He captured her hand and lifted her knuckles to his lips, the soft touch heating her cheeks. She chuckled shyly as, with a wink, Kahlym tucked her hand into the crook of his elbow and guided her toward the bubbling pools. "Many of the inhabitants of the Dantaran galaxy send their young here."

She nodded, even as her mind spun. "Kinda like summer camp?" she asked. "It's, um … where kids are sent when their parents want some peace." *Or in my case, to be forgotten.*

"Did you forget I can hear your thoughts, *ziat'xahn?*" Kahlym brushed a light kiss on her cheek. "As a sanctuary, it is where children discover their abilities, face their fears and their weaknesses. Many use this experience to chart the course of their entire lives." Her brow furrowed as she struggled to wrap her mind around kids making hard life decisions at such a tender age. He continued as they walked on. "Those who hear the voice of the Goddess Ishtanti during their meditations become clerics."

Evainne watched the tawny Ontaxian pilot cannonball into a pool with a crazed howl of joy. "Wonder what he saw here."

Chuckling, Kahlym shook his head. "I'm pretty sure he was too busy racing from pool to pool to pay much attention to his spiritual obligations." On cue, Dhaerin popped up from beneath the surface, laughing as he shook his soaked mane, raining droplets upon his sister. Zybella frowned, attempting to hide behind her raised hands as her brother frolicked in the water.

Strange night birds who called to each other took to the skies as Kahlym and Evainne approached the massive, steaming pool. The natural outcroppings functioned as both walls and steps leading to higher and lower basins. Kahlym handed her a small shoulder bag, then gestured toward a secluded corner, and a tender smile tugged at her lips as she ducked into the alcove.

Upon opening the package, she discovered what she assumed was a swimsuit and even a lightweight drape to use as a cover-up, both in flattering shades of swirled forest green and creamy ivory. He truly had thought of everything. Her cheeks cramped with a broad smile as she hastily slipped out of her gearsuit and donned the one-piece outfit. It reminded her of the ones she'd seen Olympic swimmers wear—high collared, yet open through the shoulders, giving full range of possible arm movements. She secured the front opening, then stepped out of her impromptu changing room.

A pale shade of blue radiated from the grotto's depths, though she could find no direct source of the ethereal lighting. Fragrant steam billowed from small pockets surrounding the large basin. Kahlym, resting with his elbows propped against the smooth edge, beckoned to her. Xandar and R'uan had taken up vantage points across from Kahlym, while Brel, Zybella, and Dhaerin enjoyed another spring on a nearby shelf. The rising heat tickled her bare legs and she had yet to take the plunge. *No guts, no glory.* She dipped her toe into the welcoming water and a comforting sense of peace crept into her soul.

Sighing contentedly, Evainne stepped into the perfectly heated pool. She'd asked for a hot tub; this was exactly what the doctor ordered. When her feet no longer reached the bottom of the pool, she pushed off and floated the remaining distance to the opposite side.

"I think she likes it," R'uan remarked, smile evident in his tone, while her eyes slipped closed as she settled in next to Kahlym.

"This place is amazing," she practically purred. "So much better than the baby bathtub in my apartment, that's for sure."

The more relaxed she became, the warmer the water felt, and her thoughts zipped back to her last swim. If they didn't have company, she wouldn't mind another refresher course with Kahlym....

A tap on her shoulder dragged her attention back to the present.

"Careful, *ziat'xahn*," Kahlym whispered into her ear. "These waters are the same as those in Bhaan's rejuvenating pool." She sucked in a sharp inhale and sat up straighter on the stone bench. "Not to mention"—he directed her gaze up to their companions gathered in other pockets—"these are all interconnected."

"Oh, shit," she mumbled, and she reined in her rampaging libido, curling her arms across her bound breasts, embarrassed. "Damn, I'm sorry."

Xandar shook his head. "You apologize for no reason, *learom*. This is part of the Fire that drives you. Each elemental emotion is equated to a color: Fire is red, Water is blue, Air is gold, and Land is green. If you think about the color red, it has many shades and many different incarnations. More importantly, there are positive and negative sides to each elemental emotion." He tilted his head to hold her gaze with surgical precision. "Evainne, what comes to your mind when you consider red?"

"Rage, blood," she said, listing the first two things that popped into her head.

Xandar offered her a soft smile. "What about passion, and warmth?"

Evainne looked away, her gaze drawn to her lover at her side. Kahlym laced his fingers between hers, sharing his loving strength without hesitation. Her brows drew together while her thoughts warred.

"Two sides of the same coin," Xandar stated. "Both necessary. For without them, life as we know it would be bereft of so much."

Try as she might, Evainne was unable to refute his logic.

"Let me ask you this," her teacher's voice interrupted her spiraling thoughts. "When you accessed your gifts, what were you feeling?"

"Gifts?" She choked out a mirthless laugh. "I guess that's one way of putting it." Another frown furrowed her forehead as she leaned back into the cool stones, until fingertips brushed away the deep crease, calling forth a soft smile. She remembered the first time Kahlym had chased away her aching facial muscles with a pass of his hand. Now, his gentle distraction allowed her to focus on Xandar's query. "Most of the time I was … pissed off." She grimaced. The truth had slipped from her tongue, leaving behind the sour taste of anger.

"And what happens after?"

"After?" Evainne cocked her head. "After what? You kinda lost me there."

Xandar pursed his lips. "Maybe a better way of putting it would be: what happens while you are in the zone?"

"It gets cold," Brel said, joining their pool, and the conversation, seamlessly. Evainne tore her gaze away from Xandar as Dhaerin and Zybella took a seat on the stone bench across from her.

"Nah." Dhaerin shook his head vigorously as he settled in beside R'uan. "It gets hot. When she fought with Haseunn, I thought my skin was going to melt off before she finally offed him."

Kahlym lifted his hands up. "I've felt the cold more often than the heat." His gaze darted between Evainne and Brel. "Remember when I told you about how she put dear old Mom in her place?" A wistful grin grew on Brel's face, while Evainne cringed in half-hearted remorse. "I expected to see icicles on the leaves," he said.

"This is the balance, the opposition of the emotions," Xandar explained. "When you use your gifts in anger, you draw the fire from your surroundings."

Evainne pressed her fingertips into her temples, hoping to push the pause button on her overworked brain. "Okay, so let me get this straight: When I get mad, things get cold around me. So when the heat turns up, that means I'm…" She gestured toward Xandar, looking for guidance.

"Happy" would have been the logical opposite, but she'd definitely not been tickled pink by her near-death experience at the hands of the attacking Divine. A connection sat barely out of reach, and the longer she soaked in the rejuvenating waters, the clearer and calmer her mind became. "When I fought the other Divine," she said slowly, "I was terrified … but not for me."

She scooted about on the rocky seat, angling her shoulders against the rough wall to see the gathered faces. Ethereal light reflected off of the rippling surface to illuminate her new family— protective older brothers, and now even a sister, had been added to the ranks of adopted siblings.

Yet the most important person sat on her left, bare skin brushing lightly against hers, generating heat that filled her soul. Kahlym laced his fingers with hers, a tender squeeze conveying more than any words ever would. Now, a child born of that unbreakable connection grew within her, and that thought ratcheted up the fear factor to dizzying heights.

"I didn't want anyone to get hurt because of me, like … like what almost happened when I lost it."

Kahlym shook his head and cradled her face. "*Ziat'xahn*, you are the strongest person I have ever known, and—"

Evainne placed her fingertips across his lips, halting the ego boost about to fall from his tongue. "I'm not that strong, hon. I'm a walking disaster with anger management issues that give me phenomenal cosmic powers. Not so sure that's the best combination, but it's what it is." Then an idea sparked, cutting through the static like a knife. "Wait." She spun to face Xandar. "You said balance, right? So, all those centering exercises you taught me are—"

"Designed for you to better control your Fire and temper it with Water," her mentor explained. "Opposite forces coming together. It is the nature of the Divines to be ruled by more than one elemental emotion. All you need to do is—"

The howl of approaching engines drowned out any further advice, and Evainne snapped her eyes skyward as ships blipped into existence. *Shit.*

"How the fuck did they find us?" Brel roared out as everyone dashed for cover. An explosion rocked the ground, and water and debris rained down. Evainne tailed Kahlym and his brothers, running toward the nearest alcove, while voices shouted over the blasts, confusion and terror echoing in the shattered night.

Kahlym grabbed on to Brel's arm. "Either the ship had a tracker," he said, then paused, shifting his gaze to the scrambling group beyond their shelter. "Or worse."

"We've got a spy in our midst," Evainne said, giving voice to the thought in each person's head. She scanned the pools and their scattered party. So many new faces; anyone could have been someone other than what they claimed to be. Damn. She hated having to keep watch over her shoulder among the people she thought she could trust. "Isn't this supposed to be a sacred place, or something?" she asked.

Brel produced a weapon from some hidden pocket, then peered around the corner and, using his body as a shield for Evainne, he aimed at the white-clad enforcers pouring out of the nearest craft. "Guess someone forgot to let these asshats in on the news." Light flashed from the muzzle, dropping three intruders, while Dhaerin and R'uan laid down cover fire from their protected shelter. "Kahl! Get Evainne, and get to the ship!"

Evainne clenched her teeth. How many friggin' times did she need to prove she was no weak damsel who needed saving? If Xandar believed the bulk of her power flowed from her anger, then she was sitting on a live powder keg. Time for this princess to flex her muscles.

She fisted her hands, each knuckle popping as she considered her options. Their ship was so close—just over the rise at her back—and many of their group had already scurried in that direction, when a familiar voice called out.

"What, no hello? No welcome back for your old friend?"

Warmth seeped out of Evainne's blood, her head swiveling toward Kahlym, whose cheeks paled in the dim starlight as the words from his traitorous navigator echoed off of the rocky cliffs.

Chapter 32

"Qaen."

Kahlym had spat out the single word, eager to get the taste of betrayal off of his tongue. Even amidst the chaos and the screams, the voice of his former crew member had sliced through the noise, like a spike driving into his soul. His fingers twitched as he imagined the bastard's throat clenched in his fists.

"Figured it would be you to fuck up our party," Brel shouted between directing their escape and reloading his weapon. "Don't you understand the word no?"

"Brel?" said Qaen, and Kahlym detected the hint of incredulous tone in his former nav's query. "I thought I put a hole the size of Kahlym's ego into your chest, mate? How is it you're still breathing?"

Movement off to his left caught Kahlym's eye. A quick frown drew his brows together, and he shook his head at Evainne, laying a finger across her lips. *<Do not let him know anything, ziat'xahn. If he learns what skills you possess, he will stop at nothing to retrieve you.>* His gut roiled at his own harsh tone, but he would beg for forgiveness later.

Evainne's eyes flared wide for a heartbeat, golden lightning sparkling in her deep brown orbs.

Brel was all too ready with a comeback. "Guess your aim sucks as much as your judgment, fuckwad."

<Don't you trust me?>

The world outside melted away as Evainne's words echoed in his head, leaving Kahlym and his angel at this crossroad. Her steady breathing, warm against his palm, fired up his blood, yet her pleading gaze tore into his heart. His eyelids fluttered down as he pressed his forehead against hers. *<Evainne, I will always trust you. You are my soulbond, and I will love you until my dying breath. But I would not be a male worthy of such a gift as your love if I did not protect you.>*

<But I can help. What good are these powers if I can't use them to save those I love?>

With her simple request, his heart and mind warred for a logical way to refute, but fear halted any further words. The handful of days separated from both his angel and his sanity still haunted his steps. If anything truly happened to her, nothing would be able to save him this time.

Her hands cradled his face, and in the darkness behind his shuttered lids glowed the light of her love, guiding his soul and setting his thoughts at ease.

<Have faith, kerriad. I have no desire to get dead.>

Damn her and that brilliant mind of hers. His shoulder tension slipped away as the seconds ticked by, and with a slow exhale, he begrudgingly nodded. *<How can I help you, ziat'xahn?>*

Her sexy chuckle tiptoed down his skin, and he captured her lips in a searing kiss. Time was not on their side, so the quick taste would have to tide him over until they were all safely away.

"Let me know when everyone is on board, sweetie," she whispered against his cheek before his eyelids dragged open. A wicked smile had curved her luscious mouth, and Kahlym forced his mind back to their current location. "I'm gonna create a distraction so we can get the hell outta here."

A loud boom sounded off to his right and, acting on reflex, Kahlym pulled her into the shelter of his body as he dug his shoulder into the rock wall. "Brel?"

"What!" his brother's voice echoed back in the dark.

"How close are we to full?" He turned toward the fleeing figures ducking between the clouds of steam and dust, and while he counted passing allies, Evainne shimmied out from his embrace. "Dammit," he grumbled and scrambled to his knees, intent on following her. "Evainne!"

His shouted words, however, were swallowed by a nearby explosion, and he slammed his shoulder against the sheltering stone tower. He dug into the bag slung across his back, retrieved his weapon, and provided cover fire as he chased after her. Through the haze, he spied Qaen's spiked blue-and-white hair amidst a cluster of enforcers who surrounded a couple in their contingent of guards. Kahlym growled as Qaen backhanded one soldier, knocking the man to the ground, before placing his weapon's muzzle against another's temple.

"STOP!"

Kahlym charged toward the unfolding scene, firing at the surprised enforcers, and Qaen swiveled his head around. Even as the distance shrank between them, Kahlym recognized his former nav's confident swagger, his familiar smirk knowing that victory was his. Ire threw off Kahlym's aim, and his final shot went wide of his sneering target.

A piercing whistle cut through the sound of weapon fire. "Hey, douche bag!"

Qaen snapped his stare toward the rocks, searching for the source of the insult. Kahlym peered into the smoky plumes and, taking a slow inhale, felt the responding intake of his angel. He zeroed his gaze onto her hiding spot. She clung to the walls, using the deep shadows as shelter while she taunted the bastard.

"Figured you couldn't do anything without back up," she called out. "Must be hard on the knees to play bitch to an entire legion of assholes."

She used the canyons to her advantage, voice echoing, bouncing in all directions, and the distraction gave the captured forces a window to turn against the enforcers. Kahlym hastily searched the ground for a recharged weapon as he gestured frantically. *<You have done well, ziat'xahn.>* Brel shouted something at his back, and he didn't need to pick out the exact words to get the gist. *<Hurry back to me. As much as I hate to say this, that bastard isn't worth the effort.>*

Vengeance would come. But not right now. They needed to regroup and rearm before engaging in an all-out battle. Qaen would pay for his treachery, though not at the expense of his angel.

Chapter 33

Evainne peered down from her vantage point. Not high up enough that people looked like ants, but if she lost her footing, she'd have a really bad night. She was pretty sure flying wasn't one of her new superpowers.

"Blessed Divine?" A timid voice had crept out from the shadows to her left, nearly startling her out of her skin. "I do not believe this is a very safe course of action."

She reached back and, digging her fingers into Myclen's collar, shoved him into the sheltering alcove. "Jumpin' Jesus on a pogo stick, Myclen. Are you trying to give me a heart attack?" Narrowing her eyes, she glanced over his shoulder at the craggy path she'd easily ascended. "How the hell did you follow me? And why?"

She could have sworn his gray skin had taken on an even chalkier sheen while he bobbed his bulbous head in nervous tics. "I … I … I gave my oath, and it is my duty to ensure your safety, Blessed Div—"

She lifted a hand, exasperated. "How about you let me handle this one, okay?" And she stared at him until his continual nodding clearly signaled his understanding, then turned her attention back to the unfolding battle. Kahlym crouched behind a rocky pillar, a few strides away from their ride. *Dammit. Just get your stubborn ass onto the friggin' ship.* Phantom fingers brushed against her cheek. Her brows tugged together in defiance. *I know you can hear me, so move it, bucko.*

Qaen jerked his gaze in so many directions, it was comical. Until, that is, he turned to fire at the fleeing Ontaxian guards who'd traveled with her to the sanctuary.

"Not on my watch," she muttered, and she focused her anger at the coward. A strange tingling sensation at her fingertips crawled up the length of her arms, raising goosebumps as shivers raced down to her bare toes. The night shifted from dark to a dazzling blue, and her target stood out in deep red. Her heart pounded, sending jolts of unfamiliar energy through her veins, and in an almost instinctual response, she pressed her palms onto the ground to release the pent-up power.

A small, distant rumbling grew, until it shook the entire valley. Water sloshed within the stepped pools, spilling their steaming contents onto the scattering troops. Evainne grinned as she eyed the staggered path of one certain blue-and-white faux hawk. Giving the environment an extra push, she commanded the very earth, and a stony spike exploded up from the ground, throwing Qaen into the air like a rag doll. Then her eyes snapped skyward and, picking out the enemy crafts that dotted the starscape, she sent the remaining energy through the night to fry any system she could reach.

Her mind snapped back to Saturday mornings and her favorite Japanese anime. "I'm a friggin' earth and metal bender," she said, awe coloring her whispered words. "Aang can't hold a candle to me."

She savored her victory for only a moment, though, before her arms buckled and she collapsed face-first onto the hard rocks. A pair of hands gripped her shoulders, and Evainne struggled to get her legs beneath her, vaguely aware of the surrounding muffled cries as she fought to keep her eyes open. Drunkenly, she stumbled down the narrow trail, leaning heavily on her scrawny companion. *When did Kahlym get so short?*

An uncomfortable buzz in her ears burned through the fog in her head, and a whole body ache followed the emerging clarity; edges sharpened, giving shape and meaning to her surroundings. Yet time seemed out of sync. Kahlym ran toward her as though fighting against sticky air. She reached one leaden arm toward him, stretching out her exhausted limb, eager to touch her lover.

"Blessed Divine, you must bring you to those who will protect you."

Evainne screwed up her face and glanced over at her talking crutch, confused by Myclen's strange statement. Her protector was inches away. All Myclen had to do was take two steps with her. How hard could it be? Her lips parted, then the ground separating her from Kahlym burst into a shower of fire and sand in a violent blast that threw her off of her wobbly legs and flung her lover against the rocky column behind him.

His battered body landed in a crumpled heap, and she screamed in heart-wrenching agony as her toes dug into the ground, scratching to gain her an inch toward Kahlym. Tears poured down her face, her world shattering to pieces, while voices inside her head shouted, directing her to take action.

<Evainne, hurry! There is still time, learom-xahn.> Her old teacher spoke to her, though she didn't like the unfamiliar touch of fear in his plea. She broke free from Myclen's hold and crawled closer to her lover's scarily still body.

<Toa, get out of here.> Rocks cut into her thighs, but she dismissed the pain. *<I cleared the path as best I could. Go! If you don't leave, who the hell is going to save us?>*

"Now, isn't this just the prettiest picture?"

Evainne knew that smug tone. It set her teeth on edge.

"And here I thought I was only gonna get rid of one pain in my ass," said Qaen. She ignored the bastard and continued on her mission to reach Kahlym ... until fingers clawed into her hair and yanked her to her feet. Hissing, she balled her fists together, then slammed her elbow back. An *oof* and sharp exhale over her shoulder told her she'd hit her mark, and the ground rushed up to meet her once again. Using her forearms as cushions, she blocked a second serving of dirt, then tucked her feet beneath her, legs coiled and ready to strike.

"Bitch," growled Qaen and let his arm fly, backhanding Evainne. Or would have, had an unexpected set of arms not tugged him to a halt inches before connecting with her cheek.

"To touch the sacred Divine is blasphemy!" Myclen strained to hold back Qaen's trembling limb.

Evainne never thought she would be grateful for her meddling protector, but desperate times and all that crap. Her shoulder burned in its effort to maintain the shield pose. An engine roared about ten yards behind, kicking up small swirls of dust, and she squinted, peering through the thick haze as the sleek craft zipped into the dark, navigating past the stalled armada. Qaen swept his opalescent gaze from the escaping ship, down to her, circling back to Kahlym, then returning to her before stalking away ... directly toward Kahlym. Panic set in and she clambered to her feet.

"Get your hands off him, fucker." The venom in her voice was stronger than the power in her veins, and she prayed her opponent wouldn't call her bluff. Qaen tossed back his head, sadistic laughter echoing off the high stone walls while he dragged her lover up onto rubbery legs.

"Oh, don't worry, princess." He sneered, motioning over a pair of enforcers. He pointed toward one of the waiting vessels, then passed Kahlym to them. "He'll be safe as a babe. Well, at least until I get him back to his father."

Ice chugged through her blood, and her heart dropped into her heels. "You can't—"

"Can't what? Can't collect the biggest bounty in the Seventh Quadrant?" Qaen stalked closer and knelt down beside her with a sickly grin. "Seems old Anaxar's reward for him still breathing was twice what the Thrall was willing to pay for his corpse."

Evainne swallowed hard, fear and the overpowering stench of Qaen's cologne threatening to cause her last meal to make a return appearance. She turned her face away, opting to bury her nose into her own armpit than to deal with the bastard's cloying aroma.

Misreading her current pose, Qaen inched closer and twirled a loose curl of her hair around his blood-splattered finger. "And I get another bonus for handing you over to Jhuen, as well."

"B-b-b-but I made a promise to deliver the Blessed Divine only into the hands of the rightful emperor. Only among the other Divines will she be safe."

As if things couldn't get any more fucked up. Evainne stared incredulously at her once-friend and protector. "Myclen, what have you done?"

Myclen dropped his chin sheepishly and wrung his long fingers.

"Don't blame him too much, doll," Qaen quipped as he took to his feet. "He's an idealistic fool who actually believes the emperor is the proper babysitter for the universe's freak show."

Someone new elbowed his way through the departing crowd, until he finally stepped out and stopped directly in front of Qaen. "What is the meaning of this?" he said. Evainne read the anger flashing in his green eyes and the irritated, Morse code twitch in his pencil-thin mustache. Medals and ribbons decorated the front of his soot-smudged, white uniform jacket complete with gold braided epaulets showcasing his importance.

She flipped through her memories, stopping when she recalled the officers on the space station who'd attacked Kahlym's crew, their pristine uniforms those of the station liaison. This guy was definitely some big mucky-muck in the Thrall ranks.

Groaning, Qaen rolled his eyes. "Don't get your panties in a bind, Panza. She'll end up in your father's hands, eventually. After she makes me a very wealthy male." He scrubbed a hand against his scalp, tussling the vibrant spikes of hair. "I hand them both to Anaxar, and I am set for life."

Father. If her spirit could have sunk any lower, it would have dug a hole at her feet. The man arguing with the traitor who'd tried to kill Kahlym, and nearly did kill Brel, was next in line for the Rimma throne.

She refused to give in to despair, though. Instead, she gathered her legs beneath her, forced her weary body to stand, and Myclen quickly jumped to her aid, cupping her elbow as she found her land legs. She flinched at his supportive hold, anger turning the ice in her veins to a sluggish fire.

"Please understand, Blessed Divine, I only live to—"

"If you want to live to see the next second," she snarled, "you will stop talking right the fuck now." But no sooner had she regained her balance, she was flanked by four very well-armed enforcers. Evainne shifted her glare toward the faceless guards, shaking her head sadly. "What's the matter, boys? Afraid of a girl?" She stared a little longer at her escorts, then barked out a hollow laugh as she caught the tremble of a gun's muzzle trained on her.

"Oh, they saw your little show, and we don't want a repeat performance," Qaen called out, adding her proper title, "Divine." Then, breaking off his current conversation, he strolled to stand in front of her. "In fact, I think I know how to make sure we get to our destination in one piece."

From a pocket attached to his belt, Qaen produced a strange-looking syringe, and Evainne's heart raced at the mere sight of the needle's dripping point. She'd never been a very good patient, and on more than one occasion, nurses had required extra help to give her even the simplest shot.

Myclen slunk out from behind her back to stand in front of her, acting as her shield. "She is *Dym Char'ann*," he said, "a revered and blessed Divine. I will not allow you to harm her."

Qaen blinked in bland response, then sauntered to stand at her left. Evainne narrowed her eyes, warily studying his lazy pace. "Then I guess you won't be coming on the rest of the trip with us," he replied and, with a shrug, pulled a wicked-looking blade from the small of his back and buried it hilt-deep into Myclen's chest. Evainne cried out in sharp surprise, guiding him to the ground as blood, thick and deep green, stained the front of his pale blue tunic.

Her fingers trembled as she tried to stem the flow of the warm liquid. Myclen grasped her hand, and she shifted her blurry gaze up to his face.

"P-please, forgive me. It … it was my … my honor to have m-met one … such as…"

As he fought for every word, tears spilled down her cheeks and, shaking her head, she offered him a weak smile. "Shh. Save your strength. You'll—"

His large head lolled, his last breath hissing into the night, and then … nothing.

Rage simmered under Evainne's skin, and she drew her gaze up from Myclen's lifeless eyes to the singular cause of so much destruction.

Qaen wore his mockery of a grin like a badge of honor. "Cheer up, love," he said. "I just did you a favor. Now you don't have to worry about him again."

Roaring in frustration and grief, Evainne leapt to her feet, only to be dragged to a halt by the forgotten guards at her sides, and Qaen swept in, quickly slapping the needle's fine point into the meat of her shoulder. Whatever was in the syringe sped like lightning through her body, sapping her of energy; darkness stole the edges from the rocky terrain, and her legs wobbled. Evainne fought against the enfolding black, but she was too weak to resist, and she struggled to listen for as long as she could to the voices that still argued beyond the cottony veil.

"Bring her onto my ship."

"No. I am taking her."

Sounds of a scuffle and a blast cut through, ending the conversation, then she was dragged once again, but until she was free from the drug's effects, her exact location would remain a mystery. *Please tell me you guys got away....* Silence cocooned her, drawing her into unconsciousness with hope as her only anchor.

Chapter 34

Xandar gripped the threshold leading to the pilot's flight deck, forcing his wandering mind on getting their remaining crew back to the safety of Stria space.

Evainne captured. Kahlym injured, possibly dead. Thrall forces likely screaming across the stars to Rimma to deliver both into the hands of the emperor. Dear Ishtanti, what was he to do?

The shouts at his back had grown with each passing second—arguments and angry words bounced off of the metal hull as useless and as irritating as gnats on a warm summer's day.

His thoughts circled back to the prior events. In the blink of an eye, the quiet Bashir sanctuary had been invaded, and now they were in a battle for their lives. He and Dhaerin had rushed to the ship when the ground fighting had broken out, knowing a hasty escape would be required. While the Ontaxian pilot had prepped the engines, Xandar provided cover fire as their friends made their way on board. He'd counted noses, relieved as Zybella and Brel had finally come running.

"Where's Kahl?"

Brel wiped the sweat off his forehead as he struggled to catch his breath. "I thought he was with you." He peered out into the smoky air.

Xandar shook his head, swore softly to himself. "No, I lost track of them when the Thrall troops landed."

"I can't find Evainne either," said a panicked Zybella as she gripped Xandar's shoulder.

Brel launched himself toward the open hatch, but R'uan grabbed his elbow. "Wait, he's there." Xandar and Brel followed the line of R'uan's extended arm to spy Kahlym tucked behind a cluster of fallen rocks, yards away from their location.

Xandar cupped his hands around his mouth and yelled out over the deafening explosions. Brel and R'uan added their voices, waving madly to get his attention. Evainne was nowhere in sight, but he held on to the belief that she was shielded by his brother's body. Compared to the men and most of the women in his end of the galaxy, Evainne did fall into the petite range.

When the ground at their feet shivered and shook, Kahlym was thrown to his knees to reveal only stone. *Damn. Evainne, where are you?*

"What the hell was that?" Dhaerin called out from the cockpit.

"I have my suspicions," Xandar grumbled as he spied an odd pair scaling down from the highest pools. Evainne leaned heavily on Myclen, her staggering steps uneven, and Kahlym lurched to his feet, dashed toward her. *C'mon, Kahlym. Hurry up.*

A blast between them tore through any hopes Xandar had; it sent Kahlym flying back into the rocky alcove, and Brel cried out over Xandar's shoulder, nearly climbing up over Xandar's back in his attempt to leave the ship.

<Evainne!> He focused on reaching her through their familial link. *<There is still time, learom-xahn. >*

Evainne stumbled closer to Kahlym's too-still form. *<Toa, get out of here. I cleared the path as best I could. >* Cleared the path? Xandar turned his gaze to the darkened heavens, where distant ships hung at cockeyed angles. *<Go! If you don't leave, who the hell is going to save us? >*

She was right, though the truth of it tore apart his soul. "Dhaer! Take off now!"

"You can't mean—"

"And just leave—"

Xandar slammed the hatch release, the round button leaving a deep impression in the center of his palm as he shouldered past shrieks of outrage, stopping only when he stood beside the pilot's chair. He dug his nails into the metal seat back. "Dammit, don't argue," he yelled. "Take off—NOW!"

Dhaerin had paused for torturous heartbeat before spinning back to the controls. Xandar hadn't needed to hear the tawny Ontaxian's mutters to agree with the sentiment. The sleek craft had easily maneuvered around the stalled armada, and before long, the sanctuary pools of Bashir had been left far behind.

Now, more than an hour remained in their return journey, and his headache was reaching epic proportions. He massaged his temples, praying for relief and answers, but the surrounding chaos provided no respite.

"All right. Enough, enough." Xandar turned to face the angry mob, each combatant a friend just a handful of hours ago. A sad smile touched his lips. Evainne's whistling skills would have silenced the room with minimal effort. He hadn't been as blessed, no matter how long and how hard she'd tried to teach him. Instead, Xandar reverted to the tried and true method of being louder than the rest.

"I SAID ENOUGH!" He slapped his palm against the wall, the sharp smack punctuation to his bellowed statement. Brel snapped his furious citrine eyes away from his current debate partner and leveled his gaze at Xandar, desperation pouring from his hopeless expression. Xandar heaved a deep sigh and clasped his older brother on the shoulder, then glanced over at the gathered faces. The visible wounds from their harrowing escape had been momentarily forgotten in light of fear, grief, and misery.

"We abandoned them," Ma'avi barked, flinging his arm toward

the receding planet. "To save our own skins, we DESERTED THEM!"

Xandar weakly lifted a hand to calm the young Praxxiran's growing rage. "If we had remained, all of us would have been captured. It—"

"You don't know that for sure," Zybella said, tears falling down her sleek feline cheeks. "Someone could have run and … and grabbed them … and—"

R'uan pulled his sibling into a comforting embrace as she sobbed. While Xandar wished to join in and weep for the ache in his chest, he would wait to break down once his brother and their important charge were once again safe. So, steeling his nerve, he spoke the words he hoped would help his crew understand the truth of their retreat.

"She told me to leave."

Silence cocooned the ship's interior. Xandar lifted his chin and met each astonished set of eyes. Zybella shook her head, slowly at first, digesting the news. "I know this is hard for you all to hear," he said, "but after that last blast, Evainne connected with me and ordered us all to leave."

Murmurs and gasps rose and fell in low-grade waves, while disbelief and shock drove the bulk of unintelligible responses. Xandar continued, eager to set their minds at ease. "She is the reason we were able to escape as easily as we did. Somehow, she disrupted the awaiting armada, but she did not know how long it would take them to re-engage their systems."

Grief paled the charcoal gray cheeks of one of the Ontaxian guards. "She … she sacrificed herself to save … us?"

Xandar crossed over to the frightened male and, gripping his shoulders, gave the man a sturdy shake. "No. She knew if we stayed, no one would remain to rescue them." Hope dawned in the depths of the guard's topaz eyes, and Xandar broke eye contact to include the rest of the room. "And that is exactly what I plan to do. If any of you think, for an instant, I would leave either of them to suffer at the hands of the Thrall Emperor, feel free to show yourself out." He jammed his index finger toward the airlock on his left.

R'uan's eyebrows shot toward his hairline, and Brel tipped his chin away, his hand an impromptu shield to hide a growing smirk. While Xandar was grateful for the slight decrease in tension, they were still fighting a ticking clock.

"Dhaer?" he called out over his shoulder. "Can you reach Falka? I'm gonna need her—"

"She's got *Tiamat* spun and ready to go as soon as we land." The Ontaxian bounded out of his seat, the doorframe stopping his enthusiastic momentum. "And she's already scanning the waves of every ship within ten light years of Bashir. If someone even mentions either of their names, we'll know it a heartbeat later."

Cheers filled the air as Dhaerin returned to his pilot's seat. The ship lurched forward, rocketing them toward Ontaxa at breakneck speeds.

Don't worry, kid. We're coming for you. Xandar didn't care if Kahlym actually received his message. He had to get the words out and place his faith in the hands of the Goddess. After so long apart from his brothers, he refused to give up until they were all reunited once more.

The flight back was peaceful without Panza's running commentary interrupting the trip every five seconds. Granted, Qaen did feel a tiny bit of remorse for shooting and marooning the emperor's son back on Bashir, but a deal was a deal. Anaxar Jhuen had offered far too sweet a price. All he had to do was deliver both Kahlym and the bitch into dear old Daddy's hands.

Grabbing his comm link, he sent a quick message to Kaxxahn. If she found Panza and brought him back to the emperor, it would help smooth things over with the Thrall leadership. And if his sloppy shot hadn't killed the ass, then all the better.

The ship lurched, and Qaen flailed his arms to stay on his feet. "What the hell?"

"There … I don't know, sir," came the Thrall pilot's answer. "Something is pulling the nav systems out of alignment."

Qaen gnashed his teeth, his lips curling into an angry snarl. How the fuck did that slip of a female manage to attack the electronics when she was confined? *Crap*. Another knock, and his shoulder crashed into the bulkhead.

"Get the controls back. Do not deviate from Raedyn Primus." Using the metal walls as stabilizers, Qaen bounced down the narrow corridor. The guards he had watching over their prisoners shrugged, confusion creating amusing masks. Qaen rolled his eyes and approached the holding cells. The first chamber was dark and quiet. In the shadows lay a huddled form in a sprawled heap. Kahlym was still out, but was he still breathing? A pitiful whimper caught his ear. Good. He was worth more alive than dead.

Lights flickered in the last chamber, and Qaen arched a brow, tilted his head. "Is that—"

A blinding flash illuminated the hall before the entire space plunged into darkness. In a second, the emergency lights kicked on. While Qaen's eyes adjusted, the two guards had dropped to their knees, mumbling hasty prayers.

"Hey!" Qaen called out. "Quit breaking my men, bitch!"

"Come down here and make me, limp dick!"

Should've gagged her. He stalked along in the dawning glow, shoving his sleeve up to his elbow. "Now, now, pet." He stopped in front of the unbreakable glass cell, the only one strong enough to contain their special guest. "Play nice, or things will get even uglier."

His prisoner snapped her eyes up. Strange, he could've sworn when he'd first glimpsed her curled up in Kahlym's lap, her eyes had been an unusual dark brown. But the female glaring daggers at him now had pools of glowing umber, with flecks of gold swirling within the angry orbs. Smudges of dirt and purple bruises smeared the porcelain of her cheeks, adding to her furious beauty. A faint red trail dribbled from her nose, fresh and free flowing.

"Uglier than your fucking mug?" she said. "Doubtful." Evainne crawled to her hands and knees, sniffing as she dragged the back of her hand against her mouth. The scant suit barely concealed her curves, her bare arms and legs making his mouth water.

Sleeping with the universe's deadliest assassins was his normal fare. Did he dare risking his soul attempting a one-night-stand with a powder keg of power?

One slender brow arched and she scoffed, climbing back onto the bench seat along the far wall. "Don't make me vomit. I'd sooner chew glass than let you touch me, douche bag."

"Aw, c'mon, love," he cooed, resting an elbow on the doorframe. "A free ride worth remembering while your plumbing is still tight and you can still enjoy a good fuck?"

Qaen smiled and dragged his tongue between his fingers enticingly … until his laugh expelled puffs of cool mist. Tendrils of frost crept along the edges of the thick, clear barrier as the surrounding heat drained out of the space, and the ship's engine chugged and sputtered. His grin faltered as he eased back from the volatile situation.

"Whoa, hold on, now. It was only a joke." Qaen cautiously sidestepped toward the cell controls along the wall, hands open and loose before him … then slammed his fist on the blinking sensor.

Gas quickly filled the glass cell, descending from pinhole vents in the ceiling. Qaen had learned much about the inner workings of containment protocols before agreeing to take a Thrall ship to the ambush. The noxious fumes would merely knock out problematic prisoners. Would it be strong enough to take down a volatile Divine?

"You … fucking … coward…" Her voice drifted as the surrounding temperature leveled out. As long as he remained breathing for another day, he could take whatever jabs she threw.

Triggering the comm unit, he called up to the pilot. "Everything stable?"

"Yes, sir. The mains just came back online. All systems normal."

Relieved, Qaen huffed out his breath and rolled through his knotted shoulders. As he dug his fingertips into the back of his neck, he glanced down the corridor. "Get out of my sight," he growled at the two guards, who scrambled up from their prostrated poses.

Once alone, Qaen stalked back to the hazy chamber. So the bitch knew a few tricks. No way was she some all-powerful thing that would bring the Thrall Empire to its knees. Must have had something to do with the backwater planet she'd gotten snatched from.

"How long before we reach Raedyn?"

"At current speed, we should land by moonrise tomorrow."

Qaen stared into the cell's diminishing fog as the outline of a lone figure slowly took shape sprawled out on the floor. Even in her unconscious state, Qaen knew better than to relax his guard.

"Good," he said to no one in particular. "Were the subjugo stones locked in the med safe?"

As a preemptive measure, the emperor had sent along a care package with Panza. Not all homeworlds had been forthcoming with their Divines in the early years of Thrall rule, it was said; in rare instances, tribal leaders refused to leave their flocks altogether. Because of these reluctant joiners, the first Rimmarian Emperor had needed to create a unique manacle able to contain the powers of any Divine, without damaging these sacred beings.

Qaen had heard the legend of the discovery of the subjugo stones—gems capable of absorbing, or even negating, the vast abilities of anyone who wore them—while he was still a youth. Arranged in ornate and elaborate settings, the iridescent blue fire opals worked better as shackles than even the strongest Raedynese steel.

"Sir?"

Qaen growled. "Did I stutter?"

"N-no, sir. I mean, yes, they are secured in the med bay lock-up. But do you believe it is truly necessary to—"

"Would you like to return to your family in one piece, or several?" Staticky silence met Qaen's blunt inquiry. "Then send someone to bring them down to the holding cells, because I'm pretty sure if we don't take that chance, this bitch will tear the ship apart."

Murmured confirmations bled through the link, and Qaen returned his focus to the trapped female. "And I, for one, want to be around once M'Uubair gets his prize."

Approaching footfalls echoed down the empty corridors, rapid and even, until a handful of uniformed enforcers rounded the far corner. Qaen rested his weight back onto his hip, folding his arms across his chest with a frown as the strange procession closed the final distance. With a slow and deliberate blink, he stared at the Thrall officer who continued forward from the middle of the group while rest of the group peeled off. An overly regal presentation for such a small box, but he was only a guest on board this ship of insanity.

The last straw came when the box bearer actually took a knee and extended his arms above his head. Scoffing, Qaen snatched the heavy necklace off of the exposed, black velvet liner. In an inset compartment lay a slender key on a fine obsidian chain, its release triggered when the gemstones were removed. Impressed by the level of security, Qaen tipped his chin toward the gathered soldiers and, armed and ready, he took a deep breath to steel his nerves, then faced the quiet chamber. She was still out, but didn't know for how long. His hand hovered over the door controls.

"Keep an eye on her," he said. "If she flinches, gas the room." Silence thickened and he frowned. Looking over his shoulder, he glared until one guard found his balls and nodded. As satisfied as he could be, Qaen turned back around and opened the door.

The lingering aroma was a stomach-churning blend of burnt fruit and moons-old garbage. Qaen coughed hard then swallowed back the bile rising in his throat. Kahlym's female lay face down; her thick braid of dark curls snaked along the chrome tiles. *She's helpless. Just friggin' get it done.*

The thought spun in circles as he inched closer. Right. Easy to act cocky while she was behind nearly half a foot of shatterproof glass. Within the same space, he felt his courage creep to a safer place outside of the current vicinity and, clenching his teeth, Qaen knelt beside her to slide the jewel-encrusted piece around her neck. His hands shook as he tried to avoid any contact, but he soon realized he would need to move her into a different position. He heaved a deep sigh and sat back on his haunches.

"A little help here?" he called out, and one burly enforcer shrugged, daring to enter the cell. As the man crouched at his side, Qaen gestured to Evainne's unconscious form. "I need you to lift up her head so I can get this thing on her."

The white-helmeted soldier paused. Qaen imagined his ashen face behind the shielded visor and he knocked the guard's shoulder to kickstart obedience. "Or we can wait until she wakes up and ask her nicely."

The implied threat hastened the man's response. In a second, her limp body was propped up enough for Qaen to affix the locking clasp at the base of her neck. Holding his breath, he twisted the key until he heard a soft click and, certain the gems were secured, he quickly took to his feet and followed the enforcer hastily out of the chamber. Paired rapid, shallow breathing proved two things: One, both of them were still alive; and two, the whole experience had scared the shit out of even the bravest.

"How—" The enforcer gasped, hunched over, gulping in deep swallows of air. "How long before we know if those things even work?"

Qaen rolled his neck from side to side, enjoying the sensation of stress seeping out of his body. "Trust me on this, mate. If we're lucky, we'll never need to test that theory." One cleansing breath later, he met his own reflection mirrored back from the various visors aimed in his direction. "Send for the female guards to get her cleaned up and more appropriately attired. I'm sure Jhuen will have a more lavish wrapping for this present, but first we need to show we've been good little devotees and have treated the Divine with the proper respect."

Scurrying boot heels scraped along the slick floor, each man eager to escape the close proximity of their deadly passenger. Not that he truly blamed them. Even his logic couldn't explain the vast level of power confined in the sleeping form on the other side of the glass. Would the Thrall Emperor be able to control her?

"Not my problem," he mumbled, tucking the delicate key into

his pocket as he headed back to the cockpit. "Not my problem at all."

Chapter 36

The stinging slap to his cheek dragged Kahlym out of his painful rest, making bits and pieces of memories flicker behind his half-closed lids: the pools, the explosions, the face of his traitorous former crew member … and not much after that. Where was he? Was his crew safe? Was Evainne safe?

Evainne.

From her precipice, she'd sat crouched, ready to strike, her palms pressed against the rocky surface while a pulsating pale blue glow had surrounded her. Then the ground had shaken, tremors rippling through the soil, focusing on one target in particular. He would treasure the sight of Qaen's body being tossed about like a leaf in a storm while he cried out in shock. Sadly, everything after that was fuzzy.

Voices murmured, echoing in the distance, indiscernible and garbled, until a blast of icy water yanked him into the present. Coughing out, Kahlym shook his groggy head and struggled to peel open his eyes. One lid remained tightly sealed, though, and his jaw ached. He carefully traced his tongue along the inside of his mouth, testing and counting each tooth. The number was accurate, and none felt looser than they had since the last beating. He raised his head.

"Good morning, sunshine." Qaen's overly chipper voice grated on his nerves and his first impulse was to squeeze the fucker's neck until those opalescent eyes popped out like marbles. His arms tensed, but the rattle of shackles and a burning fire in his shoulders mocked his vengeful efforts. Kahlym snarled in impotent rage, and he fought against the unyielding restraints. "Sleep well?"

"You fucking pile of tulmak dung," Kahlym growled, his still-bare feet gaining no traction on the sleek metal flooring. "There is no corner of the universe where you can hide from me. When I get out, I'll—"

Qaen threw back his head and brayed, his joyless laughter reverberating off of the low ceiling. "You'll do what? What makes you think you're gonna survive this, mate?"

Though the blunt statement drove a spike through Kahlym's mind, his heart refused to give in to despair. *Because I must live for my angel, and my child.* He mentally reached out, searching for Evainne. Even when he'd sent her halfway across the stars, he could still sense her presence; might have been nothing more than the faint whisper of a heartbeat, but he'd known she lived. Now, the sensation was different; muted, as though someone had lowered the volume of the world. She was being forcibly hidden from him. But it meant she still lived. That tiny kernel of truth buoyed his spirit and he held on to that lifeline.

Kahlym focused on Qaen. "Because," he said, "you're a limp-dicked asshole who doesn't have the balls to do the dirty work himself."

His barb struck its mark, and Qaen responded with a fierce backhand that whipped Kahlym's head about. The tang of blood filled his mouth. Knowing he'd unhinged the bastard so easily amused Kahlym, and a coughed laugh bubbled up. Another vicious punch landed, the attack only earning more bouts of chuckling.

Each strike rattled his brain, aggravated his already battered body, but Kahlym couldn't contain his maniacal laughter.

Finally, a blurry figure stepped in, halting any further abuse. Tears streamed freely, but whether from pain or mirth, Kahlym was hesitant to say. During the reprieve, he caught his breath, wincing with each inhale, biting back a groan with the next exhale. Something poked into his side as he fought to pull in lungfuls of the familiar-tasting air. The re-circulation engines found on every vessel gave the surrounding atmosphere the same tinge of charred electronics. At least they were still on board a ship.

Words slipped in from the nearby conversation.

Alive.

Bounty.

Raedyn Primus.

His heart sank. He'd fully expected to be dropped onto the Thrall Emperor's doorstep; to be given over to his own father would be a much crueler fate.

With monumental effort, he lifted up his head and peeked through the one eye still willing to work. He narrowed his focus on the Praxxiran speaking with the enemy forces. "Qaen," he mumbled, "what have you done?"

A sadistic smirk curled Qaen's lip as he angled his gaze away from his companions. "Oh, so now you're interested?" He strolled closer and wiped his bloodied knuckles against Kahlym's bare chest. "Seems dear old Dad offered me much more of an incentive than Gha'jahn," he said. "So I hand you and your little female over to him—"

Kahlym lunged forward, and his nav jerked back half a step. "Temper, temper, now, Kahlym … and then your father gets the glory of returning the kidnapped Divine to his royal fuckness." Qaen bobbed and retreated as he circled, baiting Kahlym, careful to remain just out of reach. "Plus, your public execution will make for the event of the season. So you see"—Qaen folded his arms across his chest in grand gesture—"in the end, it's an all-around win-win for me."

Qaen nodded, signaling to someone at Kahlym's back, and the energy chains suspending him gave way. At once, the floor rose up fast, and his weakened, twisted arms responded too late; his cheek kissed the cold metal a second before his hands slapped useless at his sides.

"Get him on his feet," Qaen said. "We meet the Sub-Confidant as soon as we're locked down." A hand dug into Kahlym's hair while two more sets gripped his biceps, and he was yanked unceremoniously to standing. At the sudden shift in gravity, his legs pitched and wobbled, stomach threatening to expel any contents still remaining from his last meal while Qaen added, "Oh, and put on some damned clothes, will ya? Can't have you going to your death in your drawers, can we?"

The guards jostled him down the corridor, then tossed him into an open room. His knees buckled, dumping him on his ass, and Kahlym hissed. Fluttering fabric landed at his feet, pieces scattering as more items joined the pile. A pair of boots completed the stack before the door clicked shut.

Grateful for the solitude, Kahlym closed his eyes, attempting to quiet the panicked shouts inside his head. Instead, he picked apart the hateful words of his former friend and knew Evainne was here with him. But why couldn't he touch her thoughts? Drugged, perhaps? Lost in a fog and unable to respond? The longer he pondered this, the more fear spun in sickening circles. What effects would such a dangerous toxin have on her? On their child?

Kahlym choked back a rising sob of grief. *I want to be your strength, not your weakness*—her gentle plea, spoken in the throes of passion what seemed to be a lifetime ago cut through the chaos and confusion in his soul. He would prove to her he was worthy of her gift, and even if Ishtanti demanded his life, he would give it gladly, knowing his angel and their child, created through the purest love, would go on.

Steeling his spine, Kahlym retrieved the borrowed attire, then crawled to the bench seat along the wall, where sweat poured off of his face as he gingerly finished the painful task of dressing himself. He figured Qaen would only provide loose, unarmored garments, and he was not disappointed. The gold, silken tunic and deep obsidian trousers were at least the correct size, as were the knee-high black boots. A stray thought made him carefully run his fingers along the boot's top cuff. Sadly, he found no forgotten blade tucked in the hidden pouch.

Deciding he was reasonably presentable, Kahlym rose. He needed no reflective glass to know he wouldn't be winning any prizes today. His appearance was not meant for him, though, nor was it meant for the company to whom he would soon be subjected.

Head held high, he waited as the door opened for one and only one person. His Evainne, his angel. If this was to be the last time she saw him, he made certain she would be proud of the man she'd chosen as her soulbond.

My heart and my life are yours, now and always, ziat'xahn. And he strode out to meet his fate with words of love in his heart.

———————————————

Chapter 37

———————————————

Light flooded into the cold room, drenching the space in an all-too bright glow, and Evainne cringed, slinking away from the painfully blinding visual alarm clock. Her limbs felt leaden, muscles trembling in an effort to scuttle into the receding shadows.

"*Dym Char'ann*, we have been sent to prepare you for your presentation." The new and reverent voice had barely carried past the threshold, and Evainne sifted through her foggy mind, attempting to give the words meaning. What had happened to her? Her hands patted down her body. She no longer wore the damp swimsuit. Instead, she had somehow, while unconscious, donned a baggy tunic and a pair of booty shorts.

Awesome.

She remembered the short insult session with the purple-skinned moron who'd once tried to kill Kahlym, and had nearly succeeded in killing Brel, then the glass chamber being filled with knockout gas. How long ago, she could only guess. She wanted to attribute her lethargy to an aftereffect of whatever had been piped into the room, yet … something else, something more sinister, had congealed in the thick oil chugging through her veins.

Levering herself into a seated position, Evainne swung her gaze toward the open doorway, where three exceedingly tall and slender girls waited, heads bowed and fingers clasped below their waists.

"Great," Evainne grumbled. "More kowtowing. Just what I wanted this morning." She groaned as she struggled to get her legs beneath her, only managing to plop onto the metal bench jutting out from the far wall. A glance down at her hands gave her another interesting tidbit: Gone was the fight evidence across her knuckles. Her brows pulled together and, curious, she reached for her hair. Sure enough, during her downtime, someone had washed, combed, and restyled her wild waves.

Closing her eyes, Evainne sucked in a deep, centering breath. *What the fuck was in that shit?*

In her personal darkness, her mind called out to Kahlym, but the silence that answered was so complete, so absolute, her heart skipped a beat. Panic began to rise, and she tried again. Not even an echo in the emptiness.

The drug. It had to be the reason she couldn't find him. She pressed her fingertips into her temples, hoping to kickstart her brain.

"Okay, it's nothing. Breathe … relax…." She whispered the simple mantra over and over while her gaze darted around the Spartan cell. Clearly, she would find no answers here. Instead, she leveled her gaze at the silent statues still awaiting her orders and, with an annoyed huff, she motioned the trio inside. They drifted in.

Their movements were so graceful and languid, Evainne felt oafish by contrast. She tugged her brows together while her attendants busily arranged some billowing fabric into a recognizable gown. Something was vaguely familiar about these women—long hair in varying shades of blonde and copper cascaded straight down their ramrod backs, while elegant fingers twisted the fine layers of bright red silken material into a delicate toga. A girl with steel blue skin and sunflower blonde hair presented her with a bandeau top in the same scarlet color.

Evainne narrowed her eyes and accepted the boob binder, wracking her brain. Why did she know these specific people? So many planets, so many races during their whirlwind tour of the galaxy … but it was more than that. Something deeper, more visceral. Gentle hands guided her to her feet, one gossamer drape traded out for another.

"Where am I?" Maybe with some locational context, she could identify this nagging sensation.

The corresponding silence was seriously beginning to piss her off, though she took the quiet moment to contemplate her response. She was, after all, a Divine. She should have been able to command just about anyone.

You get more flies with honey than with vinegar. While she never really liked the strange phrase—who the hell wanted to get flies in the first place?—she couldn't deny its inherent logic. So, opting for the calmer approach, she laid her fingers on one hand of the assistant fiddling with the belt around her waist, while the other two busied themselves lacing her into yet another pair of strappy, heeled sandals. Her own skin appeared dull in contrast to the shimmering aluminum sheen of her companion. "Please," she said, "just tell me where I am."

When the girl with the soft amber hair raised her face, and eyes of sparkling sapphire had met Evainne's, recognition flared to life and the truth of her destination's end hit her like a punch in the gut.

Raedyn Primus. She was on Kahlym's homeworld.

"I've seen you before," Evainne said, words deliberate and accusatory, and her companions quickly scooted back away from the Divine's possible wrath. Flashes of memory played: a marbled corridor, walking with Kahlym as Brel escorted their bound father. "I've seen all of you before," she added.

The trio had sneered in disgust when their odd party had approached, but as soon as they'd seen Kahlym's fingers entwined with hers, it was game on. Hands had reached out for him, caresses aimed at whatever body part they could touch. Evainne had thought the black sapphire-haired girl would drop to her knees right there in the middle of the hall.

Their heads swung about, each looking for aid from the other, but when no reprieve was found, they quickly knelt, bowing low until their foreheads kissed the ground.

"Forgive us, Blessed Divine—"

"We are unworthy and beg for your mercy—"

"Please, we beseech you."

Their wailing pleas rose up from the floor, and Evainne scoffed. She shook her head sadly, then traced her fingertips along the gown's confining collar. Normally, the robes she had been forced to endure had more plunging necklines. Instead of fabric, though, she discovered a cold, metal chain.

Evainne jumped to her feet and, carefully picking her way around the prone forms, stopped in front of a polished chrome mirror hanging on the wall.

Broad slices of oddly iridescent blue stones were scattered across her open throat, each piece joined together and housed in a black, filigreed setting. Although intrigued by the ornate necklace, Evainne sensed something sinister about it. It appeared light and delicate, yet the feathery weight dragged her energy straight through her body. She clawed at the fine chain, searching for the clasp or a weak link, but no matter how hard she pulled or tugged, the damned thing refused to break.

"You like your leash, princess?"

Winded from her fruitless struggles, Evainne snapped her gaze up to the smirking asshole. "Bastard," she spat out.

Dressed in a long, cream-colored, high-collared military jacket, Qaen rested his arms lazily over his head. His black, knee-length, patent leather boots gleamed, and his gravity-defining hair swooped in pristine blue-and-white stripes. A thin smudge of kohl lined his eerie opal eyes, and the unearthly lavender skin practically sparkled. Clean shaven, he was definitely dressed to impress.

"Now," he said, "are you gonna behave, or do I need to gas you again?"

Evainne's jaw ached as she fought to hold back a string of profanities. She had more at stake than her pride; lives depended on her not putting herself in abject danger. Plus, she needed to find out what happened to Kahlym and the rest of her new family, which meant, in order to do any of that, she would have to play nice.

Her extended middle finger served as her answer. *Well, sort of nice.* "And before you ask: no, that wasn't an invitation."

Qaen stuck out his bottom lip in a juvenile pout. "Pity. But we don't have time anyway." He winked, and her stomach lurched. With a dramatic exhale, he pushed off the threshold and stepped away from the open doorway. "Oh," he added, "you might want to tell your grovelers to leave. If you don't release them, they will be here until the stars burn out."

Really? Evainne's eyebrows climbed up her forehead. The karmic notion of these bitches shivering on the floor forever was very tempting, and she stroked her chin, contemplating how long she would make them wait.

"Ooh, do I detect a cruel streak in the perfect Divine?" Qaen's devious and excited tone drove her toward her final decision. She wouldn't be hanging out with these young women any time soon; they were only products of their twisted world.

"Go," she said, exhausted yet firm. "And how about you try to think for yourself from now on, hmm?" She'd added the final directions while the trio nearly tripped on their flowing skirts in their haste to escape. Doubtful her words had made it through, though she'd at least made the effort.

Strike the match.

Mentally jolted back into the beautiful forested chamber on Ontaxa, surrounded by loved ones, Evainne regained her purpose.

Head held high, she leveled her stare at her captor. "Let's get this show on the road."

Qaen inclined his head, then gestured toward the open hallway. As she stepped out, several overly armed enforcers immediately flanked her. She chuckled under her breath, shaking her head. "Pussies."

Their procession continued through the twisting corridors until they reached the descending hatchway, where a puzzled frown tugged at the edges of her lips. She had assumed they'd already arrived on Raedyn Primus and were now somewhere in the vast palace of its capitol city. Apparently, though, that wasn't enough pomp and circumstance. Evainne's steps faltered as she approached the imposing welcome party waiting at the end of the ornate, mosaic runway, recognizing only two faces in the sea of haughty expressions.

When she had first met Kahlym's parents, Anaxar and Jaleen, she'd had the luxury of her lover and a slew of overly protective adopted brothers at her side. Now, surrounded by enemies, she faced them once again. She shook out the tension racing through her fingers as covertly as possible, while forcing her strides to remain steady and even. Her gaze darted around the lavish decor, and she mentally cataloged every visible exit, calculating her chances of making it to any of them alive. Not to mention, running in heels had never been her strong suit.

So, pretending Kahlym was again with her, Evainne straightened her spine as she covered the final distance. In grand, choreographed fashion, the entire gathered mass shrunk back about a foot, and women curtsied deeply, fanning out their skirts, while men bowed graciously from the waist.

"Bright blessings upon you, *Dym Char'ann*." For as long as she lived, Anaxar's voice would make the hairs on the back of her neck bristle, and when the man rose to his full height, Evainne swallowed hard against the rising bile. "We are honored by your presence."

"Honored?" She strode forward, stopping only when two guards shuttered the power couple behind their shoulders. "You are *honored* to have taken me by force from my home, my friends, all that I love and hold dear?" To outside ears, she was speaking of her life back on Earth. But all of those things—home, friends, and love—she'd only discovered after traveling halfway across the universe. She wasn't about to let any of them go now.

Anaxar splayed his long fingers against his chest, inclining his head slightly. "My apologies. If you will permit me, I would gladly return you to those who have your best intentions in mind."

"Evainne…"

She snapped her gaze toward the speaker partially hidden behind a throng of armed guards. "Oh, God. Kahlym," she whispered, quickly changing her direction. "What have they done to you?"

Even from a distance, she could sense his pain. A bevy of bruises decorated his face, and a vicious slash still wept on his cheek below his swollen-shut eye. His arms were twisted awkwardly behind his back, no doubt bound by painful restraints. Yet in his agony, he refused to bend, and while the surrounding guards took a knee, Kahlym stayed on his feet. Evainne fought against the smile tugging at her lips. He was well aware of her aversion to such gestures.

An enforcer smacked Kahlym on the back of his legs at the knees, dropping him to the ground. Anger flooded her, and she rushed to his side. "Leave him alone."

The guilty guard merely returned to his groveling kneel. "He was not showing you the proper respect, Blessed Divine."

She shifted her gaze to Kahlym, panic crawling up her spine. He was inches away, yet she couldn't feel him in her heart nor in her mind. *What was happening here?* "Are you okay?" she asked. "Why can't… Why aren't you—"

"Blessed Divine," Anaxar blurted. "I believe it would be best if you were not so close to that criminal."

Criminal? Rich, coming from the likes of that sleazeball. But if she wanted to ensure their child would meet its father, she had to play her cards right.

"Don't trust him, *ziat'xahn.*" Kahlym's strained whisper was like a dagger that drove straight into her soul. She dared not reveal the true nature of their relationship, nor the unfathomable depth of her love. If even a hint of his alleged blasphemy came to light, his execution would be swift.

She nodded imperceptibly—a short, brief lowering of her eyes —but her message was received. *I trust only you here, kerriad.* Reining in her emotions, Evainne climbed back up to her feet.

"You say he's a criminal," she stated, praying her voice traveled across the room with conviction. "What is his crime?"

Anaxar arched a brow over one cruel, red eye. "Why, kidnapping, of course," he announced with pompous certainty, adding, "For starters. Inciting rebellion. Willful destruction of property. Theft of a Thrall vessel…" Step by step, he ticked off each offense on his fingers until he stood directly in front of her, and with each new charge, tittering laughs had wafted up from the peanut gallery. "Plus, the mere fact he breathes is an affront to the good of civilization," he finished.

If she let her temper have its day, she'd knock that smirk right off of his face. Instead, she quickly filed through the backlog of lessons she'd learned during her crash course in Dantaran history. She hadn't needed to look too far; the answer practically stared her in the face.

"Too bad the prophecy won't allow you to take his life," she said, meeting Anaxar's burning ruby eyes.

"Are you so certain of that?" he muttered, so close to her ear, she flinched back to avoid contact with him.

Her blood boiled at his oily tone. "You touch one hair on his head, and I swear to Christ, they'll be sopping up your remains with a sponge."

"Bold words, Divine," he countered, with a confident sneer. "I am curious how you would follow through on your threat, since you seem to be under my control."

Control. Evainne brushed her fingertips across the cold stones hanging at her throat. "If you think these rocks are gonna hold me back, then think again, asshole. I will punch a hole through the entire universe to find you. This"—she tugged at the jeweled collar—"is temporary. My wrath, however, will be legendary if you hurt him."

The light of victory flickered and then dimmed in the blood red orbs, while the edges of his mustache twitched in unchecked rage. Evainne clenched her jaw, prepared for the backhand soon to be flying her way. Yet the staring contest only continued.

"Do it," she muttered, loud enough for only one pair of ears. "I fucking dare you."

Chapter 38

Anaxar held his arms at his sides through sheer willpower alone, though his palms tingled, itching to smack that bitch of a Divine standing so proudly in front of him. But no matter how justified his anger, if he even flinched, then nothing would save him from swift retaliation from the emperor, not to mention every breathing entity in the room.

"What if I promise not to kill him?" he asked.

The female barked out a sharp, unladylike laugh. "I might have been born at night, sweet cheeks, but not last night." Leaning away, she folded her arms across her ample breasts. The red of the imperial gown did not flatter her complexion, although the twists and folds did accentuate her lush curves.

Gnashing his teeth, Anaxar placed a hand over his heart and took a knee. "By my oath, and upon the honor of my ancestors, he will come to no harm as long as he draws breath."

"Make it as long as *you* draw breath."

She was intelligent; he would concede that point. He forced his head to dip for a second time. "As you command, Divine. As long as *I* draw breath."

"No," his bastard son interjected, struggling against the royal guards' steely hold. "You cannot make such a bargain."

Anaxar tilted his head, a harsh rebuke poised upon his lips, but it was the Divine who silenced his impudent son. "Not my choice, sweetie. Stuck between a rock and a hard place right now. I have to believe we can come out the other side of this alive. *Trust me.*"

She spoke his language with unusual clarity. Impressed, but not fooled, Anaxar rose to his feet.

"You there!" he called to the traitor from his bastard son's crew, before pivoting on his heel and striding away from the pathetic display of useless affection. "We were led to believe the Imperial Heir, Panza M'Uubair, was to be with you. Is that not true?"

The Praxxiran navigator rubbed sheepishly at the back of his neck. "Technically, he was. But, um … he opted to stay behind with some of the Thrall troops to search for the others who escaped."

Anaxar could taste the lie in his feeble excuse, but that was none of his concern. Given the ultimatum he received from the Thrall Emperor himself, Anaxar wondered if the leader would even care about his missing son. The concealment held a glimmer of believability, though, so perhaps it would be enough to placate M'Uubair. In the meantime, he had an important delivery to make.

"I will inform the emperor of the reason for his son's delay." He nodded toward his personal flight crew who, with bows in unison, dispersed.

Confident, Anaxar crossed the landing bay to stop in front of his wife. Jaleen pinned him with an apprehensive stare, her regal head held high, even though he was fully aware of her doubt. "We leave for Rimma immediately to return Emperor M'Uubair's prize to him." Then, leaning in close, he whispered conspiratorially to his female, "Once I have handed her over to Gha'jahn, drop that abomination into the nearest pit and seal it shut."

A sadistic twinkle sparked in her diamond orbs, and her ruby red lips curled into a knowing smirk. "I await word of your success, dear husband."

Anaxar placed a chaste kiss on her cheek and, after retreating two steps, turned to face the awaiting soldiers. Peering over at the Divine and his son, his brows pulled together in disgust. Their heads were far too close together for his liking. The sooner he dispatched her to the Thrall, the sooner he would be rid of the simpering whelp who dared to call him Father.

"Blessed Divine?" Anaxar had forced his voice to remain neutral, with the proper modicum of reverence. "It is time for you to embrace your destiny."

She mumbled something indiscernible, and the phrase brought an odd smile to Kahlym's face. A great part of him wished to ask what had been said, but she'd already retreated and gracefully strode across the room. "Let's get this show on the road before I change my mind," she said and stalked past him, power walking directly toward the awaiting craft, leaving kowtowing forms in her wake.

"As you command, Blessed Divine." And Anaxar quickened his pace to catch up to her.

Within moments, they'd boarded his personal craft, and the hatch slid into place, locking them safely inside. His passenger sat in the most secluded seat, back pressed into the corner, which gave her complete view of the ship's interior without the fear of anyone approaching from behind. Normally, he chose that particular vantage point. Fuming, yet forcing a pleasant grin, he inclined his head and found another chair.

"The trip should—"

"If you value your balls, you won't speak to me. Like, ever again."

Anaxar's jaw dropped, shocked by her blunt words. *Thank the Goddess this trip will be short.*

Chapter 39

Xandar white-knuckled the controls, pretending his death grip would encourage the ship to fly faster. It had only been one moon-rising since their party had been force-fully split. Through the phenomenal hacking skills of Kahlym's Shee Va'an tech, Falka, they'd been able to track Qaen's vessel as it sped toward Raedyn Primus. When the final destination had been determined, Dhaerin had sworn eloquently, his harsh words mirroring the thoughts of all.

His impetuous brother, along with the youngest Ontaxian, had hoped they could give chase immediately after departing from Bashir, but more logical minds, namely his own and R'uan's, clearly stated that a larger force would improve their chance of success. Not to mention, Xandar refused to give voice to his heart-breaking fear of failing both his missing brother and his former student.

<Xandar?>

Xandar's spine snapped straight. "Kahlym? Where are you? Are you okay?" A rapid series of taps on his shoulder pulled his attention toward his frantic copilot, whose striped orange-and-brown eyes peered hopefully at him. Xandar offered him a soft smile and a slight nod.

<Find Evainne.>

Xandar slipped out from behind the driver's console, confused, and handed the reins over to the eager Ontaxian. Now free to move around, he quickly stepped into the main chamber. "Kahl, what do you mean find Evainne? Isn't she with you?" Brel pinned him with a curious stare before dropping his shoulders and rolling his eyes with a frustrated growl.

<She … she was. Father took her. She … they did something to her.>

"Okay, *xahn'cal,* slow down." Xandar plopped down into the nearest seat, closed his eyes, and massaged his temples to dismiss the next growing headache. A choice. Why did it have to be a choice? "Let's start with what you know. Why do you think they did something to her?"

A centering hand gripped his shoulder, and he raised his gaze. R'uan's optimistic expression gave Xandar a boost of confidence. Needing another mind on this, he widened the link to include Brel and R'uan.

<When I saw her … I mean before that bastard loaded her on board a ship bound for Rimma…> The rumble of anger in Brel's throat voiced the sentiment perfectly. *<She … I couldn't reach her.>*

"Reach? You couldn't link with her?"

<R'uan?>

The Ontaxian nodded. "I'm here, *kherdes.* How far away was she?" he asked, while Brel paced, then moved into the cockpit with purpose.

<If I could have reached out, I would have touched her.>

"Ask him if Qaen is still with him," Falka called over. Her strange question drew all eyes to her like a magnet, and she frowned, setting two of her three hands onto her hips and gesturing to the group with the third. "What? The tracker is on him, not his ship. I had Yhan'tu dart that fucker with a tracer while he got stitched up before all this shit hit the fan." With a shake of her long green hair, she headed back toward the engine room. "Never did trust that bastard."

Xandar chuckled lightly. "You've got one hell of a crew, Kahl, I'll give you that much. Falka wants to know if—"

"Wait." R'uan leapt to his feet, gaze distant, focused. "Kahlym, was she wearing some kind of blue gem? It would have been set in black chromium."

The silence deepened, and Xandar's stomach dropped. *No*, he prayed, *please not that.*

<*Yes. I'd never seen her with the necklace before…. R'uan? What is it?*>

Xandar and R'uan locked eyes, both struggling for words. After all, how did one explain that their only hope for freedom was being contained by the strongest power-dampening device ever created? R'uan dropped his gaze to the floor, while Xandar, with a deep inhale, prepared to deliver the bad news.

"Raedyn Primus in two klicks," Dhaerin said, his enthusiastic voice cutting through the tension.

"Kahlym, we are moments away from you. Show me where you are and—"

<*But Evainne—*>

"No." Xandar rose as he issued the sharp response. "*We* will all go for her—together." He strolled into the nav chamber and peered out at the approaching planet he'd never expected to see again. "Kahlym, I made her a promise to save you both, so don't make me disappoint her and not have your ugly mug greet her when we arrive at the emperor's home on Rimma."

The surrounding stars grew faint, less frequent, until the familiar, swirled skies of jade-and-fuchsia greeted them. While he had always enjoyed the kaleidoscopic sunrises and sunsets of his homeworld, they did not hold a candle to the simple joys he'd discovered on Evainne's bright blue-and-green planet.

Xandar pushed aside his reminiscence, waiting in silence for Kahlym's answer, while on gut instinct, he directed Dhaerin toward the mountainous barrier at the far end of the Jhuen family estate.

As a youth, he'd learned the best ways to sneak in and out of the palace and he prayed the sensors had not been improved during his long absence.

An image of the east landing bay appeared in his mind, along with an exact count of the awaiting guards and a handful of departing dignitaries, his mother among them. Xandar blinked past his visceral rage. Their mother never had one kind word for her youngest son, and soon, she would pay for her lack of love.

He called out the coordinates to Dhaerin, along with the proper course heading to keep them safely hidden in the shadows.

"Got it," Dhaerin called back.

Now for the hard part. "Kahlym, you said she was wearing a strange necklace you'd never seen it before," Xandar said. "That necklace has a key needed to unlock it. Which means—"

Kahlym's growl reverberated through their link. *<Qaen has it, doesn't he?>*

As they made the final approach, Xandar scanned the secluded landing bay. Seems his personal hangar had remained off the grid. Engines whirred to a halt, and silence engulfed the ship. "If he is with you," said Xandar, "keep him there."

<My pleasure.>

Brel slapped a blast rifle into Xandar's chest. "No arguments, brother. We're gonna need everyone packing on this one."

With a sharp nod, Xandar accepted the weapon, then donned the battle helm. Actions were now the currency of the hour. Time for his treacherous parents to pay for their crimes against him and his brothers.

<Hang on, xahn'cal. The cavalry is coming.>

Chapter 40

Hope filled Kahlym's heart for the first time since his enemy's armies had swarmed the sanctuary moon of Bashir. Swallowing hard, he closed his eyes to collect his rampant emotions. With his traitorous nav still acting as his personal chaperone, Kahlym had to keep up the air of defeat, lest he betray his family's coming to his rescue. Qaen's voice drilled into his mind like a nail, though, the pompous ass prattling on and on as they walked the maze leading to the holding cells.

"You know," Qaen droned on, "if you had let us nab you back at Graey's, you could have been spared a whole lot of pain." He gave Kahlym a helpful shove down the hall.

Kahlym refused to rise to Qaen's mockery, and he shuffled his feet, hoping his movements would read as broken and downtrodden. *<Xandar, you better get here soon before I do something to ruin all your plans.>*

"But I have to know this, mate." Qaen grabbed Kahlym's hair and yanked him to a halt. Kahlym hissed out as he dug his heels into the slick tiles. "It'll be our little secret," he said. "You know, between friends."

Kahlym scoffed and was rewarded with another eye-watering pull on his warrior locks. "What the fuck do you want?"

Qaen's cloying scent enveloped him, and Kahlym choked down the rising bile as the man pressed against his back.

<*We're in. Kahl. Keep Qaen close.*>

Close? How much closer could the bastard get?

"Was she worth it?"

Kahlym's blood ran cold at his lecherous inquiry, yet a hint of anticipation in the few words had told him all he needed to know. She'd rebuked the male's advances once again. "You will never know," he finally replied.

Alarms rang out, shattering the intimate silence, and a confident smile tugged at the corners of Kahlym's lips.

Shouts and small explosions echoed in the corridor, and Qaen eased his grip. At once, Kahlym smashed his head back into Qaen's, connecting with a crunching sound, and as Qaen reeled from the sharp blow, Kahlym struggled to keep his balance, still bound. Instinct and self-preservation combined and he ducked, spinning about, and kicked Qaen's feet out from beneath him. The Praxxiran, still stunned by the first strike, tumbled to the ground, groaning as he cradled his broken nose. Kahlym lowered himself to the floor, wincing, to sit on Qaen. Distant voices rose and fell, and Kahlym picked out his name among the chaos.

"Dhaerin! Brel!" he shouted, adding each crew member until he spied a pair of enforcers escorted forward by the barrels of three blast rifles. Sighing in relief, Kahlym further drove his elbow into Qaen's gut, hearing the ongoing complaints as the familiar Chandaran blue battlesuits came around the corner. The trio of figures traipsed down the corridor in a wedge, their shoulders too broad to pass three abreast. Kahlym had never been more relieved in his life to see Brel and the Ontaxian denmates.

"You ready to get the hell outta here, bro?"

Kahlym nodded tiredly. "Thought you'd never ask."

R'uan guided him back to his feet, while Brel and Dhaerin

dragged Qaen onto his knees. Deadly, dangerous tension oozed from his brother as he trained his weapon on their former crew member, and before Kahlym could ask, the restraints at his back were loosened. Blood flowed back into his numb fingers.

"Are you having a damned family reunion or what?"

Kahlym frowned, quirking a brow at the comm link. "Falka?"

"At least you still remember my voice. Now, everyone get back to the ship. I don't know how long the door is gonna stay locked."

Kahlym turned his narrowed stare toward Qaen. "Be there in a heartbeat."

Qaen barked out a harsh laugh, and a crushing punch from Brel knocked him back down to the floor. "We need one thing, and only one thing, from you, dog." The pure, unadulterated hatred in Brel's voice sent shills along Kahlym's spine. "Give it over now, and your death will be quick and painless."

"I don't know what you're talking ab—"

Another fierce blow cut short the lie. R'uan locked his arm around Brel's cocked elbow. "We are losing precious time."

Kahlym laced his fingers around the crisp collar of Qaen's Rimmarian uniform jacket. "Where is the key?"

Blood dribbled from his crooked grin. "Key?"

"Ugh. Just check all his pockets." Falka's exasperated tone and obvious directions spurred them into a frantic search, and Qaen shouted and squirmed as four pairs of hands rifled through his clothing. Kahlym caught snippets of his tech's grousing. *"Lady Evainne was right; none of you males have a working brain among you."*

"Got it." R'uan dangled a fine chain with a slender key as proof, before handing it over to Kahlym. There, the answer lay in his palm, surprisingly light. Tightening his fingers into a protective fist, he turned to face his brothers. Dhaerin had already dispatched the guards, leaving the path clear.

"Did she scream for you, too?"

Kahlym froze as gurgled laughter crept along his back. "Yeah,"

Qaen continued. "Gotta love the ones who put up a fight. Makes things hotter, don't you th—"

Qaen's head disappeared in a shower of bone and brain. Brel stood tall, arms trembling as he clutched the blast rifle. "No need for that bastard to breathe any longer," he said.

Kahlym rested his hand on his brother's shoulder, and Brel blinked a couple of times, color returning to his pale cheeks. Though shadows still haunted his citrine eyes, the darkness began to recede with each passing second.

"And he was full of shit," Dhaerin added. "He still couldn't handle the fact she shut him down. The ego on that douche."

Kahlym chuckled weakly. "Why did everyone glom on to that specific word?"

"And do any of you even know what it is?" R'uan chimed in as he led everyone back to the landing bay. Kahlym limped along, each inhale sending out a wave of agony. Dhaerin ducked his bushy head beneath Kahlym's shoulder, and in tandem, they chugged along with purpose. He shoved aside the pain with every step, his focus on one target currently speeding its way into Mordan's realm itself.

"Guess we'll all ask her when we see her again."

The sooner, the better. Kahlym kept these final words to himself, though, even if they were shared by all who raced toward *Tiamat's Revenge.*

Chapter 41

Grand Emperor Gha'jahn M'Uubair paced the length of his receiving hall, his languid footfalls steadily keeping time as seconds ticked on. His soldiers had sent word that the Divine had been located and was now being transported by Anaxar du Jhuen on board his personal vessel. The male must have been desperate to regain his seat on the High Council if he was willing to bring the female himself.

In preparation, he'd ordered for his standard retinue—a full garrison of high enforcers dressed in formal garb—to flank either side of the ornate, mosaic pathway. Gha'jahn shifted his gaze to the sharpshooters tucked into shadowed corners. With the flick of his wrist, these few soldiers would destroy any threat.

Certain all security measures had been put in place, he returned to his troubling thoughts.

Raedyn system to Rimma. *How long could that truly take?* Growling with impatience, he peered over to the awaiting Divines. When his father had ruled the Thrall, the royal chamber had been lined with Divines from every corner of the Seventh Quadrant. Now, only two remained, both old and feeble. The Healer, Qi'tan, and Hollix, the Seer, huddled together, their bald heads bowed close in conspiratorial whispers. The ancient males had consulted every tome and scroll in their library, but they were no closer to discovering any more about the nature of their forthcoming member.

However, the words of a long-forgotten prophecy had been spinning like a whirlwind Gha'jahn's mind. Perhaps because they also centered around the youngest son of the Sub-Confidant of Raedyn Primus, Kahlym cal Jhuen.

Narrowing his eyes, Gha'jahn stroked his trimmed goatee with the back of his knuckles while he mentally shuffled the puzzle pieces around. If the female was indeed a Fury, she could birth an entire legion of powerful pawns … and his mouth watered at the prospect of controlling a female Divine Fury. From reports filtering in from across his realm, she was a creature of rare beauty, so why one such as her chose to waste her time with the prophesied abomination was beyond him.

"Sire? The Perredon *requests permission to land."*

The clear voice interrupted his useless pondering and brought a smile to his face. "Granted," he said. "Send them to the Moondown pavilion." His grand chamber overlooked the designated landing bay, giving him the perfect vantage point to survey the incoming party. He smoothed down the front of his official waistcoat, the deep crimson jacket piped with ivory and gold and only to be worn on majestic occasions such as weddings … and surrenders.

Whirring engines wound down beyond the domed arches, announcing the long-awaited arrival of his mystery guest. Blackened chrome with the fiery red comet emblazoned along the hull, the sleek vessel settled onto the platform, and within seconds, the hatch opened to allow through a small entourage, the handful of guards surrounding a slight figure dressed in crimson robes.

Not wanting to appear too eager, Gha'jahn crossed the marbled floor and sank down into his low-backed, bentwood throne. His palms touched the armrests, while the resounding strike of boot heels against the slick stones echoed off of the high ceiling. *The game begins.*

The twin doors at the far end of the hall were flung open, admitting Anaxar and his party. Gha'jahn stared, stunned, as each of his trained, hidden assassins dropped to a knee as the petite, red-clad female passed them. He narrowed his eyes, struggling to catch a glimpse of her from between the close-knit barrier of armed guards, and he spied the twinkle of the subjugo stones draped over her pale ivory throat.

Even muted, though, she carried enough power to bring even the strongest to heel. His final victory over the Stria was guaranteed.

"Emperor M'Uubair," Anaxar announced and bowed deeply at the waist. "May the Goddess Ishtanti shower bright blessings upon you on this day."

Gha'jahn tilted his head and searched the party's faces for in one particular. "We thought our son would be returning with you."

The Sub-Confidant dipped his chin and placed his hand solemnly over his heart. "A thousand apologies, sire. The Heir Apparent continues to hunt down the rebels who escaped on Bashir. I have been joined by another instead; one of great value to the Thrall."

"If you are presenting our stolen treasure to us, then we shall be pleased, indeed." Gha'jahn eased back, stretching out his legs. The mere thought of her was enticing enough to draw him out of his seat. Now to see the female, himself.

Anaxar stepped back, and with a flourished gesture to his soldiers, the wall of armor parted to reveal the Divine.

Defiance gleamed in her dark brown eyes, and he arched a brow in curious appreciation. *This one will need breaking.* Waves of ruddy burgundy tresses had been bound up in an ornate, plaited knot, accentuating her defined cheekbones and plump lips, although the tempting round globes of flesh barely contained by the unflattering scarlet gown's plunging neckline drew his attention.

A strange, sharp shriek split the air, and he jerked his stare back to her face.

"My eyes are up here, jackass." A deep furrow had creased her ivory brow, and she folded her arms across her ample chest. "And if you even think about correcting me"—she snapped up a finger in warning toward Anaxar—"I will feed you every piece of your anatomy you are so overly fond of."

Willful was an understatement; she was pure fire contained in a shapely bottle.

"Emperor Gha'jahn M'Uubair, may I present to you the Lady Evainne, Divine Adept from the Terran realm."

The thinly veiled displeasure in Anaxar's tone spoke volumes of his opinion about the newest addition to the flock. "Adept, is it?" Gha'jahn said.

"Yes, sire," the Sub-Confidant stated, chin dipping smartly. "Time and again, she has shown her ... skills in hand-to-hand combat, as well as a passable degree of military strategy."

Another unladylike sound came from the unusual female. "Gee, hope you didn't hurt yourself with that one there, sweet cheeks."

"Curb your tongue, *Dym Char'ann*," Gha'jahn growled under his breath, and Evainne's furious glare slid in his direction. The impulse to bow and ask for forgiveness battled with his desire to strip her bare and take her forcibly on the floor of the great hall. "High Council Jhuen only did his sacred duty by bringing you safely to us." He stalked closer to the headstrong female, tempering his conflicting urges.

To his surprise, she held her ground, eyes never wavering. He circled behind her, ogling her hidden curves. She would be sweet indeed, and he would ravage her first before handing her over to the doddering ancients.

As he stood at her back, he glanced at the remaining Divines, both males nearly drooling in anticipation as they approached. Hollix and Qi'tan eyed up the prickly female, muttering and grinning, though notably avoiding contact with the potent stones hanging at her throat.

He leaned down and inhaled deeply, savoring her unique fragrance. "You might want to show a little more gratitude," he whispered into her ear, trailing a fingertip along her creamy skin hidden beneath the twisted straps of royal gown. "This will be your home for the rest of your days, Divine."

Klaxons blared in the distance as explosions cut through the air. Gha'jahn frowned, shifting his eyes to the fidgeting lines of soldiers, while the captive Divine tilted her head, a devious smirk tugging at the corners of her ruby lips as she glared at him over her shoulder.

"I wouldn't bet the farm on that."

Chapter 42

Kahlym ran on, forcing the jarring pain from each stride into the back of his mind. Laser focused, he dashed along the maze of corridors, turning right and left with complete confidence.

The moment he'd set foot on his ship, strange events had begun to unfold. At first, simply seeing his crew alive had filled his heart with joy. Yhan'tu had immediately gone to work on his injuries, while Dhaerin and Xandar made short work of slipping through his homeworld's lax defenses. Apparently, the mere mention of Evainne's name had been enough to get them a direct pass through any security gate, and once they were safely in the hyperlanes, R'uan had reached out to all Stria ships, requesting aid for their upcoming assault on Rimma.

While Kahlym did his best to be a model patient for his blustering medic, a soft voice echoed in his mind, though not speaking to him in words he could understand. Instead, it conveyed sensations and emotions, images and ideas, and he struggled to make meaning of the unfamiliar presence until his forehead ached from frowning. Yet, there was no denying the strong sense of urgency and defined course across the stars presented through the messages.

"Am I hurting you?"

Kahlym shook his head and, rising to his feet, he waved off Yhan'tu's inquiry. A strong hand pressed him back down, and he trailed his gaze up the locked arm until he reached Brel's face.

"Let Yhan'tu do his job, *kherdes*. We are gathering allies as we speak. In total, twelve warships will be joining us on the attack on Rimma. It should take about an hour to coordinate things and—"

"No." Kahlym fought against his brother's hold, struggled to stand, shook his head. "That's too long. Brel, I can't explain it, but we have to go. Now. If the others meet us in Rimma space, we can figure things out there."

"Kahl, you look like hammered shit and—"

"Please." Kahlym grabbed on to Brel's shoulders and stared deeply into the cautious citrine eyes. "Get me to Rimma," he said, "to the dark side, near a white-capped mountain range." Brel leaned away, screwing up his face in confusion. Kahlym groaned and dropped his shoulders. "I don't know how I know this, Brel. But please, trust me."

Seconds ticked on. For a moment, Kahlym feared he would have to go the route alone, until Brel sighed and gave his head a slow shake, his long warrior locks swinging back and forth. "Dhaer? Tell any Chandaran fighters to meet us on the far side of Rimma." Brel threaded his fingers through Kahlym's knotted hair and pressed their foreheads together. "And tell that female of yours not to have all the fun this time."

Kahlym swallowed hard and nodded. *If only I knew the messages were from her, I would.*

But the identity of his informant remained a mystery for the duration of their journey to Rimma. He'd asked Brel for his trust, and in return, he gave his crew a wide berth, allowing them to bring them all safely to their destination. Emotions poured in, frantic and desperate, as his ship slipped through his homeworld's atmosphere. Circling the vessel below the sensor array, Dhaerin found the exact spot Kahlym had seen in his mind and touched down, the deep shadows of the surrounding peaks offering excellent cover. A direct path, clear and bright, blazed like a beacon in his waking eyes, and without taking a step, Kahlym knew this line led to his angel.

"Captain?"

Kahlym blinked back to the present, a bit shocked by his sudden company. "What is it, Falka?"

"*Fallen Grace, Victorious,* and *Devil's Armada* are all waiting in the hyperlanes beyond the comm range of the Thrall." She stood in full battle garb, weapons strapped to her thick legs, and three streaks of deep blue trailed from ear to chin along her left cheek. "How long will it take us to reach the palace?"

"Us? Falka, I've never known you to jump into battle."

His tech dropped her gaze and stared at her booted feet for another heartbeat before once again raising her topaz eyes to his. "For the Lady Evainne."

Nothing else needed to be said. Grateful and humbled, Kahlym rested his hand on her narrow shoulder. "Tell the captains to give us until moonrise. Then unleash the fury."

"Moonrise?" Dhaerin quipped as Falka gave a sharp nod and turned on her heel. His Ontaxian pilot sidled around the fleeing Shee Va'an, confusion contorting his tawny features. "Bro, no way are we gonna make it to the palace gates in that short amount of time."

Kahlym held his friend's panicked stare. "We have to, Dhaer."

"We got a plan?" Brel asked, sliding his last blade into its wrist sheath.

As Kahlym glanced around the room, he met the eyes of his crew. His friends. His family. All of them were willing to put their lives on the line to rescue his reason for living.

"Yeah," he announced, clapping Dhaerin on the back. "Keep up with me and don't get dead."

Dhaerin answered with a toothy grin and holstered his last weapon. "Outstanding. Guess it's hero time."

"Hang on." Xandar grabbed Kahlym's arm as Kahlym headed toward the opening hatch. "Do you even know where we're going?"

Aside from hell? He kept his glib remark to himself. "I have a feeling. I know, I know." He waved off the impending lecture. "Just … just follow me. Please."

His plead was the last word said. At Kahlym's stern nod, he and his crew began their trek, led by his ethereal guide. From the secluded landing platform to racing down deserted corridors, it appeared Ishtanti had truly blessed them, and while he was grateful for the open pathway, the lack of resistance began to tug at his already frayed nerves. Something of immense importance must have been pulling all of the populace of the Thrall stronghold into one place.

Only a formal presentation would warrant such a room clearing. His father must have arrived. Whether or not the male drew breath at the setting of this night, Kahlym was unwilling to lay odds.

He chugged on, forcing his blood to return to his limbs.

"*While I'm enjoying the quiet,*" Dhaerin whispered through the comm link, "*any idea where everybody is?*"

His guide shouted to him, and Kahlym raised a fisted hand above his head as he skidded to a halt before the final bend in the corridor. While he slipped his weapon from his thigh holster, he fought to catch his breath, and between the thundering pulses of blood pounding in his ears, he picked out the familiar clicks and scrapes as his crew armed themselves at his back.

"*On the alarms, we go.*"

"Alarms," Falka croaked. "What al—"

The ground shook, rocking the walls, and the explosive boom mingled with the whine of the defense sirens.

"Anyone else thinking that's a little scary?" Dhaerin mumbled, sliding his gaze toward Kahlym.

"Don't care," Brel replied with a crazed grin. "I just think that's my new favorite sound."

While Brel chuckled at his own joke, Kahlym bolted around the corner, where a handful of startled enforcers staggering to their feet blocked the massive double doors. With deadly precision, Kahlym squeezed the trigger and made short work of the dazed guards. A comforting warmth stirred in his chest. His angel waited beyond the barrier.

Howling with primal purpose, Kahlym blasted the locked handles, then slammed his shoulder against the sagging doors. All heads swiveled his direction at his abrupt entrance, yet his own gaze was drawn to the emperor and the red-draped figure immersed in his shadow.

"TAKE YOUR HANDS OFF HER!"

Rage coursed through his veins as he raced into the serpent's den, and the object of his attention immediately vanished in a sea of white, armored uniforms. Roaring, he fired until his weapon clicked empty. His crew followed his reckless lead, and the room exploded in pockets of small skirmishes. Kahlym dropped the useless blaster as he continued to drive forward. Flashes of crimson fabric floated through the chaos, and he glimpsed the emperor fall to the floor, though he only had a moment to savor the scene when a spike of fiery pain pounded into his shoulder, knocking him to his knees.

"You've ruined *everything*!"

Kahlym spun about to face his father, whose unchecked rage had twisted his mouth into a hideous snarl, his eyes wide and wild. Anaxar lifted his weapon, but Kahlym easily ducked the slipshod shot. Then he kicked up off the ground and tackled his father around the waist. This fight had been brewing since the first day he'd drawn breath, and he was going to savor the battle.

Something solid thumped into his back, jarring his aching ribs, and his legs buckled. Kahlym hissed as he dragged in a breath and released his tight hold to stumble out of arm's reach. The distance wasn't far enough for his father; the man swung sloppily at Kahlym's head. Kahlym bobbed back and countered with a bone-crushing cross, while Anaxar, snarling, spun with the force of his attack, his elbow connecting with Kahlym's temple.

Kahlym staggered, shaking his head to settle his fuzzy mind, until a pair of hands dug into his shoulders. He reacted quickly, threading his fingers into his father's short hair and yanking down, driving his knee into Anaxar's gut before he slammed his laced fists between Anaxar's shoulder blades. The man dropped heavily at his feet, but Kahlym was far from satisfied. He raised his foot, prepared to slam it down onto his father's exposed neck. Only the timid touch of an invisible hand on his own stayed the killing blow, its calming presence brushing away the hate that had darkened his heart for so long.

Centered once again, Kahlym lifted his gaze to the surrounding melee. The cobalt blue of the Chandaran Stria had begun to outnumber the white-and-crimson clad Thrall enforcers. But he had lost sight of his angel.

"Evainne!" he called, though his repeated shouts were swallowed by the sounds of struggles and the groans of the dying. Frantic, he retrieved a discarded blast rifle dropped by a lifeless Thrall and limped toward the dais where he'd seen her last. His blood-smeared fingers fumbled with the small pocket at his hip, finally opening it, and he slipped the all-important key into his palm.

I am coming, ziat'xahn.

Chapter 43

Evainne had played nice throughout the shuttle flight over, biting her tongue until it bled. So when she'd arrived in the presence of the high-and-mighty of the Thrall, she shifted her teeth to the inside of her cheek.

The whole planet had an unwelcoming aroma, air bitter, acrid. Once she was out of there, she vowed to return to the beautiful forests of Ontaxa or to the lush gardens on Raedyn Septicon. Anything away from this barren, mechanized land sprawling out beyond the thick glass. She held her chin up as she marched the gauntlet of enemy forces leading her straight to the feet of the Thrall Emperor.

She assumed he was head asshole, since only he was sitting, while two wizened men stood off to his left, whispering and pointing. Great. Those must have been the other Divines. No way would she let those fossils touch her. Her stomach flip-flopped at the mere thought.

After a quick mental inventory of any and all doors and possible escape routes, Evainne returned her focus to the man occupying the throne. Confidence oozed off of him and spilled down the marble steps leading to the raised dais, where he surveyed the scene. His hair appeared to have a red sheen, but it was plastered to his head, so it was difficult to determine the true color. He'd been in power for many years, she guessed, evidenced by his paunch threatening to pour over his belt line.

Yet she knew better than to underestimate him. He might have had others doing his current dirty work, but that didn't mean he wasn't capable of throwing down if needed. She read this in his unearthly lavender eyes. Violence had brought him to his current position; yanking him off of his high horse would take some doing.

With a hard swallow, she pushed down her doubts and fears, mustered a brave facade, and strode forward. During the fiasco-of-a-presentation, she'd remained cool as a cucumber, being pawed at by the lecherous leader and his drooling cronies. In her very bones, she felt this situation was temporary.

Yet when the first explosions had rocked the palace, she hadn't realized it would be quite that short. The bastard believed he had a Divine Adept on his hands; so that's exactly what he'd gotten. As the emperor turned to face the splintered, battered-down door, she'd used his distraction to her advantage. Cupping her hand around her fist, she'd twisted and drove her elbow into the side of his head—a blow strong enough to knock him off balance—and then she'd tried to run.

Too bad her heel had gotten snagged in the hem of her long skirt, and she tumbled down into an embarrassed heap. "Oh, for fuck's sake," she muttered and attempted to scramble back up, huffing in exasperation and gathering up handfuls of fabric. She gave standing another shot. Fingers grabbed her ankle, and she jerked her gaze toward her attacker. Wild purple eyes glared at her from above the snarling maw of the Thrall's head honcho.

"You bitch," he spat. Without hesitation, Evainne coiled her other leg then thrust out, the pistoned kick landing square in the center of his distorted face. The pointed heel tip stabbed into his golden-skinned cheek, splashing her with warm blood, and he shrieked.

"Pal," she said of his comment, "you have no fucking idea." She clawed at the slippery floor, scooting out of reach of the howling emperor, growling in irritation. If only the skirt had been a separate piece.

She scanned the nearby bodies, finally spying a short dagger dropped beside a fallen guard and, grumbling, working fast, she hacked off about two feet of the bottom of the ridiculous gown she'd been trussed up in like a Christmas turkey. Her heart pounded behind her rib cage as she yanked off her heels. She fought better barefoot, and she needed every advantage while this albatross hung around her neck.

Another hard tug on her shortened gown wrenched her away from escape, and she flopped onto her belly, spun the exposed blade to lie flat against the inside of her forearm, allowing herself to be dragged closer to her enemy. She focused on her breathing as her heavier opponent pinned her beneath him. During her feigned struggles, she'd tucked her knees and elbows up underneath herself, waiting for the right moment to strike.

"I will take you right here on this floor, and there is nothing you can do about it." The crazed voice of the emperor had poured into her ear, spittle raining down onto her cheek. Gritting her teeth, Evainne slammed her head backwards, and as the man howled in agony, she arched her spine and shoved against the floor with all her might. The sudden force was perfectly timed, and her fleshy blanket went flying. She sprung up from her crouch, then dashed away from the dais.

Free for a moment, Evainne searched the growing crowd for a familiar face. The blue uniforms continued to pour in, all protected with armor and helmets, though one shape stood out among the bipedal, two-armed fighters. She had to give the girl props. Falka moved like lightning, each of her three arms wielding weapons with deadly accuracy. Evainne headed toward the ship's tech; if she stuck by her side, they'd likely meet up with Kahlym at some point.

An enforcer stepped in and leveled his long-barreled weapon at her, only to immediately drop to his knees. Confused, Evainne glanced around for the source of the timely shot, though no blood or protruding bone marked a wound on the man's back.

"A thousand apologies, Blessed Divine," he said, offering her the gun in his outstretched arms.

Unexpected, but she wasn't about to look a gift horse in the mouth. She snatched up the unused rifle, muttering her thanks in reply while she slipped his knife into the braided belt at her waist. Yet the devotee refused to budge. With a shrug, she let the man hang out in his prostrated pose, jumping over the odd speed bump, and continued toward her visible friend. Firearms, especially shotguns, had never been her thing, but she'd seen enough movies to know to brace the butt against her shoulder. Sighting down the barrel, she squeezed the trigger, and the enemy at Falka's back vanished in a puff of black smoke.

The serpentine head swiveled toward Evainne, and she could have sworn a smile warmed the alien's face. But the expression melted as something at her back grabbed Falka's attention. Evainne ducked, stepped back, and swung the rifle like a bat toward the pussy who dared to attack from behind. The slashing blade sliced a long furrow across the meat of her bicep, missing the killing blow. But the rifle's stock cracked against the fragile rib cage of the ancient Divine with bone-crunching force. The old man cried out, collapsed at her feet.

"Wow," she huffed out, wrapping her fingers around her arm, blood dripping off of her fingertips. "Does this mean you don't want me to be part of your club?"

"A ... a Divine does not ... take life," he said, struggling to hiss out the words, blood bubbling up with each exhale.

Disgusted, Evainne knelt beside the hypocrite. "Then what were you going to do with that knife? Tickle my fancy and ask nicely?"

She scoffed as he blinked rapidly, his confusion morphing into embarrassment, and she rose to her feet.

A figure flashed to stand before her, shouting just as a blast knocked the pair of them to the ground. Evainne scooted out from beneath Falka … and the world around her slowed. *No.* She fought against her tears as she pressed her hands against the gaping opening in Falka's chest.

"Hang in there, sweetie," she croaked out. "I'll get you outta here and—"

But Falka only shook her head weakly, her four long fingers covering Evainne's bloodied hands. "Save your skills for another," she whispered. Evainne opened her mouth, but a gentle squeeze to her hand stalled her tongue. "It is time for me to join the rest of my race in the annuls of history."

"But we need you—I need you." The right words were stuck in her throat, and Evainne choked on them as they poured from her lips, tears coursing down her cheeks. "You can't leave me to be the only voice of reason on board that ship of idiotic males."

Her feeble attempt at humor brought a pained smile to her friend's face, but color was draining quickly from her complexion. Falka lifted her earthy topaz eyes to peer directly into Evainne's heart. "You have restored *my* faith in the Divines, Evainne. Now, go ignite the universe."

One shuddered breath escaped, and then Falka was gone. Frozen in grief, Evainne watched as a fine spiderweb of cracks appeared on Falka's skin, black tendrils spreading in all directions until they engulfed her entire body. Then, with an invisible gust of wind, she simply disintegrated, returning to become the stuff of stars.

Evainne gasped, emotions swirling at the heart-wrenching moment. Every possibility coalesced into a new source of power, and fire coursed through her veins. She lifted her gaze, rising to her feet as she reached up for the cold metal draped across her open throat. Locking eyes with the smug emperor, the killing tool still in his hand, she wrapped her fingers around the necklace and poured every ounce of anger into her palm.

One smooth tug was all it took, and the chain melted.

Murmurs of shock and disbelief rose up as she stalked toward the Thrall leader, his face contorted in panic. She wrapped her fingers around the twisted remains of the once-ornate piece, while from the corner of her eye, she saw the gathered armies tripping over themselves to take a knee as she moved onward with purpose. Only a small handful of blue-clad warriors dared to pick their way through the reverent forms.

Sharp edges cut into her palm, but she dismissed the dull ache, her cool tears doing little to extinguish the agonizing blaze in her heart. When she finally stood directly in front of the cowering emperor, she extended her arm and released the useless hunk of charred metal and crushed gems from her fingers. It dropped ... then clattered onto the floor, shattering the eerie silence.

"I thought you'd want your leash back," she stated flatly. "Fucker," she added as punctuation.

"It ... it cannot be." At the hushed whisper, she swiveled her gaze over to the two Divines, who wobbled to their knees. "The ... the legends are ... are—"

"Are true."

Chapter 44

With those two words, Kahlym forced his voice to carry through the immense chamber. His heart ached at the raw and devastating loss of his dear friend; Falka's sacrifice to save his angel had been the ultimate price.

Earlier, he'd fought his way toward Evainne, but the mystery presence in his mind had warned him to pause. The air had stilled; the universe had held its breath in anticipation. Confused, Kahlym stopped to witness the true birth of a Paramount Divine.

Evainne slowly tucked her legs beneath her and smoothly rose to her feet, while shades of blue pulsated, coursed around her body. Yet her eyes held his main focus—the deep brown orbs he'd fallen into all those moons ago were now laced with gold-and-silver bolts of lightning, proof of the mighty tempest within. Somewhere inside that firestorm, though, lay the soft presence that had guided him there: their child, blessed with bond of prophecy, had ensured his finding her across the stars once again.

Buoyed by this newfound knowledge, Kahlym had lifted his chin with pride, while a quick tug of Evainne's hand had torn the stones from her neck, unleashing her full force.

As the groveling began, Kahlym nodded to his crew, and they closed the distance. He reached out along his private link with Evainne, sending out waves and waves of love. He sensed her sorrow, her anger … so many different emotions rose and fell as she stood proudly before Gha'jahn.

When the Thrall Divines fumbled for words, Kahlym stepped up to shoulder her burden. Blood and grime had darkened her face, while thin, silvery trails washed clean streaks down her cheeks. A nasty gash had laid her arm open nearly to the bone, but the pain reflected in her eyes touched him more deeply than any of his own wounds. "A Paramount Divine has come to the Seventh Quadrant," he announced with a warm smile as he reached out toward her. "And she is the answer to my Soulcry."

"NO!" The emperor lunged to his feet. "The Divine belongs to me!"

And before anyone could react, Evainne snapped her fingers, and the Thrall leader exploded into bits of flesh and gore. "No," she said. "I belong to myself, and myself alone." Nothing but the sound of breathing dared to disrupt the sudden, heavy silence.

Dhaerin whistled low, impressed. "That was one hell of a neat trick, *learom*," he declared with all the tact of a bomb. "Can we go home now?"

Kahlym rolled his eyes and, shaking his head, he captured Evainne's cold fingers. He rubbed his thumb against the back of her stiff hand, encouraging her warmth to return. "The decision is yours, *ziat'xahn*. By rights, you could remain here and rule the Thrall."

"Grand Divine, you must stay with us," Hollix pleaded.

For a heartbeat, Evainne peered over at the cowering ancients before raising her gaze to meet Kahlym's.

"*Kerriad*, take me home," she said. "They made the mess; they can clean it up." She flung her arm toward the groveling masses. "The ruling days of the Thrall are over."

At her simple pronouncement, the Chandaran forces jumped to

their feet, cheering and whooping in celebratory shouts that filled the stale air with a much-needed sense of joy.

Careful of her wounds and his, Kahlym wrapped an arm around her shoulder, pulled her close. "Then home it is," he said. He pressed a chaste kiss on the crown of her head, then rested his cheek against her bound, bloodwine tresses and drew in a deep, centering inhale. Grief still clung to her, heavy and agonizing. <*We will mourn Falka, ziat'xahn.*> With her face buried into his side, she nodded and sniffled back the tears that dampened his battlesuit.

"This is not over," said an enforcer, and Kahlym halted to peer over his shoulder at him.

"Do you want to try your luck?" Kahlym asked. The male held his gaze for only a moment longer before ducking his chin and melting back into the surrounding reverent throng. Officers in Stria blue stripped weapons off of the remaining Thrall soldiers, then herded the males toward awaiting cells.

Certain the clean-up was in good hands, Kahlym saluted with his working arm to the other captains. Lev tossed back his head, his bellowing laughter lost amidst the raucous festivities, and Kahlym chuckled softly, savoring the joyful scene. A gentle knock against his shoulder dragged his gaze toward his gathered crew.

No—more than his crew. His family.

Xandar tipped his chin toward the path leading back to the landing bay. "Come, *kherdes*. I believe home was requested."

"That it was," he replied and, brushing his lips across Evainne's hair, he leaned in close, whispering into her ear, "Where would you like to call home, Grand Divine?"

A quick jab into his ribs coupled with a weak laugh brought a smile to his face. "Can we go back to Ontaxa?" she asked.

"See?" Dhaerin beamed proudly. "Told ya it's the best planet in the system." He took a couple of steps before wheeling around, an impish twinkle in his eye. "Hey, and maybe on the way back," he said, "you can tell us all what a douche is."

Xandar groaned, dropping his face into his palm. "Why did you have to teach them *that* word?" With a stern hand on Dhaerin's shoulder, Xandar spun round the cackling Ontaxian, pointing his nose toward the gaping exit.

As a group, they wove their way through the rubble and debris. Kahlym lagged a step behind the others, and once they were safely outside the chamber, he paused and eased his angel out of his embrace. "Evainne, while you were—" He swallowed hard, searching for the right words. "Locked away from me, I was guided to you by another."

Her eyebrows tugged together, and he trailed a thumb across the deep furrow. "Who could've known where to find me?" she asked.

"Only one who was always with you." And with his honest statement, he rested his palm low across her belly. Closing his eyes and lifting his chin, he recalled the words of the wise woman from his dream so long ago. Evainne covered his hand with hers, and he savored the peace he'd fought for his whole life.

"If this kid's a handful," she said, her voice thick with barely restrained tears, "I'm blaming you."

Kahlym dropped his head down and laughed, the sound squeezed out between his still-broken ribs. "I take full responsibility, and gladly, *ziat'xahn*."

Tucking his angel back beneath the shelter of his arm, Kahlym guided her after his brothers back to the ship and on to a place he thought he would never find.

A real home.

HAVE YOU MET THE
GUARDIANS YET?

Enter a completely unique world within the realms of paranormal romance, with new rules and fresh stories. In lieu of vampires and shape shifters, readers discover the Guardian Warriors, immortals who protect mankind from agents bent on pure chaos. Amid the battle of good and evil, love that transcends time grows, connecting souls and leaves readers wanting more.

Here is a sampling from the first book in the Guardians series, *Spirit Fall...*

"Find something you like?"

The deep voice behind Voni caught her completely by surprise. She scrambled to pull the headphones off, catching her hair in her haste. Twisting around, she found herself facing a broad chest. She raised her eyes to come face-to-face with her late-night Samaritan.

Black fabric stretched taut against his sculpted chest, and one bronze arm braced on the wall well above her head. The black T-shirt melted into black jeans, finishing in black boots. His hair, though partially slicked back, fell to tantalize her senses, enveloping her in his amber-and-musk scent, pure male and pure sex. His crooked smile brought out a devilish gleam in his ice-green eyes.

My own personal dark angel of mercy. Her tongue and her brain seemed to have a difference of opinion. While her mind fought to make some intelligent response, her tongue seemed only interested in resuming its unfinished battle with his and stumbled over the simplest sounds.

"Oh, wow. Um, hi. I mean," she stammered, fumbling with the bulky plastic headphones and the cord currently tangled in her hair. The more she tugged, the stronger the snare became. *Shit. Great, Voni. Just great! Can't you for once not make him think you're a complete clod?*

Her words rang through Kai's mind, filling his heart with emotions unfamiliar to him, compassion and sympathy. He smiled warmly as he slid His fingers into the thick curtain of dark chestnut softness, sifting through the silken strands to help loosen the offending cable. The scent of jasmine and lavender, laced with vanilla and spices, assaulted his senses, dizzying, intoxicating. He fought to keep his distance, to maintain his cool, when every fiber of his being screamed at him to kiss her. It would be so easy to dip his head, close the final distance, and claim her lips.

"Sorry, I did not mean to startle you," he said smoothly, his hand still buried in her tresses. The cord fell free, and he begrudgingly released the softness but not before he trailed his fingertips gently against her cheek. Not wanting to leave her, but knowing she needed a little space, he pulled back to his original resting place. "So, what are you listening to?"

"It's, ah, Apoca—a, something," she said, flustered as she searched for the now-invisible case. "Where did that go? It was just —hang on." She turned abruptly to face him, stopping mid-search. "How did you know where to find me?"

He opened his mouth to respond, but a quick wave of her hand stopped him cold.

"Wait, never mind." she paused, looking up at him. "I guess last night really wasn't just a dream," she muttered. "Now, the real question is, why did you even want to find me?"

"I would think that would be the easier question," he replied, a devious smile curling his lips.

Spirit Fall is available in paperback and ebook.

Author's Notes

Thank you for allowing my stories into your life and I hope you stay along for the ride. Without readers like you, my characters would only live in my own imaginations.

Keep Believing in Magic!

And don't think for a minute that you've seen all from the Seventh Quadrant!

Never miss a new release or
sale!

BE SURE TO SIGN UP FOR MY NEWSLETTER
AT WWW.TESSAMCFIONN.COM

Connect with me!

www.TessaMcFionn.com

tessa@tessamcfionn.com

Twitter: @TessaMcFionn

Instagram: @tessam2112

About the Author

Tessa McFionn is a very native Californian and has called Southern California home for most of her life, growing up in San Diego and attending college in Northern California and Orange County, only to return to San Diego to work as a teacher. Insatiably curious and imaginative, she loves to learn and discover, making her wicked knowledge of trivial facts an unwelcomed guest at many Trivial Pursuit boards.

Her love of the fantastical began at a young age while her mother read to her and her brother such classics as *The Hobbit* and *Rikki Tikki Tavi*. She continued this love, devouring Terry Brooks, J.R.R. Tolkien, Ray Bradbury, and Isaac Asimov as well as comic books galore. Romance entered the field in the guise of Anne Rice's *An Interview with a Vampire*, and during college, she discovered the works of Sherrilyn Kenyon and Christine Feehan, and the rest is history.

Her first novel, *Spirit Fall*, came to her as she looked over the edge of a very dark place. Since then, she's added three more tales to the world of the Guardian Warriors and *Spirit Bound*, Book Two in the series, was awarded the 2016 Write Touch award for Paranormal Romance from WisRWA. But she never lost her love for science fiction and began a space opera, The Rise of the Stria, in March 2018 with the release of *To Discover a Divine*. After the original publishing house went under, she has now decided to continue the series on her own, releasing the second in the series, *Divine Challenges* in December 2019.

When not writing, she can be found at the movies, hiking in the local Southern California mountains, or at Disneyland with her husband, as well as family, friends or anyone who wants to play at the Happiest Place on Earth. She also finds her artistic soul fed through her passions for theatre, dance and music. A proud parent of far too many high school seniors and two still living house plants, she also enjoys hockey, reading and playing Words with Friends to keep her vocabulary sharp. She has served as Treasurer, President-Elect, and President of the San Diego chapter of Romance Writers of America and loves spending time working with such amazingly intelligent and creative writers.

Also by Tessa McFionn

The Guardians

Spirit Fall, Book One

Spirit Bound, Book Two

Spirit Song, Book Three

Spirit Shattered, Book Four

The Rise of the Stria

To Discover A Divine, Book One

Divine Challenges, Book Two

"Wishes & Whiskey," a short story

Storybook Pub